THE CASABLANCA QUARTET

III. RESISTANCE
&
IV. FREEDOM

THE CASABLANCA QUARTET

III. RESISTANCE
1953–1954

&

IV. FREEDOM
1955–1956

Based on true stories

JOSH SHOEMAKE

Opium Books

The main character of this novel is Casablanca in the years between 1942 and 1956. It is a life of its own, through which other lives move, changing it in ways both subtle and significant, only to return again like memories, strengthening the connections between them until patterns emerge, melodies and refrains, a discovered symphony – a life.

Like the city of Casablanca itself, those characters are based on real people, now mostly forgotten, and here reimagined. The facts of their lives and deaths, to the extent that they are still known, have been respected to the best of my ability.

PERSONS REPRESENTED

Victor Tessier (b. 1925) – French pilot

Franklin Sidney Felton (b. 1914) – American vice-consul (COI/OSS/CIA)

Arkady Zubov (b. 1910) – major in the NKVD, Soviet secret police

Camille Morin (b. 1923) – French girl from Dakar
Madame Morin (b. 1902) – her mother

Tommy August (b. 1918) – American Navy pilot
Lucy August (b. 1922) – his wife

Mike "Mag" Magursky (b. 1918) – American Army supply sergeant
Lieutenant Stec (b. 1907) – his superior

Josephine Baker (b. 1906) – American singer, dancer, actress

Abdelwahed Chaoui (b. 1911) – actor, producer, journalist,

businessman, Nationalist
Zina Chaoui (b. 1916) – his wife
Touria Chaoui (b. 1936) – their daughter, pilot, Nationalist
Salah Chaoui (b. 1944) – their son

Ahmed Touil (b. 1922) – driver, resistant, cop

Aziza Benayiche (b. 1911) – Jewish businesswoman, owner of clothing shop
Suzanne Benayiche (b. 1934) – her daughter

Fadila (b. 1928) – a prostitute
Jean Bart (b. 1922) – her *patronne*

Jacques Lemaigre-Dubreuil (b. 1894) – industrialist, politician, writer
Simon Castet (b. 1928) – male model, friend of Lemaigre-Dubreuil

Albert Forestier (b. 1929) – journalist, soldier, policeman

François Avival (b. 1920) – manager of La Gironde, former boxer
Antoine "Tony" Méléro (b. 1929) – policeman
Congos (b. 1928) – policeman
Jean "the Gypsy" (b. 1928) – policeman

Rémy, Jean "le Footballeur", Omar "le Sheik", Michel "le Juif", Andre "El Negro", François, and other members of the Red Hand.

Captain Fillette (b. 1909) – director of Action Service of the SDECE, French foreign intelligence agency

Saadia Taibi (b. 1934) – nurse, resistant

Zaïm (b. 1908) – resistant

Directeur Martin (b. 1905) – French director of the flight school at Tit Mellil
Lieutenant Noguera (b. 1922) – French pilot, instructor at Tit Mellil

Haj Alaoui (b. 1906) – businessman connected to the Sultan
Hajja Aliya Alaoui (b. 1912) – his wife, a philanthropist
Haj Driss Alaoui (b. 1930) – their son, a businessman
Hajja Hiba Alaoui (b. 1916) – her sister

Major Sartout (b. 1907) – French police officer in Affaires Indigènes, newspaper director
Antoine Mazzella (b. 1916) – French newspaper editor

Mohamed Zerktouni (b. 1927) – resistant

III. RESISTANCE
1953–1954
JOSH SHOEMAKE
F-AIUL
F
THE CASABLANCA QUARTET

THE CASABLANCA QUARTET

III. RESISTANCE

1953–1954

Based on true stories

JOSH SHOEMAKE

Opium Books

WAR
LANDING
1942
Victor Tessier
Franklin Sydney Felton
Mike "Mag" Magursky
Tommy August
Lucy August
Franklin Sydney Felton
Jacques Lemaigre-Dubreuil
Camille Morin
Tommy August
Mike "Mag" Magursky
Tommy August
Victor Tessier
YELLOW MAGIC
1943
Camille Morin
Mike "Mag" Magursky
Abdelwahed Chaoui
Franklin Sydney Felton
Mike "Mag" Magursky
Touria Chaoui
Aziza Benayiche
Ahmed Touil
GENTLEMEN CALLERS
Mike "Mag" Magursky
Fadila
Camille Morin
Mike "Mag" Magursky
Victor Tessier
Fadila
Tommy August
ANIMAL KINGDOM
1944
Mike "Mag" Magursky
Ahmed Touil
Jacques Lemaigre-Dubreuil
Camille Morin
Franklin Sydney Felton
Tony Méléro
Victor Tessier
Mike "Mag" Magursky
Camille Morin
Mike "Mag" Magursky
Albert Forestier
Ahmed Touil
Abdelwahed Chaoui
Aziza Benayiche
Suzanne Benayiche
1945
Touria Chaoui
Mike "Mag" Magursky
Aziza Benayiche
Camille Morin
PEACE
THE ANGLE OF ATTACK
1948
Abdelwahed Chaoui
Touria Chaoui
Zina Chaoui
Salah Chaoui
Tony Méléro
Abdelwahed Chaoui
Albert Forestier
1949
Touria Chaoui
Franklin Sydney Felton
Camille Morin
Jacques Lemaigre-Dubreuil
Fadila
Suzanne Benayiche
Touria Chaoui
Tony Méléro
1950
Abdelwahed Chaoui
Victor Tessier
BLUESHIFT
1951
Touria Chaoui
Victor Tessier
Abdelwahed Chaoui
Suzanne Benayiche
Victor Tessier
Touria Chaoui
Fadila
Suzanne Benayiche
Touria Chaoui
Abdelwahed Chaoui
HANDS
Tony Méléro
1952
Aziza Benayiche
Touria Chaoui
Hajja Aliya Alaoui
Tommy August
Lucy August
Camille Morin
Tony Méléro
Albert Forestier
Victor Tessier
Suzanne Benayiche
Albert Forestier
Aziza Benayiche
Abdelwahed Chaoui
Suzanne Benayiche
Albert Forestier
Hajja Aliya Alaoui
Touria Chaoui

RESISTANCE
EXILE
1953
Jacques Lemaigre-Dubreuil
Fadila
Tommy August
Lucy August
Victor Tessier
Tony Méléro
Touria Chaoui
Jacques Lemaigre-Dubreuil
Saadia Taibi
Abdelwahed Chaoui
Jacques Lemaigre-Dubreuil
1954
CIGARETTES
Saadia Taibi
Victor Tessier
Ahmed Touil
Lucy August
Franklin Sydney Felton
Ahmed Touil
Saadia Taibi
Abdelwahed Chaoui
Saadia Taibi
Albert Forestier
THE BIG SCREEN
Camille Morin
Jacques Lemaigre-Dubreuil
Tommy August
Saadia Taibi
Ahmed Touil
Victor Tessier
Lucy August
SHORT CONTROLLED BURSTS
Touria Chaoui
Aziza Benayiche
Suzanne Benayiche
Camille Morin
Albert Forestier
Ahmed Touil
Albert Forestier
1955
Albert Forestier
FREEDOM
DJINNS
Lucy August
Tommy August
Victor Tessier
Suzanne Benayiche
Touria Chaoui
Victor Tessier
Hajja Aliya Alaoui
Touria Chaoui
Tony Méléro
Jacques Lemaigre-Dubreuil
INVISIBLE LINES
Touria Chaoui
Aziza Benayiche
Tony Méléro
Saadia Taibi
Hajja Aliya Alaoui
Victor Tessier
Mike "Mag" Magursky
Aziza Benayiche
Ahmed Touil
Touria Chaoui
Mike "Mag" Magursky
Fadila
Tony Méléro
THE BIRDCAGE
1956
Ahmed Touil
Mike "Mag" Magursky
Touria Chaoui
Fadila
Suzanne Benayiche
Suzanne Benayiche
Aziza Benayiche
Hajja Aliya Alaoui
Touria Chaoui
Tommy August
INDEPENDENCE DAY
Lucy August
Salah Chaoui
Tony Méléro
Tony Méléro
Saadia Taibi
Tommy August
Aziza Benayiche
Abdelwahed Chaoui
Fadila
Victor Tessier
Mike "Mag" Magursky

EXILE
1953–54

Jacques Lemaigre-Dubreuil sat at his desk in the penthouse apartment of the Liberty Building and picked up his pen. From this desk he controlled Lesieur Oils and shaped his political future, which again looked promising. The revolts since the Sultan's August exile had made him a prominent voice in the North African debate. In September, he had met outside Paris with opposition leader Mendès France to chart a new course for the protectorate, and now perhaps even the post of foreign minister was in play.

A storm lashed against the plate glass windows, making concentration difficult, but also mercifully drowning out the sound of Simon flamboyantly packing his suitcase. Where did the boy imagine he was going? To Paris for another tentative modeling job? At this time of night? In this rain? Simon was young, but no, youth was no excuse. At his age Jacques had already been named captain to the military staff of the French High Commissioner in Constantinople. Now the boy was shouting for a missing sock as if it was a poodle trained to come. Jacques shook his head and put down the pen.

The fight had started, as it often did, with Jacques's proposal to spend the weekend together at the country house on the Bouregreg River. Simon had never been, although Jacques drove up the coast to stay a night as often as he could. The landscapes along the Bouregreg reminded him of his hometown, Limoges, with its green hills, wide fields, and deep rivers with quick currents. He loved to swim the river and ride horseback along its banks. His body was as fit as it had been at forty, and he wasn't yet sixty. For a few months he could still say that to Simon with total honesty. He was in his fifties. But he was bored with Simon. The boy did nothing with his life, and yet apparently the thought of a weekend in paradise filled him with dread. Casablanca was where his friends were, he always said, but did he actually have any friends? Sometimes he went out, but he had never brought anyone around to the apartment, and Jacques couldn't remember him mentioning anyone specific.

"Who are these friends?" he had asked earlier.

Simon had exploded. "A man from Dakar! I'm meeting him tonight!"

This had been their joke. Twice after they had met, Jacques had called home to tell his wife that his return to Paris had been delayed by a meeting with a man from Dakar. Did Simon miss those early days of passion too? Was he jealous maybe? Or merely cruel?

Jacques sighed and picked up the pen again. He needed to finish the editorial for *Le Monde*, and now he was impatient for Simon to be gone. Clearly the Sultan had needed to go. The decision hadn't been an easy one, but his anti-French rhetoric had become too strident, and anyway, wasn't France constitutionally opposed to despotic rule? Unfortunately they had ended up having to replace Mohammed ben Youssef with Mohammed ben Arafa, the feckless cousin whose addiction to kif they had radically underestimated. At least he was malleable.

"Simon?" He turned in his chair. The room was empty, except for furniture and the Limoges porcelain covering every flat surface: glazed plates, hand-painted with exotic wildlife and set on wooden stands, gold-footed eggs, intricately patterned and made to open with a clasp, his mother's collection of brooches, and uncannily accurate miniatures – a tea set, a living room suite, a piano.

"Simon?"

Had he actually left? Never mind. He would return soon enough, hat in hand. Jacques put pen to paper and wrote:

On August 20, 1953, the French Resident General in Morocco found himself forced to inform Sidi Mohammed ben Youssef of his removal from power for the safety and tranquility of the empire.

This act, while regrettable in itself, was unfortunately made inevitable by circumstances, and should not, despite its perfect execution, prevent us from pointing out the true, underlying causes of the crisis.

The political folly of a sovereign who undoubtedly confused the appearance of power with actual power, one who was counseled by an overly young and impetuous prince, gave hope to an opposition which he tacitly supported.

The former Sultan, a theocrat, went to the U.N. espousing democratic values, and then refused to relinquish any authority at all. Some suspect this was a clever political defense of his own economic interests. Never mind. France has exiled a sovereign whose actions had definitively shown that he was its enemy and has gathered incontrovertible evidence that the former ruler was serving himself at the expense of his own people. We are still in the process of uncovering the immense fortune he had amassed, but the deposed Sultan will never return.[1]

Simon had come into the room. Jacques could feel him standing there, hovering at a distance like a wounded poodle. He willed himself not to turn around. All it would take was a few kind words, but he needed to break that pattern. He wasn't the boy's father.

The door clicked shut, but even then Jacques didn't turn. How silly. Without even saying goodbye. That was unexpected, and rather cold.

o

---

1   *Le Monde* – 10/30/1953

Fadila sat once again in an office of the Spectacles and Morality police. The office looked identical to the one in which she had sat a decade earlier, when an angry girl of fifteen had been sent to the brothel at Bousbir. The same metal desk, the same high window behind a sneering officer, the same gray cement walls. Could there be dozens of these identical rooms with dozens of identical officers sitting across desks from dozens of girls like her? No, no girl could be like Fadila, because she was the angriest girl in the world.

In the year since she had fled Bousbir, she had been sleeping on the streets and trying to avoid cops, which had become especially difficult after the Sultan's exile. Any woman walking alone was suspect, especially if she was beautiful. They would take her in, test for diseases, and put her to work. Even the unbeautiful ones were regularly stopped and questioned. Fadila knew this because she no longer believed she was beautiful. The men no longer approached her. She needed to approach them, and every step was terror. Once upon a time she had been a magician, but now she was a monster.

To hide her tattoos, she had worn long kaftans covering even her wrists, but nothing had changed. She was still a monster, and men could see the tattoos in her eyes. But men get desperate, and there had been a few over the months. In the summer she spent nights on the benches of Parc Murdoch, staring up at the black knives of palms against the sky. The cops came hunting there too, but in the park they wouldn't arrest you. They would spread your legs beneath the black knives and then let you sleep until another came along to spread you. In the winter a Moroccan had put her in his garage. Every afternoon he came out to work on his car, leaving grease streaks on her thighs, which smudged the wings of her angels. Food was brought every couple of days, and she didn't complain. She didn't say anything at all. In the garage she was no longer so cold. And it wasn't Bousbir.

"What shall we do with you, Fadila?" The officer's voice seemed to be coming through a thick wall. She looked up at him with dull, unfocused eyes. Maybe he was in another room speaking to another girl. "As you may be aware, it has become increasingly difficult for us to place young women at Bousbir. Your *Nationalists* claim the quarter is 'an attack on their moral values', and they have demanded its closure. They were your biggest clients, of course. But there is someone else I would like you to meet."

She looked across the desk. The officer had disappeared. Now he was coming through the door again. Was it starting all over? Was she caught in some loop? No, this time he was accompanied by a second man. This man's uniform was different, although he otherwise looked the same as the others. He paused to look at her body. During this part she never knew what to do anymore. She pulled the hem of her dress down over her leg tattoos and stuck out her chest.

"I am Major Sartout," the man said. "I work in Affaires Indigènes, and I would like to give you an opportunity. Fadila, how would you like to serve your country?"

For a long moment she didn't respond. Then she burst into laughter.

"Should you accept," the man went on as she laughed and laughed, "you will be formally enlisted into the French Army along with twelve other women. Together you will form a BMC, or Bordel Militaire de Campagne, which will travel to Indochina so that your services can be provided to our soldiers stationed there. You will be paid, and when you return, you will be rewarded with the right to install yourself in the bordello of your choice."

Fadila was still laughing so hard that she must have misheard the man. Or he had gone crazy in his head.

"Should you not accept, you will be sent to the Senegalese barracks here in Casablanca."

Fadila just laughed.

○

Jacques was pleased that he had resisted the temptation to acknowledge the boy. Now he stood, walked over to the bar, and poured himself a cognac. Cooperation was what was required. Perhaps not an entirely equal partnership at this time, but a shared vision for the future based on the shared history of the two countries. France must be clear-eyed, and if it succeeded, as it must, Lemaigre-Dubreuil himself would have provided the vision. The rain had subsided to a drizzle. He gazed out across the gray city before sitting back at the desk.

Many Frenchmen feel that the Moroccan question is settled. It isn't at all. The changing of the Sultan is not even the first act of this new play, which with the help of Moroccans, we must perform. It has been merely a prologue, and an unusually easy one. I say this without diminishing the challenges faced by recent police operations, which although hastily organized, have been smoothly conducted, with remarkable results.

It should also be pointed out that nationalism as it has been conceived by many Moroccans is obsolete. No nation can live in isolation. What is needed is the creation of a Franco-Moroccan Union, which will make up part of a European Union certain to emerge sooner or later.[2]

○

They had rolled out of Fez at dawn, and the truck was now moving through the Taza Gap between the Rif and Atlas

---

2   *Le Monde* – 10/30/1953

Mountains. Thirteen sullen BMC recruits sat on backpacks in the bed of the truck. Later when the day grew warmer, they would stand braced against the metal slats that hemmed them in, just as they had the previous day. Otherwise the truck got too cramped.

They didn't speak. They hardly made eye contact. Sometimes one would sing for a while, but otherwise each stayed lost in her own thoughts. They were headed for Oran, the soldiers had said, where a boat would sail them to Vietnam.

Fadila had never been on a boat before, but she longed to look around her and see nothing but ocean. She felt alone, but she had felt like this for years. The feeling was now who she was. How long would they be on the boat? Days? Months? She didn't care. Anything was better than Casablanca, and little by little she was begrudgingly acknowledging a twinge of excitement. Today would not be like yesterday, and tomorrow would not be like today. They had asked her to serve the country. Maybe they would even give her a uniform. She hid a smile behind her scarf.

2

CENTRAL MARKET BOMBING IN CASABLANCA LEAVES 19 DEAD AND 28 WOUNDED

The explosion occurred at 11:36am. The Christmas Eve crowd was even denser than usual inside the market. Many were thrown to the ground, displays were shattered; panic seized the crowd, which pushed towards the exits. Bodies piled up: two were beheaded, and many of the injured were severely burned.

The police officers dispatched to the scene could hardly collect any evidence in the hours after the explosion, as witnesses were still in a state of shock....

The shock soon gave way to indignation and anger. While ambulances transported victims to the Hospital Colombani, Europeans attacked Moroccans on the scene, and the police had to intervene.

Terrorism has become rampant in Casablanca, but this is the first organized attack on the European zone. Never have we seen such a high number of non-Moroccan casualties....

General Guillaume vowed to do everything humanly possible to fight the terrorists.[3]

○

Tchaikovsky's *Nutcracker Suite* played softly on the hi-fi. The orange bulbs of electric candles glowed in the windows. In the living room a crooked tree had been decorated with flashing lights, as well as the cardboard snowmen Lucy had

3   Le Monde – 12/26/1953

cut and colored with the kids. Someday they would laugh about that pitiful cypress chopped down along a country road. They'd done the best they could.

The season had also transformed the houses of the Augusts' new neighbors along Echo Court. Makeshift wreaths of gray eucalyptus and palm fronds hung on doors. The Lyles had glued together three beach balls to make a rainbow-colored snowman that leaned against their lamppost. The houses were all single-story cement block constructions with flat roofs. The Augusts' was the largest of the three available blueprints. Entering through the front door, you had the living room to the left, the dining room to the right. Beyond the dining room was a large, well-equipped kitchen. Another door led out to a small yard planted with wiry grass, and the gravel driveway. In that spot Tommy was eager to build a sort of carport to protect the Caddy from the African sun. Probably he'd just go ahead and make it big enough for two cars. Then back inside the house, beyond the living room were three small bedrooms and two baths. Out those bedroom windows was the Pickerings', with garlands of flashing lights the size of softballs hanging from their cement eaves. The lights were too much, Lucy and Tommy had agreed. They flashed through the night, so that the Augusts slept in rooms dyed green, red, yellow, blue. Green, red, yellow, blue.

Late that afternoon the high school choir had come around caroling. On the front steps they had all done *Good King Wenceslas*, even the kids – Jimmy already ten, and Mary seven. Now Lucy was in the bedroom freshening up, Fatima was in the kitchen making last preparations, and Tommy was humming and pacing around the living room with a Budweiser in his hand. *When the snow lay round about, deep and crisp and even.* Every couple of bars he glanced out the front windows. With security tight after the morning's market bombing, he'd made a special point of calling the guard on duty at the front gate to give him Vic's name. For the moment, however, the street was quiet. People were probably starting to ladle out the eggnog, or preparing to make their way over to the Jacksons, who were apparently giving a party.

The Augusts' dinner would be small, but that couldn't deflate Tommy's excitement. More than a year after the base meeting where he'd reconnected with Vic, he'd finally tracked down the kid. He'd simply driven out to the Tit Mellil airfield one Friday afternoon, having decided to invite him for Christmas dinner. Hadn't Vic mentioned his family had left Casablanca? In any case, Tommy was eager to catch up, and hear about his years as a pilot, in the war and afterwards. They had a lot in common, and not only those three crazy days in 1942. Maybe there was a girlfriend, and of course she'd be welcome. Knowing Vic, she'd probably be pretty attractive, plus Lucy would have another woman to keep her company. Luckily Vic had just come down from a training flight when Tommy had arrived, and he had accepted the invitation. Apparently there was no girlfriend at the moment.

From the kitchen Fatima called for Lucy. The Moroccan had been with them since the family's arrival, and although they had never employed a servant, here they were so affordable that it was foolish not to, and now she was like family. From the beginning they had decided that Fatima should call them by their first names rather than Madame or Monsieur August, but Fatima routinely ignored this request and hardly ever referred to Tommy, especially, as anything other than *Monsieur*. If she was being insubordinate, he had decided to let it go for now.

Lucy sashayed in from the bedroom smelling of perfume, her pantyhose pleasantly swishing. She wore a red skirt and white blouse with her gold reindeer brooch pinned to her chest. Her dark blonde hair was curled, just the way he liked it. She moved past Tommy into the kitchen. Seconds later she called for him. He knew that voice. Something had gone wrong.

Earlier that day Fatima had arrived in tears, having just heard the news about the terrible attack on the Nazarenes. And so in honor of the Nazarene feast, she had insisted on cooking her special fish recipe, and once Fatima got an idea in her head, it was a fool's errand to get it out. Tommy set down his beer and walked into the kitchen, where Lucy was smiling tightly at a platter. Fatima had boned the fish, then had mixed the flesh with mayonnaise and some of her secret spices – whole cartloads of coriander, no doubt – into a sort of patty. This patty she had molded back into a fish shape before arranging the head, tail, and fins, which she had kept aside, into their original positions. Lucy looked up at him with moist eyes, her smile rapidly fading. "Looks like somebody took a perfectly good fish and ran it over with a dump truck."

Tommy took up her smile as if he'd caught it falling and neatly delivered it to Fatima. "Ah, Vic won't care," he said through his teeth, rubbing Lucy's back. "I'm sure it'll be delicious. Although maybe she could be convinced to remove the...parts." Heck, Fatima didn't speak a word of English anyway. Just clean it up, and nobody would know the difference. It was Christmas. Sometimes Lucy could get so worked up over the smallest things, and he wondered vaguely whether she did it to get back at him. But get back at him for what? She had been happy to come to Morocco. Never mind. The doorbell had rung, and he kissed her on the cheek. "That must be Vic!"

"Or Pastor Collins. He's bringing dessert. At least that won't be a disaster."

o

Victor had brought champagne. "This is a very special kind of French wine, kids," Tommy said.

"We should probably wait for Pastor Collins, honey."

"The pastor?" Tommy was already fiddling with the foil around the cork. "Heck, the pastor doesn't even drink. First you take off this little cap, am I right?" Victor wore an elegant suit and had shaken the children's hands rather awkwardly, Lucy felt. Then stepping towards her, after a brief hesitation he had kissed her on both cheeks, very French, and maybe she'd blushed a bit. He was handsome enough, although not especially personable, with faded blue eyes, hollow cheeks, and a crooked, unnatural smile. As she went off to the kitchen again in search of fresh glasses, she heard Tommy warning everyone to stand clear. A loud pop quickened her step.

o

Pastor Collins arrived not long afterwards bearing an impeccable lemon tart. He was about fifty, solidly built, with a pitted face and small, dull eyes that appeared to have been pressed into his head like a snowman's. A widower, he had been grateful for Lucy's friendship, Tommy knew, and the dynamism that she had brought to their little church. Growing up in Texas she had often rebelled against her preacher father – her first pregnancy being the most scandalous example – but here she had become increasingly involved with the church, and that afternoon she and Tommy had bickered over whether they would make that night's eleven o'clock service. "It's important to me," she had said, as if that were enough. "Well Vic's important to me," he'd replied. Once upon a time, his life had seemed to have a divine plan. Now it felt somewhat directionless, or at least immune to any intervention.

Tommy liked the pastor well enough, but he did feel there was something inconsequential about Collins. And he could never entirely respect a man who befriended women without arousing even the slightest bit of jealousy from other men. Once he had invited the pastor to play golf, but he didn't own any clubs. Even Tommy's offer to lend a set hadn't gotten him out on the course. Probably some sports like golf were sins, although the pastor and Lucy never spoke of "sin". Things were "crass" or "indecent" or "wasteful" or "impolite". Never sinful. Still, he was glad those two had found each other. Lucy needed a vivid social life to thrive, but because of Tommy's odd position on base, she hadn't been invited into the Officers' Wives Club, or even the Corps of Engineers' Wives, although she had made friends, of a sort, with Mrs. Jackson, who lived to see her social life in the People section of *The Minaret*. Lucy's southern beauty always lent some glamour to the snapshots of her *fêtes*.

Surprisingly the fish was a hit. A bit too mushy for Tommy's taste, but Vic took seconds. Tommy winked across the table at Lucy, who finally seemed pleased. Happiness made her radiant, and he remembered then how easy it was to make her happy. A strand of hair had fallen onto her flushed cheek. She was laughing at something the pastor had said, her pink lips parted to reveal her perfect white teeth. She was still his mermaid. But their international life had given her more sophistication, he sensed. She was even learning French, which he found not only seductive, but practical, since somebody was going to have to figure out how to communicate with Fatima.

Unsurprisingly the talk turned to the morning's bombing. Its message was clear: after the exile of the Sultan and other Nationalist leaders, every foreigner was a target. The presumed architect of the bombing was a twenty-six-year-old former soccer player named Mohamed Zerktouni, who led an armed branch of Istiqlal called the Secret Organization. The bomb had been loaded with metal scraps, and now police were banging on doors throughout the city hunting for suspects. Some Christmas Eve.

Lucy frowned and stood to clear the dishes. "I'll bring

out dessert so the children can get off to bed. Mary, Jimmy, why don't you two give your mother a hand." The children obediently stood. "You can leave the glasses, kids," Tommy said, reaching for a bottle of white. "The men will have something more to drink. Wine, pastor?"

"I'm afraid I still have a sermon to preach tonight," the pastor said, smiling stiffly.

"Anyway," Tommy continued, refilling the other glasses, "I hope they get the cowards and string them up. I mean what sort of barbarians kill innocent women and children? But isn't the French administration still pretty hopeless, Vic? No offense, but remember those officers during the landings? They were too worried about themselves to organize breakfast, much less a war. Among those in power now, are there any men of character? What do you think?"

○

Victor swallowed some wine and shifted in his chair. "What do I think?" He was thinking that he was desperately bored, and already overcome by the prospect of the next hour. What did Tommy want from him? Without him Victor might never have become a pilot, but now he couldn't begin to locate the man. There was nothing at all to say about Tommy August. Really Victor couldn't think of anything. How did she stand it? "I don't think character has anything to do with it. I think France does what's best for France in the moment. The Moroccans do what's best for them in the moment. And the United States does what's best for it in the moment. Ideals get attached to history afterwards. Surely it's naïve to think otherwise."

"Come on, Vic," Tommy groaned. "You don't really go in for that Machiavellian stuff, do you?"

Pastor Collins nodded in agreement, the most assertive gesture the man had made all evening. "I agree, Tommy. If we don't strive to live according to our ideals, then what value can life have at all?"

"Life has no particular value in the first place," Victor replied. "Of course one can experience love, hatred, passion, devotion, generosity, and all the rest, but these also exist only in the moment, and to work towards such moments is to pervert them entirely. Men are comically incapable of plotting their own futures. So why should we imagine that nations of millions are any better at it? What France does, or how the Moroccans and Americans respond, will have little to do with peace or democracy or any other ideal, no matter what we call it in the end. Each will act according to its own needs with a limited perception of the present."

Lucy had appeared with the tart, flanked by the children. Tommy and Pastor Collins simultaneously cleared their throats, glancing away from Victor, who grabbed his glass and silently cursed himself for attempting to transform the moment into something he could bear. He regretted having accepted the invitation. He dreaded all dinner invitations, because dinner invitations always disappointed, and already he knew that nothing would occur to connect him more profoundly to these people. Time would pass, that was all. Wouldn't anything else be preferable – to punch one another, rip off one's clothes, scream?

"Vic has just been making some real interesting points," Tommy mumbled as Lucy set down the tray. "What do you think about France's role in Morocco, honey?"

"I think it's Christmas Eve," she said, smoothing her skirt over her hips before sitting, "and our guests might like to talk about more pleasant things."

They watched her cut the tart in silence, and once the plates were handed round, they immediately dug in. "Man oh man," Tommy groaned through a mouthful. "That is one special lemon tart, pastor. Nobody get me anything else for Christmas. I'm done."

The children giggled. "*Très bon*," Victor agreed. Lucy glanced across the table at him and smiled. "I love hearing proper French," she said. "My dream is to go to Paris someday."

"Lucy's been taking lessons. Say something for him, honey."

"Oh, I'd only embarrass myself." She blushed. "I can read a bit, but my pronunciation is simply appalling."

"I doubt it's as bad as you imagine," said Victor, who had resolved to become a blank for the rest of the evening. It was their Christmas. The game was now to reveal nothing. "In any case, a little accent is quite charming."

"Well *you* don't have any accent, Victor Tessier!" she cried.

"Not much," he said, "but I also lack charm."

"Try him, honey," Tommy interrupted. "Give him a little *voulez-vous. Où sont les toilettes?* The trick to French pronunciation is unconditionally surrendering before you reach the end of the word. Right, Vic? *Restauran....Boulevar.... Cha....* What's that one, Mary?"

"That's cat, daddy."

Victor made a smile. He had actually felt betrayed by this version of Tommy, he realized, which had annoyed him the most. If he was honest with himself, he had looked forward to receiving those postcards. But now it seemed ridiculous, even perverse, that Tommy had taken the trouble to hide them in envelopes. What a perfect metaphor for Tommy August, he thought, and then his smile became real. A postcard in an envelope.

"That's right, my little kitty cat," Tommy said, clapping his hands. "Now you and your brother go put on your peejays and brush your teeth, and then you can come back out and say goodnight to our guests. Bring your trumpet, Jimmy, so you can show Pastor Collins how you've improved."

After the children scampered off, Tommy explained to

Victor that the boy was talented and in two years would be eligible to join the Nouasseur Band. "You still listening to Stravinsky?"

"Occasionally."

"I miss the composing, and using that part of my brain, but I've had some ideas recently, and I'll get back to it someday. As you can see, though, at the moment I've got quite a few other responsibilities."

Victor nodded.

"You know Stravinsky's an American now, right?"

Then Jimmy came out and puffed through *Jingle Bells*. Victor couldn't look at the boy.

○

They sat in the living room beside the tree drinking another bottle of wine. Pastor Collins had left for his service. Victor wanted to leave too, but sensed it would require an enormous effort. He would have preferred to become furniture. A hat stand. A stool. Tommy was saying he rarely got the chance to fly anymore. Victor asked Lucy if he had ever taken her up.

"Oh no," she said, sitting pertly on the sofa's edge. "I hate flying. Heights give me vertigo. Just walking across a bridge, I go dizzy.... I guess I'm afraid I'll jump." She giggled. Had she caught him looking at her body? For at least half an hour he'd been imagining her tied naked to the couch with her ass in the air. "So how do you like your life in Casablanca?" he murmured.

"I really, really like it here."

"Really?" Tommy said. "That's the first I hear of it."

"Well you've never asked it quite that way before," she said, and after an uncomfortable pause she described her work with a couple of women's associations, which was giving her a chance to meet some remarkable Moroccans. One association was teaching practical skills to young local girls, while another run by the U.S. military was committed to eradicating malaria. They went into communities near American bases, including Nouasseur, showed the population how to dig drainage ditches, and convinced them to put little mosquitofish into the open wells. The mosquitofish ate mosquito larvae in the wells. "They're not the sort of fish you can eat," she said awkwardly, and Victor watched the story drain from her face.

"Now isn't that fascinating, Vic?" Tommy said.

God he hated that nickname.

○

"I'd better go wash up a bit and let you boys talk," Lucy said, rising from the couch to walk a little unsteadily towards the kitchen, looking down at her heels criss-crossing along the wall-to-wall carpet. As soon as her back was turned to the men, she felt a chill down her spine. She was deep in a well, submerged in dark water as mosquitofish nibbled at her skin. She turned back to the two men, head spinning. "I forgot to mention the snails. In summertime they just invade this place. They cover the grass, the telephone poles. They're white and can climb to the very tops, covering the poles completely. So we've also formed a group that's trying to do something about the snails."

○

Somewhat later, Tommy and Victor stood outside in the driveway, shivering in the cold. Their exhalations changed colors under the Pickerings' lights. "Hey, I almost forgot your leather coat," Tommy said. "I kept it, you know. I always knew I'd get a chance to return it to its rightful owner. And look at us now."

"Please keep it," Victor said, his face yellow, blue. "It's my Christmas gift."

"You sure?" Tommy had hardly ever worn the thing, and it wasn't likely to fit anymore.

"Keep it," Victor insisted.

"Okay then," Tommy said with a chuckle. "Thanks. Hey, let me show you the Caddy before you leave. How much do you know about American cars? This one's a 1953 Eldorado Series 62 Convertible Coupe. I would consider getting yourself one when that Peugeot finally kicks the bucket. No finer automobile in existence, in my opinion. I might even be able to get one shipped over for you through my connections. Not cheap, I'll warn you. This one was 7750 dollars, but worth every penny."

"Another time, Tommy. I need to leave. Thank you for inviting me tonight. I guess it was my first American Christmas."

"Heck, Vic," Tommy said hoarsely, suddenly overcome with emotion. "You know you're always welcome here. We'll do it again soon." Vic shook his hand, climbed into the Peugeot and puttered off through the neighborhood. Even after his taillights had disappeared, Tommy kept watching. He wished he hadn't mentioned the price of the Caddy. That had been in poor taste.

The children would be up at dawn, but he wasn't ready for bed. Some dissatisfaction still gnawed at him. At a certain point the night had turned. Vic's character had surprised him quite a bit. Was he really so cynical? Maybe Tommy had lost some of his own idealism, but he still believed that America, and France, stood for certain values, and he refused to believe that Vic didn't share at least some of those values. As the pastor had said, otherwise what was the point?

Had Lucy drunk too much? These days when he was with her, he sometimes felt as if he had become a statue. Sometimes he couldn't even speak. Shivering again, he decided on a quick stroll. The night was probably the coldest so far of the year.

At the church the service had let out, and the parking lot was empty. The lights still burned in the pastor's office, however, and Tommy wondered if God could really relieve a man of his loneliness. Heck, he didn't know what he'd do without Lucy. She was a good girl, still beautiful, and he was probably just worn out after a year of facing one deadline after another. It wasn't any way to live.

He walked until the runways appeared. Tonight the bombers were sleeping, the B-29 Superfortresses, the B-36 Convairs, and the swept-wing B-47 Stratojets, their bodies pale silver in the moonlight, like the surface of a lake. As he crossed the runways, he felt small and exposed. Quickly he moved past the refueling stations towards the western fence. Out past the fence was what the locals called Little America, a vast Moroccan slum of tin shacks and open trash fires subsisting mainly on cast-offs from the base. On weekends they set up a sprawling market, and people drove out from town to buy broken radios, mismatched Tupperware, faded blue jeans. Tommy put his fingers through the chain link and listened. They were drumming out there, intricate rhythms rolling into one another towards a pounding consonance, then coming unstuck. He imagined the arms of the drummers flying, bodies whirling into trances, and he thought of his two Spahis, so many years ago. Back then he'd felt he was someplace. Now he wasn't so sure.

Walking back across the runways, he heard laughter from the barracks of the enlisted men. Women's laughter. Probably some of the boys had scrounged up a couple of secretaries for a Christmas party. Holding up rosemary and calling it mistletoe. His eyes fell on the massive building still publicly called the ordnance dump, purpose-built by the Sandia Corporation out of Albuquerque. Tommy had been brought in to consult. The windows were fake, and all night spotlights blasted the walls, which were seventeen feet thick and surrounded by an electrified double fence topped with coiled barbed wire.

Inside the walls was a secret in a locked igloo known as the "bird cage".

That secret within the bird cage, he knew, was a nuclear bomb.

Laughter sounded from the barracks again. Or wild dogs in the distance. Tommy shivered.

3

MOROCCAN TERRORISM SHARPENS ITS METHODS

By Jacques Le Prevost

Rabat – Over the past few months, Moroccan terrorists have struck with increasing boldness, especially in Casablanca, where attacks occur almost daily.

Now the attacks are accompanied by anti-French propaganda which may be less violent, but is no less worrying: boycotts of French products, including tobacco, shoes, and sugar; intimidation of domestics employed by European families; and the banning of the djellabah for Moroccan women, which is intended to force them to wear the traditional haik. By thrashing their assailants, as it happened last Saturday in Casablanca, the women have at least shown that they do not approve of these instructions. Men, however, are more willingly obeying – in the cities and in the countryside, in private and in public – the order to abstain from smoking....

This is a showdown...and the Casablanca police claim to have insufficient men to monitor a city of over 550,000 Moroccans....[4]

○

The phone call came in to the commissariat that morning around ten. At noon Tony Méléro was expected at the Residence in Rabat.

Congos snickered as he hurried past. Tony had a

_____

4   *Le Monde* – 04/13/1954

girlfriend who wanted sex all the time. That was the story. A classy woman, a little older – experienced – real stylish, short skirts and silk stockings. Tony didn't like lying, but duty came first, and at least Congos and the Gypsy no longer wondered where he'd been.

Neither did anyone else in the department, but as Tony rushed out to his car, a major in Affaires Indigènes, of all places, pulled him aside. Somehow he knew Tony's name. Tony only knew the man by reputation. Supposedly Major Sartout had been stationed in both Algeria and Indochina. He was a big man, tall and distinguished, with a well-tended mustache. And now he wanted to discuss the weather, in detail, with Tony standing there dying to speed off towards Rabat. Yes, it really was an extraordinarily humid summer day, he agreed, attempting to appear relaxed. No, he hadn't made it to the exhibition match of Roches Noires, the European soccer team, but he heard they'd won, and the squad looked strong that year. The Peugeot 203? Extremely pleased with it, highly recommended. Finally the major let him go, and Tony drove off as calmly as possible. What an odd character. And what had that been about? Or was he being paranoid?

On the drive Tony contemplated the increasing challenges faced by the men of the Red Hand in the aftermath of the Central Market bombing. Untrained gangs of armed Frenchmen now roamed the streets, ignorant of the complexities. Informal militias like the Ultras, the Organization for Anti-Terrorist Defense, and even the La Gironde crew were identifying their own targets and speeding past Moroccan cafés spraying machine-guns. Tony shared their frustration, but unfortunately the attacks had also led many Nationalist leaders to request French police protection, and so now Tony and his Action Unit often needed to get past their own cops to strike a target. Sometimes Tony even knew the guys. That's how ridiculous it had gotten. People needed to calm down and let the professionals do their jobs.

Two hours later he sat in the office of Captain Fillette, who confirmed that the whereabouts of Mohamed Zerktouni, the bombing's mastermind, were still unknown. Fortunately intelligence gathered from the scenes of recent actions had provided a new list of prime targets, mostly businessmen and lawyers associated in various ways with the Nationalists. Some actions in this new phase would need to be carried out in native quarters, where any foreigner was suspect, and so the risks would be compounded. At the top of Fillette's list, in fact, was a medina-dwelling factory supervisor who had attempted to unionize employees. Was Tony up for the challenge?

Tony fingered his cufflinks and looked up at the captain, in whom he now felt he could confide. His service had been exemplary, and their interactions had become more relaxed. Not exactly casual, perhaps, but founded on a mutual respect. Still, Tony resorted to the old trick as he began to speak. He fixed his eyes on an invisible spot on the captain's forehead, a spot he had targeted so often that it was now practically visible. "I would like your permission to recruit my own team for this one, captain. They know the medina, and they speak fluent Arabic. They will approach the target without drawing attention to themselves, in a way that Rémy and the others, at least on this occasion, cannot. These are childhood friends, captain, and I trust them with my life. They are good men, but have lacked guidance."

For a long moment the captain remained silent. He stared at Tony until the invisible spot on his forehead wavered, then vanished. "You will have to answer for them," he finally said. Tony nodded sharply.

"And why will they help?" the captain continued. "We can offer them nothing."

"Because they love Morocco," Tony said huskily. God, didn't they all. More than anything.

"Fine," the captain replied, snatching up a single page from his desk, already onto next business. "You have carte blanche to form your own team, but I'll want their names, and you and I will meet again here in exactly two weeks."

That evening Tony sat on the rocks near Ain Diab watching the sunset with Congos and the Gypsy. They drank warm wine from a bottle while eating slices of the season's last watermelon. The bottle was their second. Upon returning from Rabat, Tony had found his friends leaving the station, and still exultant at the confidence Captain Fillette had placed in him, he had proposed the wine.

They were good guys, Congos and the Gypsy. As Tony watched the fishing boats motoring towards port at the end of a long day, he thought back on all the times they had shared. Casablanca had been such an extraordinary place. Kids playing soccer in the streets, hawkers selling their wares, each with his own distinct call, men with ancient faces sitting in tattered djellabahs beneath the shade of plane trees, the singing, the sun, the fish tajines at the little market restaurants. This was the real Morocco, and by God they would keep fighting for it.

"On Christmas!" Tony said through gritted teeth. "Christmas!"

Congos grunted and swigged more wine. Later that night with Avival they were planning to feed some little birds, if Tony wanted to join. Tony looked at him blankly, so Congos angled out the mouth of the bottle and pivoted it around making a machine-gun sound: chun-chun-chun-chun-chun. *Feed some little birds.* Tony shook his head and straightened his posture. "We have to keep our heads, *mes amis*. Now more than ever. We can't stoop to their level. What is required is *justice*, not revenge. So I need you to listen very carefully."

They listened for hours, until Tony was unquestionably their leader. He hoped he wasn't making a mistake, but even when they had been boys, he had known his time for leadership would come, and it was his responsibility now to instill in his friends the discipline of the Red Hand.

Meanwhile the sun dipped into the ocean, scattering

flecks of firelight across the waves. A last fishing boat, its blue hull sharply curved up into the pale horizon, puttered around the lighthouse as the men on deck dragged together heavy nets to heave ashore. The surging water tossed translucent seaweed over the rocks, where it slivered down into their dark crevices. A lone seagull circled overhead as a muezzin climbed the spiraling staircase of the nearest white mosque. Everywhere was astonishing beauty, entirely unaware of the three young men plotting glories on the rocks.

4

Three weeks ago in this column we denounced with a heavy heart the rot that eats at this country. Since then we have had two attacks on mosques, multiple daily bombings in the major centers, acts of terrorism of the sort we were told would soon stop.[5]

Jacques sat in his office at the Lesieur factory in Roches Noires. Night had fallen, and through the walls the machinery had shuddered to a stop. He wrote by the light of a single desk lamp. Everyone had gone home except his secretary, whose voice he occasionally heard through the door, murmuring into the telephone. Had she finally found a boyfriend, or was it her horrid mother again?

For several weeks he had been in the habit of writing at the office, often staying late. At home the view had become distracting. From up so high, the city sometimes seemed as distant as a postcard, a memento of a place he'd once lived. The total silence was also distracting, and he would play loud opera from the stereo until very late, then wander off alone to bed. From his desk at the factory, however, he could feel the heartbeat of his machinery, hear the whispers of activity, and sense the necessity of his existence at its center.

Simon had come and gone again. He had come for a night and had stubbornly insisted on cooking dinner. Inedible omelets and cheap wine, Jacques thought with a smile. The boy could be wonderfully tender, but he was lost. Often Jacques dreamed of spending a whole month together up at the Bouregreg villa. They could ride horses and swim rivers and nap in the sun. But there would be no time for that at the moment. Jacques's political role had become too important. Casablanca's streets were now like a nervous system threading out from his fingers. He knew everything

---

5   *Le Monde* – 03/12/1954

the city felt, and France must be spurred to feel the same.

o

Around noon, two Frenchmen in a black jeep had pulled up to the little grocery across Rue Bonaparte. After climbing down from the jeep, they had crossed the street to the garden door of La Frigoulette, the modest house where the Chaouis had been living. With the children older, the family had needed more space, and the neighborhood was quiet and suburban, away from the city's dangerous center. But now two suspicious men knocked at the garden door. They were probably cops, although they were not in uniform, and ununiformed cops had become Moroccans' worst nightmare.

Nobody answered the knock. The men pushed open the unlocked door and slipped into the garden. Soon one appeared just over the wall atop the three steps to the front door. He knocked for a long minute or two, loudly, and then the men slipped back out onto the street, both smoking cigarettes. The grocer pulled down his shutter, but before he could escape, they approached and asked when Chaoui would be home. The grocer mumbled that he hadn't seen the family for a while. The Frenchmen glared for a long moment, then climbed back into the jeep and drove off. This was the story the grocer had told Abdelwahed when he arrived home later that afternoon. Neighbors gathered, talking animatedly on the sidewalk. Others had also observed the incident.

Abdelwahed was tired. Work had been busy, and they had been trying to live as normally as possible. The house had provided them greater anonymity, and Zina and the children, especially, had been happy there. He wanted to believe that this was just another tiresome threat. He really wanted to take a nap before Zina and the children returned from their aunt's.

But the family had been threatened enough times for him to suspect that this was something more dangerous. The black jeep was concerning. That was a police vehicle, and from the grocer's description, the two men had known what they were doing. After some further discussion, the neighbors decided to band together and move the Chaouis out of their house.

They fetched boxes and blankets. The grocer loaned a wheeled cart. One neighbor owned an empty garage at the end of the street. The family's belongings could be stored there for the time being. A close search of the garden found nothing suspicious, but every trip into the house was fraught with tension. They moved furtively, like thieves, expecting at every moment to be split apart by a bomb. They carried chairs, tables, boxes of clothing and books. The beds came out, and most of the dishes. There were blankets tied full of shoes and the family tea set. At some point Monsieur Girardin came along and saw the commotion. He owned the Hotel Bonaparte down the street and offered the family rooms for the night.

The others eventually arrived. Horrified, Zina demanded an explanation while the children watched wide-eyed. "We have to move," Abdelwahed said. "At least for tonight."

Touria didn't ask questions. She already knew she was the answer.

○

The virulence of the resistance after the Sultan's exile had been surprising. Jacques had expected greater leadership from Nationalist figures like al-Fassi and Balafrej, but they had been ineffective, and ultimately lacked ideas. Now they were exiled too. Perhaps that had been a mistake, but at the same time those men had enabled the armed resistance, which was now orchestrating violent attacks almost daily, many of them,

Jacques suspected, backed by communist allies. Moderates had left the debate. There were no longer peaceful Arab voices to remind the people that France's role in Morocco was inevitable, and should continue to be mutually beneficial. This was the only way forward.

Unfortunately the most positive symbol of Morocco's extraordinary relationship with France was still only a girl: Touria Chaoui, the aviatrix trained by the French at Tit Mellil. Jacques had followed her story with great interest, as had Simon, who especially admired her style, but besides the handicap of her sex, she was still too young to be a spokeswoman, and the Nationalists had already rashly pushed her as a symbol of independence, rather than as one of mutual cooperation, an ideal she so clearly embodied. New ideas were required.

A line darted into his head, and he put pen to paper. "Revolutionary situations require revolutionary measures." Yes, that was effective. For several minutes afterwards, however, no further words came. He slapped his cheeks, took several deep breaths, and called out to his secretary, who pattered to the door. He needed coffee.

"Will that be all?"

"Just coffee," he snapped. He knew she disliked staying late, and recently he'd asked her to do it often, but these were no ordinary times. This was a war, of sorts, and Morocco now depended on Jacques Lemaigre-Dubreuil perhaps more than any other man.

The coffee arrived, and he winced at the first sip. Even coffee stretched her competence. Was he all alone? He snatched up the pen:

In recent months Istiqlal has gained the upper hand... proving to Moroccans that the former Sultan's departure has in no way diminished the power of the independence movement. Instead, it has only strengthened the movement's determination, giving birth to terrorism. Despite police crackdowns, in people's minds terrorism has gradually replaced the notion of force represented by the State. This can only be remedied by the application of force on multiple fronts, which should remind a majority of Moroccans that a better-armed State always calls the shots.[6]

○

Around midnight the neighborhood was startled from sleep by a blast that shook bedposts and the heavy covers of manholes down the street. Lying next to Zina at the Hotel Bonaparte, Abdelwahed had not been sleeping, and he was dressed by the time Monsieur Girardin knocked at their door. Without a word he followed the Frenchman into the night, Zina close behind him, already weeping. Together they took the long walk down Rue Bonaparte, coughing through clouds of dust. The same neighbors who had helped them empty the house that afternoon were already gathering, their features indistinguishable in the haze. A woman wailed. Men angrily muttered. As the dust settled, Abdelwahed and Zina watched anxiously for their house to be revealed. It never was, although they waited and waited. Nothing remained of anything. Their house was now an empty lot.

And so the next plan was quickly set into motion. Touria, still sixteen, drove the family through the night to Madrid, where Istiqlal had arranged a safe house for six months. Abdelwahed didn't have a license. He'd always said he was too jumpy behind the wheel. Salah sat in the backseat watching the nape of his sister's thin neck. For months she had been having nightmares in the room they

---

6   *Le Monde* – 03/12/1954

shared, waking him with her screams.

She understood now. It couldn't be clearer. People wanted her dead. All she could do was drive and drive, locked in on a low straight line as stars swarmed overhead. She couldn't fall apart.

5

The door to the clinic burst open, and two men with stocking caps pulled down over their faces staggered in carrying another with a gunshot wound in his thigh. Without a word, Saadia Taibi flicked on the light and led them into the examination room, where they dropped him on the table. The wounded man's mouth had been stuffed with a rag so that he wouldn't scream. She patted him once on the cheek, then hastily plucked out the rag with two fingers. She wasn't especially pretty, she knew, and couldn't afford to lose a finger. The man's jaw locked shut, and he groaned.

Dr. Ouarzazi then came into the room, glanced down at the table, and told Saadia to cut off the man's pants. This one wasn't even wearing underwear. The other two men glanced over, but she didn't care. She had seen it all before. Setting down the razor, she peeled the pants clear of the wound. Then she went over to the metal table for the hydrogen peroxide. That was the next step.

Nineteen years old, Saadia had been nursing for Dr. Ouarzazi for five months and six days. The doctor had never said what they were doing, but she knew, and he had trusted her from the beginning. An ordinary clinic during the daytime, at night it catered to members of resistance organizations who came to have their bullets removed. Usually they were hit in arms and legs, often the legs. The French gangs mostly used machine guns and fired wildly. Sometimes, though, one would come in with a hole in his chest that gurgled like a baby's mouth. They had saved a few. Dr. Ouarzazi was one of the best surgeons in the city. The ones they couldn't save were bundled up to be taken back to their mothers. One night a man had even come in with his eyeball hanging out. He had been beaten by policemen, and Saadia hadn't let it bother her, but sometimes in her dreams she still saw the eyeball hanging by a bloody cord. If the clinic was ever discovered, they would all go to prison, but they never spoke of that.

Saadia had no formal training and had initially struggled to keep up with the doctor, but she had learned quickly and now could even understand most of the words he used, many of them in French. *Aorta. Suture. Tourniquet. Hydrogen Peroxide.* Nothing in her life had made her prouder. "You're an intelligent woman," the doctor had said one night. "I can only imagine what you would have done if you'd gone to school. You could have been someone."

But school had never been an option. She had been married off to her first husband at age ten. From day one he had beaten her because she liked to sleep in. At twelve she had given him a son, and then the baby died. They got divorced. She found a new husband. She rode a bicycle and sewed her own dresses so that she could have modern clothes. She cut her hair short, had big teeth that sometimes got in the way of her words, and was four-feet-seven inches tall, but with strong legs. That was from the bicycle. The new husband had repudiated her at seventeen. She was pregnant, and in the hospital she had met a young woman studying medicine. The woman carried this big book around with her everywhere. Saadia didn't know it was a book about medicine, because she couldn't read, but that's what the woman said. Saadia couldn't believe her ears. Here was this woman studying medicine. Then after her daughter was born, Saadia gave the baby to her husband and found Dr. Ouarzazi. He had heard her story from the woman with the medical book and needed someone.

This was around the time they had taken the Sultan away, and Saadia had listened to everyone until she was angry too. Her father had always talked about the Jews who took Palestine, even sometimes when he beat her. In Tunisia, the French sacrificed Muslim children instead of sheep for Aïd. These were things that were happening. They said police had come to the house of Mina the washerwoman, who lived down the street, to take her daughters away. Then they had thrown the children in the ocean. But you were a fool if you believed everything Mina said.

Now the resistance was stronger, and the nights were busier and bloodier, but the more men Saadia and the doctor patched up, the stronger the resistance became. At dawn she never wanted to leave the clinic. She loved being with the doctor, the surprises in the night, the pleasure of performing new skills, and the company of men who treated her respectfully, not as their daughter or wife. She was proud, and wanted to do more, but she didn't dare tell anyone, so for the moment she had decided to just keep going like this.

6

Opera blasted from the speakers, *La Traviata*. Simon had not appeared for lunch as promised, and Jacques was dejected. He had actually shaved twice that morning and felt like a perfumed fool. He couldn't write. He'd poured himself another cognac and stared south through the curving windows of the seventeenth floor. He didn't want to fight anymore. Why couldn't they be happy together? He thought of Simon's long fingers, the scruffy hair at the back of his neck, the way even a few notes of music could make him cry. Increasingly it seemed that nothing was more important than these specific details, and they consumed Jacques's thoughts, invoking other details. A trace of dried sea foam on his shoulder, his utter concentration when he tied his shoelaces.

Had Jacques been too unforgiving, too stern? If the boy felt trapped, he could have his freedom. He could have whatever he wanted. If that made Jacques a fool, then perhaps he could accept being a fool. Perhaps everything was worth seeing Simon tie his shoelaces. Out the windows starlings were massing. Then a murmuration formed and moved through the blue sky like a thumbprint. In that moment Jacques longed to shed the weight of his existence and move among them.

The words of his last editorial for *Le Monde* had echoed for days in his mind. The piece had been the most difficult he had written for the paper, revised so many times that it was committed to memory.

Every day the situation grows more serious. We understand the difficulties facing the government. Obviously it cannot yield to the dictates of the mob, but here, as everywhere, we must seek the cause of evil, examine our responsibilities, and if required, correct our mistakes.

Can we continue to pretend that this violence is

36

caused by some foreign influence? Can we continue observing effects without acting upon their causes? Can we still imagine that in ignoring the real cause of the current riots, we will somehow stop them? Or, even worse, do we think that brute force can solve a problem that for months we have refused even to discuss?

Ignoring a difficult question does not answer it.[7]

For the first time since the increase in violence, Lemaigre-Dubreuil had begun to doubt his approach. The politicians in Paris had always been shortsighted, and he had sought to guide them down a clearer path, but now he questioned the whole notion of the protectorate. This last editorial, especially, had raised eyebrows. Perhaps the Sultan should not have been exiled. Those words had been difficult to write, but if he was not brave enough to speak the truth, then who would?

Should he ask Ahmed to buy champagne? Simon loved champagne, because it fizzed like Coca-Cola.

Whether our official representatives like it or not, the revolution brewing in Morocco began with the question of the Sultanate....Ever since the exile dictated by France in August 1953...the issue of the throne has increased unrest with every passing day. Why can't we realize that our policy benefits the enemies of France, who seek disorder in Morocco for strategic reasons, as well as those who would internationalize Morocco for purely financial reasons?

It occurred to him that he hadn't seen Felton in over a year. Perhaps they should meet to discuss the Americans' increasingly aggressive intentions. He knew that Simon hadn't liked Felton. Perhaps he'd viewed him as competition, which was laughable.

7   *Le Monde* – 08/09/1954

Isn't it time to grant Moroccans the sovereignty that we have long promised? It is up to them to choose their ruler – a willing ruler, under conditions guaranteeing full independence.

The role of France will be to ensure, through law enforcement, the free expression of different opinions, replacing the current political situation with an interim provisional government.

The era of feudalism is over. The first duty of a people entitled to freedom is to debate all ideas freely, without killing one another.

The piece had apparently outraged the Resident General. They said Jacques had become a liberal. But his words still sounded clearer and truer to him than anything he'd written in years. Surely independence was now the only option.

There was a noise at the entrance. He rushed over to the stereo and lowered the volume. "Is that you?"

It was.

CIGARETTES
1953–54

Lunch was usually a circle of bread and a half tin of sardines. Sometimes a hard-boiled egg. Saadia ate quickly on a bench in Place Lyautey, then sat studying passing faces, wondering if their secrets were as big as hers. One day a stooped waterseller smoking a cigarette came along jangling his metal cups. She closed her eyes to listen to the sound, but immediately heard a shout and looked again. A crazy young man in an oversized suit swooped up, flipped open a pocket knife, and cut the cigarette from the waterseller's face. The crazy man's bloodshot eyes gleamed, and he ran off with another shout, showing yellow teeth. The waterseller spit out the severed butt and shuffled off with his metal cups jangling. Saadia sat for a while longer, her heart pounding as she felt her big teeth with her tongue.

At the clinic that afternoon, she couldn't stop thinking about the crazy young man in the oversized suit. Why had he done that to the waterseller? What was his secret?

That evening she went back out to Place Lyautey. Again on her bench she admitted to herself that she had come looking for the crazy young man. Her new husband was better than the other two, but he was Algerian and did business in Oran, so she rarely saw him. Which was good, because she never could have explained why she worked at the clinic at night. But she hadn't been with a man in months and felt the itch. She wasn't ashamed to admit it. That's the way it was. Okay?

Maybe it wasn't even the man with the knife she wanted to find. But walking past the big Nazarene church that looked like a Nazarene wedding cake, the church that was supposed to be the sacred heart of Jesus, she spotted him strutting towards Rue Curie. Most Moroccan men no longer dared draw attention to themselves, but he did. Maybe the knife in his pocket gave him that swagger. A little bald spot showed on his head. She hadn't noticed it at noon. Maybe it made him look more distinguished. Was he looking for another smoker now? She kept her distance as she followed him along Rue Curie.

He stopped to wave at something. Maybe he'd seen a friend, or maybe he really wasn't too right inside the head. She stopped too, and when he set off walking again, she followed. He bent down to tie his shoelace, and she wondered if he'd seen her through his legs. She pretended to look for something in her purse. She felt like one of those detectives from the movies, except usually they smoked cigarettes. She challenged herself to memorize every detail about the man. His head bobbed back and forth as he walked, like he was hearing music. His elbows stuck out, and he was bow-legged, although his trousers were so wide you hardly noticed it. But she did. He wore a big watch on his right wrist. He probably had a job.

She studied him so hard that she stumbled on a cobblestone, and then he stopped too. He couldn't have noticed. Once he set off walking, she tested this by stopping again. He stopped. So he had spotted her, or she was going crazy. Heart thumping in her chest, she ran up to the man. "Please," she gasped. "I want to talk with you."

His face was swollen and serious. "What do you want?"

"I saw you in the park today. I didn't dare talk to you then, but then I decided to find you."

His bloodshot eyes no longer gleamed. "It wasn't me."

She made two fists. "No, it was you."

"Okay," he said. "So where are we going now?"

She couldn't think of a place. The Cinema Vox was up the street. "I was going to a movie."

"Then go into the theater," he said, "and come out the back exit."

She nodded and set off walking. Her first thought was

that she really was the crazy one. Her second thought was that she would have to spend her last francs to get into the cinema and out the back. But she did it.

The cashier said the movie was almost over. "Give me the ticket," Saadia said, and in the theater she moved down the aisle, the light of a kiss flickering in her eyes. She didn't stop to watch. None of this was real.

In the alleyway by the exit, he was leaning against a dirty wall with his legs casually crossed. She strode over to him and asked a dozen questions. Who are you? Why did you cut away that man's cigarette today? Is that some kind of fancy watch?

Smokers were traitors, the man explained, smiling crookedly. They defied the Nationalist boycott of the Régie des Tabacs, the French National Tobacco Company. And the waterseller had been lucky. Sometimes he split a lip or took off a piece of a nose. He didn't care. Maybe sometimes his aim accidentally wasn't all that good. She nodded. This made sense, and although the name of the fancy watch was something in English she didn't understand, she nodded at that too. The man didn't mention his name, but then neither did she.

"So what do you want to do now?" he asked. His eyes no longer wanted to hurt her, she didn't think.

"I want to help my country," she cried. "I can't stop thinking about it!"

"Okay. Tomorrow night we meet here at ten o'clock. I'll take you someplace."

He left her then, snapping his body off the wall to swagger down the alleyway. That night she couldn't sleep. Her nightgown kept getting twisted up around her strong, short legs. The next day at the clinic she unspooled half a roll of bandaging before realizing what she'd done. Thankfully no one noticed, and she swiftly rolled it back up, crooked at the edges. She was a fool for even considering meeting this man tonight. With the doctor she was already doing her part for the resistance. This man seemed more dangerous, and she dreaded what he might ask of her. Which was why she needed to go.

The alleyway was deserted like the night before. The hour was the same, the movie too. She knew that inside two big faces had just kissed. He was waiting for her, wearing a different suit and the watch with the funny name. He nodded and set off walking. "At least tell me your name," she cried. "I'm Saadia!" But he didn't answer. She huffed and hurried after him.

They walked and walked and walked, all the way down the length of Route de Medouina until they approached Bousbir, where the prostitutes had been. Now everybody probably thought she was the prostitute, walking with this strange man whose name she didn't know. At first she had tried to make conversation, but she had given up on that. He hadn't said a word, and she was furious now.

Eventually they came to a garage filled with buses and broken trucks. The man walked into the garage and led her down a narrow gap between two buses. She concentrated on breathing as slowly as possible, which is what she told wounded men at the clinic to do when the doctor dug for bullets in them with his forceps.

The man opened a door at the back of the garage, and they walked into a small office. A bare bulb overhead illuminated walls of shelves filled with stacked papers and auto parts. Two other men stood beside a desk, along with a young woman wearing fancy earrings and carrying a purse. Saadia sneered. The woman looked down at the floor. What was that one doing here?

The men whispered to each other. Only her man wore a suit. The others wore djellabahs and looked exhausted and unclean. Saadia just stayed standing there. After a while her man announced in a hoarse voice that the women would now take the sacred oath. "Where is the Koran?" he asked the others. It wasn't on the desk, so they slid open the drawers. In the bottom drawer one located a mechanical guide to Ford trucks, but still they couldn't find the Koran. Saadia's man was furious. They had done sacred oaths only a few days before. Where had they put the Koran? One suggested they do the oath with the mechanical guide to Ford trucks. Surely any book could work, at least in special circumstances.

Her man grabbed that man by the throat and pushed him up into some shelving. His face went red, and his arms flapped in the air. Saadia thought he would die. But then her man released the other and stormed back out into the garage, where she heard him opening truck doors and slamming them shut. Eventually he returned with one of those pocket Korans long-distance drivers hung from their rearview mirrors for good luck. Her man held it in his hand, and when she covered it with her own to repeat the sacred oath, you couldn't tell there was a book between them.

"Repeat after me." His voice was scratchy like the cheap wool blankets she had slept under at her first husband's house. "This a promise to Allah and the nation" – she repeated it – "that I will be true to Allah and my people."

"And my Sultan," another interrupted, and she repeated it.

"And that I will be true in all things. I will sacrifice myself. I will sacrifice my father and my mother if I find that they have strayed from the path." She repeated it. Gladly. Her father was dead, her mother hated her.

"And I will keep the secret of what I have seen here tonight or else suffer really terrible punishments," added the third man. She repeated it.

"And I won't ask too many questions," said her man, and she repeated it.

"This has been your sacred oath," he announced, and she nodded solemnly before lifting her hand from the pocket Koran.

Was she different now? She closed her eyes and felt blood rushing through her veins, from the tips of her fingers to her toes. Yes. She was. The sacred oath had worked its magic, and she was a resistant in her own right now, not just an assistant. Now she could fight.

Then they gave the oath to the other woman, which Saadia resented. Women who wore fancy earrings and carried purses shouldn't be resistants.

Afterwards she followed her man out of the garage. "So now can you tell me your name?"

"Ahmed Touil," he said with a grin, and in the faint light his eyes were as yellow as his teeth.

She thought he might want to talk some more, but he told her that they would contact her when they were ready. She was disappointed, but the next evening Ahmed met her coming out of the doctor's clinic. They had decided the sacred oath hadn't been properly administered, he said, so she needed to come back to the garage and take it again.

But if the sacred oath hadn't been properly administered, then how did that explain her happiness over the past twenty-four hours? That day at the clinic she had worked with boundless energy, not even stopping for lunch. If that hadn't been real, then she couldn't imagine how she would feel when it was.

This time they did it with a full-sized Koran in front of a man Ahmed called the president. Afterwards they explained that the resistance was organized into three-person cells. Ahmed would be in her cell, but she would have no information about other cells, so that if one cell was compromised, the infection would not spread to the rest of the body. She nodded. Dr. Ouarzazi, for example, would have no knowledge of her role, and she needed to keep that secret at all costs. The thought of another secret excited her tremendously, and that's when she knew the second sacred oath had been the good one.

VOX
AGENT

2

Franklin Felton sat at the radar console at the American AC&W station at Saddle Rock. It was two in the morning, and he was alone. The circular green screen was blank. No sound had been transmitted through his headphones since he had come on duty at midnight. Nothing to report. Nothingness to report.

But at some point – in the next hour, or years from now – there would be something to report, and that moment, whenever it came, would be ecstasy. The key was to be ready for the moment. Because someday the Russians would come, a deadly dark green blip on a lighter green screen. Only this eventuality could make any sense. Otherwise the green circle was just a blank bull's eye with Franklin perpetually at its center. Why *bull's eye*? Were a bull's eyes especially round? Rounder than a human's? A donkey's?

Casablanca had seen him grow old. Perhaps. In any case, it was too late to start again. The fact of those years must be justified by the present, which was still Casablanca. For a long time his father had expected him to return to America before it was too late to *become something* – to leap from his platform onto the train just before the doors shut. But even his father had abandoned that hope. It was too late. The train had left the station, carrying his former classmates from Groton and Columbia towards their destinations. This was what was known as success. Good for them. Franklin had chosen freedom. What he hadn't expected was that freedom didn't always feel like unbridled joy. Sometimes it felt more like abject failure. Or was it even freedom at all?

Now he voluntarily took the night shift so that he could smoke kif until the empty green circle became pregnant with possibilities. Any second now, any second he would see the deadly blip. Years ago when he'd dreamed of being a poet delivering missives from darkest Africa, he had believed in the soul, but now this was his soul: a blipless green screen at a radar station someplace south of Casablanca. Years ago he had also believed in love, and had walked arm-in-arm with the one and only Josephine Baker through the North African night. That love had been meant to transform his life into one of historical significance, but it had not, and that experience had been followed by a series of working-class Moroccan girlfriends, exotic in theory but never especially satisfying. His most notable victory was that he had assimilated, living in a humble flat in the Moroccan quarter of Habbous, wearing a djellabah out in the neighborhood, eating couscous on Fridays, cooked by the maid. He had become fluent in two Arabic dialects, Darija and Fusha, in which he had read the Koran. Now if asked by a Moroccan, he would say he was Moslem, and although he couldn't be seen attending mosque, he prayed on his own, briefly, five times a day, most days, when it didn't make him too sad. Sometimes, however, brushing off beggars on his filthy street, or discovering that the maid had pilfered yet another shirt, he had a vague notion that he had never much liked any Moroccan.

A mouse darted across the cement floor beneath the machinery. The continuous construction out at Nouasseur had displaced all sorts of critters, and mice especially were a problem here. They could gnaw through anything and had shown a taste for electrical systems. Franklin didn't mind them so much. They reminded him of Joe, the way she'd let them crawl all over her, the time she'd given one to Zubov, which he'd never mentioned again. What had they called it? Flaky? Franky? Maybe the Russian had fed it to one of his famous slender-billed curlews. Franklin still often wondered about the slender-billed curlew, although he was no longer a birder. He hadn't noticed birds in years. Birds never even came up on the radar, which had surprised them at first. The technicians had suspected a malfunction, at one point even blaming the mice. But after consulting with radar operators at bases all over the world, Felton had discovered that the phenomenon was common. Radar stations could scramble birds' navigational systems, throwing off migratory patterns, and whole flocks had been known to vanish into thin air. They were somewhere, but you would never find them.

After sunrise Felton's replacement called in sick, so he willingly took the morning shift. Nothing awaited him at home. The only inconvenience was that once the Air Force men from the 736 AC&W squadron arrived, he would have to smoke his kif outside behind the trash bins on break. Other than that, the green circle was always the same, although blips might appear at any instant. Something was out there. He was certain of it. The Soviets never slept, and so neither would he. Most people had no idea what an enemy they faced.

Before leaving the station that afternoon, his head fuzzy, he used the phone to call Zubov. He wasn't entirely sure what he was doing, but the act made him feel smug, then annoyed that he still remembered the Russian's home phone number. Of course Arkady picked up. After lunch he always returned for a nap to the little room he rented down the block from the Transatlantique. Arkady never changed. He would be napping according to schedule.

Franklin proposed a drink, trying his best to sound friendly. Of course Zubov never drank alcohol, and of course he pedantically explained this for the nine thousandth time, but nonetheless he would be eager to see his old friend. It had been years.

"Wonderful," Felton said. "Let's say the bar of the Transatlantique in an hour."

On the road into town he passed an immaculate black Cadillac Eldorado convertible. Didn't it belong to that American contractor out at Nouasseur? What was he called? The name of a month. May? August? Even though the man was no longer military, he still dripped with self-satisfaction, always so eager to please. A lot of the AC&W guys were like that too. None of them could accept that these days it was men like Felton who occupied the front lines. Wars would now be fought from behind radar screens and radio control panels. Spycraft was outdated. These days the men you met on the ground were hardly ever of any use. The ones who mattered were the ones you never saw.

In town he parked down the block from the Transatlantique, across from Zubov's building. With no spots available on the street, he bumped up onto the sidewalk. The Moroccans did it in Habbous, so he could too. The sun had faded his red Pontiac Torpedo to a fleshy pink, and rust ate at its edges. Once he had been so proud of that car, and he thought back to those first nights with King and Reid, driving like outlaws to the next champagne party. He cut the engine, pulled a joint from his shirt pocket, and lit it while keeping an eye on the rearview mirror. Zubov would be exactly on time, and Felton pitied this too, snickering when the Russian promptly appeared and marched up the sidewalk. Arkady hadn't changed a bit. Even the uniform. Perhaps another medal or two, but still impeccably pressed. Zubov probably pressed his twenty-franc bills. That was funny. Franklin looked down at his own shirt and pants. Toothpaste had spattered his shirt, and dirt lined the creases of his khaki pants. So maybe he'd slipped a bit, but given the state of the world, did it matter? His mouth was dry, and he tried to lick his lips, but his tongue was like a roasted slug. He attempted to move it up and down, left or right. Where did it belong? He was thinking too much, but what a funny thing a tongue was.

Zubov had entered the hotel. Felton stubbed out the joint in the ashtray and burst from the car, reeling in the sunshine as if it had struck him on the head. Once his eyes adjusted, he crossed the street to the entrance of Zubov's building, not even slightly nervous. He had done this so many times in his mind that he was practically bored. To remind himself that he was alive, he bit his tongue.

The name was on the mailbox. He took the stairs to the third floor, two by two, turning dizzily at each landing. In the elevator he would have risked meeting someone. The hallway was shabby, and 3B was marked on the door. Could he still pick a lock? We would find out. Not that pocket. That was the miniature camera. Spycraft, actually. That was funny. From the other pocket he took a small flathead screwdriver and a bit of wire, which he inserted into the keyhole and wiggled. These old buildings tended to have simple single-lever locks, and he'd picked a few before the war. Now, however, his wire didn't recognize anything, much less a lever to notch aside. Annoying. But did it matter? He removed the wire, took two steps backwards and kicked the door until it splintered open. Zubov wouldn't be coming back anytime soon, not as long as he expected Felton to show up at the Transatlantique. Felton shut the door behind him, more or less.

The room was even more spartan than he had expected, like a Groton dorm room, but set in Soviet Russia. Bars of light raked through closed shutters, striping yellowing wallpaper, a small wardrobe, a desk, a chair, and a single bed. That single bed was possibly the saddest thing Franklin had ever seen. Arkady really believed: discipline, fastidiousness, self-abnegation. The communist religion, although all the prophets were dead, even Stalin if you wanted to assume he'd ever had the faith. Now the church was run by corrupt priests. Only sheep could still believe in such a religion. But you underestimated sheep at your peril. Look at the Rosenbergs. Most ordinary Americans could never have conceived of such treason. Or look at the Sultan of Morocco. Ever since he had formed alliances with local communists taking orders from Moscow, his position had become untenable. The threat was real, and Felton often thought back to his conversations with Lemaigre-Dubreuil. Crusoe, the old goat, was everywhere these days, and had certainly been right about the communists. They threatened our whole way of life.

Glancing around the room again, he walked over to the lone frame on the wall. The image appeared to be a religious icon of sorts, but obviously it couldn't be that. As he came closer, he saw that it was a drawing, primitive, perhaps of an angel, although the creature had several sets of wings, so maybe it was more of a dragonfly. It was only a child's drawing, but he felt an intense revulsion to it and turned away from the wall. It didn't fit with everything else he knew about Arkady. But he was wasting time. He had come looking for intelligence.

In the desk drawer were stacked at least a dozen of Zubov's little black notebooks. Felton flipped through them, moving back in time. The script was Cyrillic, but he could read the dates, and only in 1948, 1947, did sketches of birds start appearing. Zubov had apparently given up the hobby too, which was somewhat surprising. Or maybe after 1947 he had kept his birding notes separate. Whatever the case, the sketches were remarkably accomplished. He had even painstakingly shaded them with colored pencils. Then 1942, the critical notebook. Slowly he flipped through towards the end of the year, September, October, the Americans still not fully committed to the war in Europe, Operation Torch a secret, Franklin Felton a young man. And in October he found it. The slender-billed curlew, unmistakably. He slumped down into the desk chair. Could Arkady have copied it from another guide? Of course he could have, but what would have been the point of that in one's own private diaries? Franklin took the miniature camera from his pocket, held it over the page, and clicked the shutter, sick with shame.

Afterwards he stood for a long moment in the middle of the room. He saw nothing. His mind was a blank. Then, finally, he understood that he had failed, and that it was time to go back to America.

o

3

Victor drove slowly along the coast on Boulevard Calmel, his elbow propped out the open window in the sun. Gulls swooped in lazy patterns, and he lifted his untanned face to watch them through the windshield. Total freedom in flight. Yet surely our every terrestrial movement could be the same. The turn of a wrist, the shift of a hip, always unrepeatable, freedom if we could ever see it that way.

Turning right onto Avenue de la République, he fell into traffic and noticed a black Cadillac convertible several cars ahead. Blonde hair streamed in the wind. Was that Tommy August's famous car? Eight months had passed since their Christmas dinner. What was her name? Lucy. Yes, she sat behind the wheel. He switched lanes, accelerated abruptly, cheated a stoplight, and edged closer. Definitely Lucy, the Texas girl with the pert ass and the strained blouse. He pressed closer to her bumper.

Maybe her eyes shifted to the rearview mirror. She had become conscious of him, at least, and accelerated. But apparently she hadn't recognized him, or hadn't wanted to. Wrapped around her neck, a red scarf licked back at him like a tongue. Faster. *Mon dieu*, now he understood the appeal of a Cadillac. She leapt forward as easily as a cat, while the accelerator of his battered Peugeot was already stuck to the floor. A fine automobile was one of the few luxuries he hadn't permitted himself. But why? Because Tommy had suggested it? He hoped not.

Lucy, Lucy, speeding back towards Nouasseur and linoleum and American God. She needed more than she knew.

○

She hadn't been able to stay as long as she would have liked. The children would be getting home from school, so she had needed to get back to the base. The association meeting had been another animated one, the women so eager to discuss politics these days, although she hadn't got a lot of the specifics. Her French was progressing, however, and she understood a lot more than before. Her problem was vocabulary, and especially with women like Hajja Aliya, who was becoming a real friend, she wished she was capable of more intimate conversation. Although Hajja Aliya spoke English well, so maybe she shouldn't worry about it so much. What was important was the wonderful work they were doing for all those poor Moroccan girls. Lucy felt strongly that if those girls could only learn to read and write, and maybe learn a few household skills, then their lives could be immeasurably improved. It was all so inspiring, and that was about as far as her politics went. Hajja Aliya was inspiring too, and also so stylish. Lucy admired her, and was secretly proud of having made her first real Moroccan friend. Apparently she also knew a fabulous dressmaker in town, whom Lucy was just going to adore. That's where she bought those super stockings.

She was humming an old hymn. *Faith of our Fathers.* Throughout the meeting she hadn't managed to get it out of her head. Why was it always the hymns that stuck in your brain? Maybe it was because she had sung them throughout her youth, or maybe it had something to do with musical structure. Tommy would know. Oh boy, would Tommy know. Were they getting old? Had he lost interest in her? Maybe it was inevitable, but really she had no cause to complain. She still loved him so, even if every once in a while she longed to wander off somewhere and have all her responsibilities swept away. Sometimes even the Sahara Desert sounded pretty enticing. Just stop it now, Lucy August.

Her scarf was just flying all over the place in this wind. That's how people strangled themselves. Remember the dancer Isadora Duncan? Sort of glamorous, sort of grotesque. Not to mention what the wind was doing to her hair. But she just couldn't bear to put up the top on such a beautiful day. She lived in North Africa, under the desert sun, and she let her hair fly in the wind. She imagined herself saying that to her high school girlfriends back in Corpus Christi. Too funny.

Now what was that crazy car doing? Casablanca drivers were nuts. This was one of the first observations she had sent home to Daddy on a postcard: *Daddy, you just can't believe how people drive over here. Remember Uncle Tipsy? They're worse!* She glanced up at the rearview mirror again. Some Frenchman in a uniform. The face looked familiar. Was that Lieutenant Tessier? She was almost positive. After their dinner he had disappeared. She blushed then. Her postcards to Daddy hadn't been like his. Tommy had told her all about them.

○

He drew level with her and veered close. Large round sunglasses, a sleeveless white blouse, and the red scarf licking the wind. She turned and briefly smiled, a flash of recognition, then the smile vanished in the slipstream.

Traffic lightened as they approached Sidi Maarouf, so she was easy to follow. The Peugeot shuddered. His hands gripped the wheel. He imagined that she would be soft and ready to be seen, and then she would want to show him everything.

What would her reactions be? Again he attempted to overtake her. Past the American listening station at Saddle Rock, eucalyptus trees lined the country road. An occasional truck stacked with bales of hay, and otherwise only the two of them dueling. In his mind he saw the collision, steel crumpling into steel, bodies merged through shattered windows. Better to die in a car crash. Fighter pilots met solitary deaths, suicides,

57

not suicide pacts. *Lucy August*. What a ridiculous American name. Inexperienced, she would pitch towards the extremes, and overwhelming guilt would become overwhelming passion. He knew. Too well.

○

She wondered if he'd forgotten her. He had turned to look, but she had seen no recognition in his face. She pressed the accelerator and pulled ahead. What a nut! This wasn't some kind of game.

Again she glanced in the rearview mirror. Was it his intention to follow her all the way home like some racecar driver? He was unbearable, arrogant. What would Tommy say? Actually, Victor – *Vic* – probably didn't even care. You know what they said about Frenchmen and their fancy manners? Well she simply hadn't found that to be the case. Most of them were perfect louts.

She could go faster. You could always say *that* about this ridiculous car. She could leave him behind. Honestly, he was everything she disliked about this country. The cold privilege of the French colonizers. She shouldn't have lowered the roof. That sun was just blazing. Perspiration trickled down her spine. Her thighs stuck to the seat, and the snail dream played in her mind as if she was really dreaming it. The snails that covered the base in the summertime, climbing up the electricity poles to coat them like barnacles. In her dream they were suctioned over her body, nipping gently at her skin. She dreamed it almost every night, and when dawn came she would burrow beneath the sheets and try to keep the dream there in the cave warmth. The dream was so strange. It made her feel like some forest goddess worshipped by rivers and vines.

Stop being such a complete looney, Lucy. Her eyes were

moist. Look at that, she'd let herself get all worked up. Time
to lose this creep. She couldn't be pulling into the base with
a French officer on her tail. He and Tommy were friends, of
course, but those PTA ladies would never be content with
just one explanation. They tended to develop three or four,
particularly where Lucy was concerned. No, she would take
the back way in, down the dirt road past the shantytown they
called Little America. He wouldn't be expecting that. She
would leave him in the dust. Ripping the wheel to the right,
she skidded off the main road onto the dirt and grinned. The
countryside came on faster. Would he follow? She couldn't see
anything with all the dust churning up in the rearview mirror.

○

She was gutsier than he'd expected. He wasn't even sure
anymore what game they were playing, but he raced onto
the dirt road after her, the Peugeot rattling as if it had left its
suspension behind. Get too close, and the dust blinded him, so
he kept his distance. Where was she taking him? He laughed.

Then out of the gray cloud a lash of red appeared,
drifting closer as he sped ahead. He slammed on the brakes
and watched the scarf ease down to the dirt. The dust faded
as he descended from the car and stepped over to the scarf.
He stooped to picked it up. Silk, smooth between his fingers.
Her cloud receded. He stood with Lucy's scarf in his hand,
watching her grow smaller and waiting for her lights to turn
red, but they didn't.

○

4

"We want you to go into combat," Ahmed said. Saadia walked impatiently with him through Place Lyautey. If he ran off again with his knife to try and chop off somebody's cigarette, she swore she was going to strangle him. He got like a dog after a bone. Did he think she was impressed? "But you have to quit your job."

"No, I'll keep working at my job, and at the same time I'll be with you."

He grabbed her arm and spun her around into his chest. Honestly, she wasn't impressed. "Say yes or no," he growled. She snorted.

The third member of their cell was a resistant named Zaïm. Recently released from prison, he had been tortured, and they needed Saadia to tend his wounds at a safe house in Derb Carlotti. She now belonged to the Black Crescent, an armed branch of the PDI, the Party of Democracy and Independence, formed by dissatisfied members of Istiqlal. Previously they had been called the Black Hand, Cinema Rio branch, but they liked the new name better. Saadia just shook her head.

"Bring only a mattress and your clothes," Ahmed said. So that night she moved into the safe house. Her husband was still in Algeria. Only her mother might ask questions. "Don't come looking for me," Saadia said. "Just wait till I'm back." Her mother didn't care.

In the house were three men: Ahmed, Zaïm, and a guy living in a room upstairs who belonged to a group called the Sword of God. Before that he'd been in the Vengeful Hand, and before that the Lion of Liberation. He wasn't very talkative and tended to hog the bathroom. They gave her the poison pill and told her to keep it on her at all times just in case. Then they made her swear another sacred oath on the Koran and showed her the wardrobes, which were filled with

61

guns and grenades. One of her responsibilities would be to guard the wardrobes.

"What do you want to call yourself?" Ahmed asked. She looked at him blankly. "You need a fake name."

"Farida," she said.

He looked surprised. "Why Farida?"

"I don't know," she said. "Should I choose something else?"

"Okay, Farida," Ahmed sighed and left her with Zaïm, who lived on the couches in the ground floor salon. His feet had been ruined by the prison beatings. The *falaqua*. The French had stolen it from Moroccan schoolmasters, turning it into a brutal torture method. They tied up your feet and beat your soles with a stick until they bled. Zaïm's feet looked like hunks of bloody meat cut from a sheep on Aïd el Kbir, but Saadia washed and bandaged them. Even if she had never seen such damaged feet, she had done similar work at the doctor's clinic, and already she was impatient. This did not seem like combat to her. But Zaïm was kind and told her long stories about his battles against the French, treating her like a man, as if the stories were ones she could understand. Before prison he had been a weapons trainer, and Touil had been his driver. He admitted that Ahmed was too hotheaded for his own good, but Zaïm still loved him like a son. They had been through much together, and he told her the stories, how they had passed messages written in onion juice, which you held to a light to read, and how they had learned to test pistols by taking them out to the southern beaches late at night, where they fired them softly into the sand. Occasionally Ahmed would bring them an international newspaper smuggled in through the British Post Office in Tangier, and by candlelight Zaïm would read to her about the Nationalist movements in Egypt, Turkey, and other parts of the Middle East. Most evenings it was just the two of them in the house, but she imagined thousands of other houses like this filled with other cells, all over the country. She never felt alone with Zaïm.

He was in his forties, older than her father would have been. His feet were healing, but still he could not move from the couch, and she was the one who removed the pot when he went to the bathroom. She washed his djellabah once a week, sliding it up over his shoulders and then back down again. She had insisted he let her wash the rest of his body. With a warm rag and soap she gently bathed him then, making sure not to miss a spot. His body was sinewy and strong, with a long scar across its chest. She had never washed a whole man like that. She even cooked, and enjoyed it, although the results were often disastrous.

More than anything she liked watching Zaïm's face, deeply lined and thoughtful. One day he caught her staring, and although she quickly glanced back down at his feet, it was too late. "What's on your mind, Saadia?" He never called her Farida.

"Nothing. The resistance." He smiled at her softly, and she wasn't embarrassed then.

Ahmed brought more guns. Other times he took guns away. Hiding them in wardrobes was stupid, she thought, so she got more creative, hiding some in the ashes of the fire. They gave her a few of the old American banknotes from the war. Passing these back and forth was how resistance members identified themselves to one another, but she needed to be careful. The police were aware of the trick and had jailed one of Zaïm's associates for carrying the American bills. Zaïm said they had charged him with "beginning the execution of an act whose nature would disturb public order".

"What do you think about that, Saadia?"

"I think I don't want that old money. I know how to make myself clear."

Above all he told her never to trust women, especially not the upper-class ones associated with the Nationalist parties, who despised the working-class women of the armed resistance. He made her knock at doors with the butt of a pistol until she could recognize the sound. If one day she heard a sound like that, it was the gendarmes or the police. They always knocked with the butts of their guns, and these days they were raiding neighborhoods like Derb Carlotti. They needed to be prepared, but she was. At night she practiced with a pistol she kept stashed beneath her mattress. She knocked on the walls and the floor and recognized the police in her dreams.

By now the neighbors assumed she was a prostitute, so she used disguises when she went out for supplies, often dressing like a man. She had found a pair of golf pants she liked, which she wore with a suit jacket liberated from one of the wardrobes. She rode her bike everywhere and never left home without her poison pill. The secret of the pill gave her power. Nobody could ever touch her if she had the pill.

Back at the house she would change into her normal clothes again to take care of Zaïm. Most days she couldn't wait to get home to him. He let her wash him regularly now, and she even learned to make the foods he liked. "You're a wonderful woman, Saadia," he said one evening. Probably she hadn't heard him right, but still she blushed.

Ahmed had an apartment in Monastier Alley, in nearby Derb Sultan, and he rarely came by the house except to move guns, although sometimes he also tried to pull Saadia down onto her mattress. She just laughed. The guns were meant for Black Crescent missions, but Saadia suspected he also sold a few around town. She also knew he ran his own operations, targeting traitors who hadn't donated to the Black Crescent. These were mostly owners of restaurants and shops, and he personally went around every month to collect their donations. For bigger businessmen he went "on patrol", which meant he wore a mask and grabbed them off the street, giving them an hour to come up with twenty thousand francs or else. She knew this because one night she heard Zaïm yelling at him downstairs. She had never seen Zaïm angry and crept over to the top of the staircase to listen. Ahmed was insisting he always took the money to Rizq, the group's financial controller, whose office was in Derb Chorfa. He was doing this for the resistance. Maybe true, Saadia thought, but she doubted Rizq got all the money. Ahmed's suits were endless.

The two men had other disagreements too. Ahmed couldn't stand Mohamed Zerktouni, the hotshot behind the Central Market bombing. He often talked of knocking him off, or at least knocking off some of his men in the Secret Organization. But before prison Zaïm had been close to Zerktouni and loved him as much as he loved Touil, which was the real reason Ahmed couldn't stand Zerktouni. He was always saying that Zerktouni had no *integrity*. The only reason he had joined the resistance was to sleep with female recruits.

Another of Ahmed's obsessions was the pilot girl who got all the press, Touria Chaoui. "You want to know the truth, Saadia?" Saadia nodded. "She was trained by the French, her father works for the French, he even writes in French, and she has a French lover! A French pilot! It's all true."

"How do you know it's true?" The question made him even more furious. But Saadia had always liked the girl – her haircut, her courage, and especially her uniform. Whenever Saadia saw an airplane overhead, she even said hello. *Labas, Touria?*

But Ahmed could go on for hours. "If she's so courageous, then why doesn't she speak out against French occupation? Because a deal was struck, Saadia. She gets to go up in the airplane, and they get to show the world the civilized little Moroccan they made. Have I mentioned that her father has ties to Istiqlal? Don't be a fool!" Saadia nodded. Ahmed could be persuasive, and sometimes she thought of how he had excited her that first day in the park.

But he didn't excite her anymore. One night after Zaïm had fallen asleep, Ahmed stuck around. He ordered her to make tea. She refused. He wasn't her leader, and she definitely wasn't his wife. He lunged at her then, and she saw the red veins in his eyes. With the back of his hand, he slapped her so hard a tooth broke loose.

Later he found her sitting at the kitchen table holding a wet towel to her face. "Son of a donkey," she said.

He wanted to hit her again, but she knew he wouldn't, and this knowledge was a revelation. Men had never stopped before, but her role in the resistance alongside Zaïm was now her protection. She was in a cell connected to other cells, and even if she couldn't see the connections, these other cells were her protection. Ahmed pulled out a chair and sat down at the table. His face looked even yellower in the yellow light. "You make me laugh," he murmured. "You think you're in combat? Then let me know when you've actually killed a Frenchman."

He reached into his jacket pocket and pulled out what looked like a dried prune, so small you wouldn't have put it in a tajine. He set the prune on the table. "This Frenchman, I cut off his finger before I killed him. Cut off some other parts too, but I kept the finger for a souvenir." She grinned, at least until she remembered her swollen cheek, but she didn't dare say anything. Ahmed, furious again, snatched up his prune and rushed out of the house.

She didn't believe a word of that story, at least not until the next week, when Ahmed shot Fatmi Brahma, a Moroccan who taught French, right outside his house in front of his little daughter. Brahma had been a collaborator too, he said later, a *khayen*. He had taught the language of the occupier. Saadia wondered what else Fatmi Brahma had done, because there must have been hundreds of French teachers in the city. In any case, from then on she kept her three words of French to herself.

5

On a cold February night, Abdelwahed Chaoui stood before the printing press at the Imprimerie Al Atlas. The last of the yellow run had come off the press, and before beginning the black he was waiting for the posters to dry. He was alone in the room, which was lit by two dim bulbs and smelled of paper and ink. The press was owned by Mohamed Ghallab, an old friend from the independence movement, who had gone home to dinner leaving Abdelwahed to close up. "Don't stay too long," he had said, as if Abdelwahed had anything in mind other than going home to dinner himself.

The posters advertised a bullfight featuring the famed matador Domingo Ortega, who was coming out of retirement for the reopening of the Arènes bullfighting arena. Abdelwahed had been relieved to get the publicity job for the *corrida*. The months in the Madrid safe house had nearly bankrupted him, despite the help of Istiqlal, but even if he somehow solved his money problems, the threats against his family were still unrelenting. Touria was now on the board of one of the city's most prominent associations, and although he was proud of this, the work only drew more attention at a time when the French were openly assassinating Moroccan political leaders. Her accomplishments had exceeded anything he could have imagined, but could they ever live a normal life? For his country and his family, independence had become the only solution.

His hands were stained with ink, blue and red. The machine was old and leaked. He had needed to stop it repeatedly to pour the leaked ink back into canisters. Neither he nor Ghallab could afford any extra expenses. He picked up a poster and fanned the air. The outline of a matador and bull had appeared, and after all four colors had been printed, the image would come into focus.

A while later, halfway through the black run, the door

banged open and four men barged in. They seemed surprised to see him there and drew their guns. Stunned, Abdelwahed raised his hands, and the four men gradually came into focus. Moroccans. He recognized one as Mohamed Zerktouni, whom he had met a couple of times, but whom he knew principally through the obnoxious young associate who had insisted on helping with Touria's school fees. After the Central Market bombing, Zerktouni was the most wanted man in North Africa.

"*Salam alaikum*," said Abdelwahed, tentatively lowering his hands as the guns disappeared.

"*Alaikum salam.*" Zerktouni was thin and handsome, with a smooth face and a pencil-thin mustache, like a younger version of Abdelwahed. The other men, Abdelwahed would learn later, were Hassan Sghir, Slimane Laraïchi, and the one they called Big Dahous. "We didn't mean to interrupt."

Should he warn Ghallab? Or had his friend's advice to return home quickly been more than a friendly remark? "No problem," Abdelwahed said. "I was just finishing my work. Ghallab mentioned someone might stop by." The performance wasn't his best. His voice cracked, but they fought on the same side, and Zerktouni made no comment, so perhaps Ghallab had been expecting them. Sghir switched on a table lamp and extinguished the overhead bulbs. Abdelwahed gathered up his posters, carefully stacking them so that they wouldn't smudge. The last run could wait until morning.

Meanwhile the four men got to work. From a satchel Laraïchi pulled out a photograph of the exiled Sultan and brought it over to the press. Such photos were banned, as Abdelwahed knew from experience. Laraïchi had smuggled one across the border from Tetuan, in the Spanish zone. Now he took it back into the darkroom to transfer onto a printing plate. The men knew Ghallab's press.

"That ink canister tends to leak," Abdelwahed said, "but if you're only doing black, you should be fine."

"*Shukran.*" Zerktouni nodded. "I hope we haven't rushed you. How is your daughter, by the way?"

"She's well." Zerktouni seemed much older than Abdelwahed remembered, and more commanding. How old could he actually be? Twenty-five? Twenty-six? "She's gotten involved with a non-profit association that helps young Moroccan girls."

"And Madrid was good?" Zerktouni asked, watching him closely. "You're keeping safe?"

Abdelwahed nodded. *If you can call this safe.*

"We wondered if you had lost faith in us," Zerktouni said. "Some suspected that you were no longer devoted to the cause, but I never doubted that you were always one of us."

Abdelwahed said nothing. The plate had been rolled around the cylinder, and the machine whirred to life. Fliers began spitting out from the machine's opposite end. Sultan, Sultan, Sultan, Sultan. Laraïchi would wait until he had a stack, then place it in his satchel. They printed hundreds.

Once the satchel was full, Laraïchi swung it over to Zerktouni, who hefted it up to his shoulder. "I'll take these and return in thirty minutes."

Abdelwahed glanced over at his own stack of posters, some of them surely smudged now, ruined. "I should take these back to the office and get home to my family."

"Will you stay?" Zerktouni calmly asked. "Just thirty minutes, in case there are problems with the press. Just lock the door until I'm back."

He didn't wait for an answer.

Forty-five minutes later, Zerktouni still hadn't returned, and Abdelwahed paced over to the window to stand beside Big Dahous. Nothing moved down on Rue Aviateur. Big Dahous saw his agitation. "You've got a family," he said. "You can go. Laraïchi will unlock the door."

Outside the night air was cold and bracing, and he breathed it in deeply. His hands shook, but that wasn't the cold. He had felt like a hostage in that room. Perhaps that's what he'd been. Had Zerktouni been testing his devotion? Had he even intended to return? Abdelwahed walked briskly towards his office, where he dropped off the posters, then retraced his steps back towards Rue Colbert and the *imprimerie*, the quickest way home. That's when he heard the sirens. They swarmed from all directions, from Boulevard de la Gare, Avenue Poeymirau. He expected to feel hands on him at any instant, but the sounds flew past, and he crept up to the corner of Rue Oulad Ziane, hugging the shadows of overhanging hibiscus. Around the corner, red lights flashed in the air above. He moved slowly up to the end of the wall and peered around the corner. The *imprimerie* windows now burned brightly. Gunshots sounded, and in the shadows along the street he noticed another hidden figure staring at him: Mohamed Zerktouni.

The police had received a tip that night before storming the Imprimerie Al Atlas. Hassan Sghir swallowed his cyanide pill, becoming the first martyr of the resistance to die by his own hand. Big Dahous managed to shoot a cop, and in the confusion he and Laraïchi escaped. They found refuge in the medina and lived for weeks on a parallel plane, jumping from rooftop to rooftop. Eventually they managed to disappear. Mohamed Zerktouni wouldn't be so lucky.

o

HARD-DRINK PLAN RESCUES SEAMEN

BARS AT UNITED SERVICE CLUBS KEEP DRUNKEN MARINERS SAFE FROM ROBBERS

Robbing drunken seamen has been made harder in

the world's major ports, thanks to the United Seamen's Service.

Otho J. Hicks, executive director, reported last week that the organization, by serving hard drinks in its centers, had helped to protect the inebriated mariner from losing his money to pier-head prowlers. The organization adopted its hard-drink policy after World War II.

In the center, the seaman is among friends, Mr. Hicks said, adding: "Should he lose control, and most seamen don't, he is quieted down by the rest of the crowd. If he passes out, we can put him to bed and keep an eye on him until he's ready to go back to his ship."

Mr. Hicks described the service's program at a luncheon in honor of Mme. Helen Cazes-Benatar, a member of the organization's Comité de Patronage in Casablanca.... "I cannot tell you how much this organization has done to help French-American friendship," she declared.[8]

---

8   *The New York Times* – 03/07/1954

6

Sometimes Zaïm asked Saadia to run guns too. Maybe he no longer trusted Ahmed. He had even asked her to keep the secret documents – his letters and the resistance papers – beneath the clothes in her wardrobe. So she ran weapons for him, except she bicycled them, and the golf pants were perfect, because down each leg she could hide a revolver. Zaïm counted on her now. Once he had even called her his partner.

Ahmed made fun of the golf pants but sometimes tagged along, wanting to see what she was up to. One evening she headed for a garage to get a revolver repaired. Ahmed went with her, and four Senegalese soldiers carrying rifles came along on a patrol. She grabbed Ahmed's arm and pretended to be drunk. Ahmed just went silent and slouched. He was a terrible actor and almost got them busted, but she was convincing enough to avoid a search, and the soldiers moved on. Afterwards her eyes shone with the thrill, but Ahmed, after a silent moment of relief, was angry. He was a professional, he said, and didn't need to go around acting drunk to get past some stupid Senegalese. Afterwards he called her a whore for grabbing onto him like that, but from then on he let her work alone.

She learned tricks. She would go into the houses of resistants and put henna on her hands so that when she left, anyone observing would think she'd visited the wife rather than the husband. Back at the safe house she would fix Zaïm's tea exactly as he liked it, often serving it with her *cornes de gazelle* cookies, another new skill, along with running guns. One day he told her about the fliers Zerktouni intended to make from a photo of the exiled Sultan that Slimane Laraïchi had smuggled across the border from Tetuan, where the Spanish still refused to recognize the fake Sultan Ben Arafa. She should make contact with Zerktouni, he said. His men needed help moving the fliers. But when Ahmed heard the plan, the two men fought again, and it was Ahmed who went off to help Zerktouni. Which made her furious, but then she liked it, because she and Zaïm could be alone. He smiled at her as Ahmed left, and she went off to tidy the kitchen, humming a song.

Days passed. Zaïm's feet were healing, and on the couch he was cleaning a gun. She wiped the flour from her skirt and came into the room, and at that moment the gun accidently fired. The bullet grazed her scalp. They jumped at the noise. The instinct was to panic, but they froze, staying perfectly silent. Prison was guaranteed if the police came. She felt a trickle of blood oozing through her hair.

Then outside they heard shouting. The police. Saadia sprang into action, tying a scarf over her head, then in the kitchen throwing sugar on a burner to cover the smell of the gunsmoke. A rifle butt beat at the door. She knew the sound and ran back to Zaïm, who whispered into her ear, "The papers."

She flew for the staircase and up to her bedroom, wildly determined to save Zaïm from the Nazarenes. She slipped the papers from the wardrobe, rolled them, folded them, wrapped them in a plastic bag, and sat down on the bed. She lifted her dress to her thighs and spread her legs wide. Then she shoved the papers deep inside her.

That pain she had felt twice, giving birth to two lost children. Maybe this pain was worse, because for a dozen seconds she couldn't breathe, and tears pooled in her eyes, but she wouldn't let them fall.

She stood. Slowly she walked downstairs to meet the policemen like a housewife. She called herself Farida and offered them tea. They left within a minute. She had done it. Just like with Ahmed. She had kept them safe. So then, without looking at Zaïm, she returned to her bedroom and fell back onto the mattress, staining it with the blood that flowed from between her legs.

The next day she was infected. On the second day the infection was so bad that she couldn't ride her bike. Finally she knew she had to tell Dr. Ouarzazi the truth. She couldn't tell if he was angry with her for fighting for the resistance right under his nose. He looked at her on the table, shook his head, and gave her some pills. Then he told her she would never have another child.

THE BIG SCREEN
1954

Albert Forestier walked into La Gironde.

The enigmatic soldier walked into a bar in his native Casablanca, so hardened by the vicissitudes of war that those who had remained, not heeding the call, could never have suspected his true identity.

The returning war hero strode like a Colossus into his old watering hole, preparing to greet those old friends and lovers who had gathered to celebrate his triumphal return.

That was it. Should he casually mention the machine-gun nest, storming it? Vietnamese pussy? The motley crew he had commanded with firmness but genuine affection? No one had heard these stories except himself, repeatedly, and so they had become true, or at least as close to true as anything had ever been in his life. Indisputably, he had served in Indochina, as none of them had, and he wore the uniform to prove it.

Arriving in Vietnam, he had been posted to Tonkin, and for two years had done nothing but sweat, swat mosquitoes, and hack at the jungle. Hundreds of times he'd asked to be sent to the front for some action, to no avail. But now back in Casablanca, he anticipated that glorious opportunities would present themselves to a medaled veteran of the Indochina war.

Not medaled exactly, although there was the citation from General Henri Navarre, which he carried in his pocket, wherein the general deemed Forestier "worthy of the best traditions of the French army and the gratitude of the nation". The general's signature hadn't been difficult to forge, and surely Navarre would have echoed those sentiments if he'd found the time to write them. Albert hoped the general's recommendation might get him a promotion back at *Maroc-Presse*. Perhaps as their lead sports reporter, or even politics, front page stuff. It wasn't inconceivable.

Tonight the crowd wasn't too big, so he sat at his old

table near the bar. Nobody had noticed him yet. Probably he had changed. Probably he was harder. Also, Avival wasn't behind the bar. A new girl served drinks, younger than Camille but not as pretty, in Albert's opinion. Then Avival and Camille both came out from the back, looking irritated with one another. Albert stared bravely down at his table as if remembering jungle horrors. Then after a moment he glanced back up. Avival was now behind the bar beside the younger girl and still hadn't noticed him. How surprised he would be! Camille, however, was moving towards his table, upon which he refocused with steely concentration. Ripping a pin from a grenade. Machine-gun nests. Bayonets.

"*Salut Albert. Ça va?*" He glanced up, startled from horrific memories. Two years had aged Camille. Dark smudges underscored her eyes, which were creased at the corners. Her tits, however, were still just as fabulous in a tight, shaggy sweater, and her short skirt showed off legs still firm. "We missed you, but I knew you would come back. In church I prayed for your safety."

So she'd thought of him then. He couldn't suppress a grin. "You're a s-s-sight for s-s-sore eyes, Camille," he said, feeling a little risky.

She murmured to herself and glanced uncomfortably around the bar. He figured she wasn't used to receiving compliments. After some more incoherent murmuring, she said she liked a man in a uniform, and a blush tinted her cheek. He wanted to put the little black speck on that cheek in his pocket.

"How is your daughter?" he asked.

"Oh, she's fine. Almost nine now."

"You and Avi-v-v-val must be very proud."

She blushed again and shifted on her feet. "He's not Micheline's father, Albert. I thought you knew."

Then Avival's voice was booming over from the bar. "*Putain*, is that the great war hero? Don't just stand there,

Camille. Offer him a drink!"

"A beer," Albert said softly, smiling broadly at Avival. "I lost the whiskey habit in Vietnam." She nodded and walked over to the bar, shoulders slumped like a child expecting a reprimand. Avival poured a beer and thrust it at her. Some splashed out onto her sweater, but she made no effort to wipe it off. The new girl behind the bar sighed and rubbed herself against Avival like a kitten. Forestier bristled and wanted to say something kind to Camille, but then Congos and the Gypsy burst in and spotted him.

"It's the colonel!" Congos shouted. "The general!" the Gypsy cried. "Get over here, and let's all drink to Albert Forestier!" Ecstatic, Forestier rose from the table and walked as slowly as possible over to his old friends, who really were good fellows.

"Down that beer," Congos said, clapping him on the back, "and then we'll have a proper drink together." Avival poured out whiskeys for the four of them and the new girl, and they raised their glasses in the air. "*Vive la France!*" Congos cried.

"V-v-vive la France!" Forestier shouted. The whiskey burned his throat like jungle rash, but he was iron, and forged in the fire he only became stronger. Through watery eyes, he glanced down to the other end of the bar, where Camille stood watching the scene with a blank face. He imagined her pulling the sweater over her head and pushing one full breast into his mouth.

○

Short, stocky, and tireless, *Maroc-Presse* editor-in-chief Antoine Mazzella worked impossible hours with undimmed passion, motivated solely by principles, the most important of which was his sense of responsibility for the world as it actually was, rather than for how others, whatever their politics, believed it should be. He spoke out to the best of his ability, constantly challenging French authorities, devoted to the truth.

"It's wonderful to see you, Albert, but unfortunately there are no positions available at the moment. The counter-terrorists are making it difficult for us even to publish. We are the only newspaper questioning the Resident General's hard line, and we receive bomb threats almost daily. Newsstands have boycotted us. Advertising has disappeared."

Stacks of yellowing newspapers rose from the floor around the edges of the room, smelling of dust and cigarettes. Through a glass panel at one end of the shabby office, two typists clacked at keyboards. Forestier was still nodding, although the words didn't appear to have registered. He wrote prose more suitable for romance novels and would never be a reporter, but Mazzella liked him and believed he could still be taught. Or perhaps not. Now the boy had reached into his uniform pocket to place some sort of letter of recommendation on the desk. Mazzella glanced at the page and sighed.

o

Forestier loved Mazzella. He was the father he wished he'd had, the one who had made him feel capable as a man. The editor-in-chief had given him his first job as a reporter and had patiently nurtured his talent, sometimes reworking whole paragraphs himself before publication, which as editor-in-chief was something he almost never took the time to do for others. Forestier had immediately grasped the man's good intentions, even if he didn't especially understand his politics, and he knew that Mazzella was somehow different from his friends at La Gironde.

He placed the citation from General Navarre on the desk and said, "Even if it's not a promotion, I will k-k-keep covering boxing until something else opens up. I wrote every day in Tonkin. I know I have imp-p-proved."

Mazzella shook his head. "It's not possible. But why don't you wait here. I just had an idea. Maybe you should meet someone."

Forestier sat waiting for ten minutes that felt like an hour. He scanned the newsroom through the glass panel, but Mazzella had vanished. So Albert stepped into an imaginary boxing ring and softly described his unexpected skills to himself, just as he'd done as a boy. He grew more excited. Mazzella was too clever to let a man like Albert go to waste.

Eventually the door clicked open, and the editor-in-chief strode in with two men Albert didn't recognize. One was tall, with a thick gray mustache and a head that seemed too small for his body. Forty-something, he wore the uniform of Affaires Indigènes, the military unit formed by celebrated Resident General Lyautey to gather information about natives. The other was about sixty, short and stocky like Mazzella, but while the editor-in-chief's notable paunch was often decorated by the lunch he ate at his desk, the older man looked especially fit and wore a suit that must have cost a fortune. He had a broad, smooth chin, and there was something like a bulldog about him. Forestier shot to his feet.

"That's a good soldier," said the man from Affaires Indigènes.

"Forestier," Mazzella said, "meet Major Sartout, the newspaper's director, and Monsieur Jacques Lemaigre-Dubreuil. You probably know him from his editorials in *Le Monde* and his direction of Lesieur Oils. Soon he will also own our humble *Maroc-Presse*."

Forestier shook their hands enthusiastically, impressed that Mazzella had seen fit to introduce him to the most powerful men at the paper. Perhaps there was an executive position available that the editor-in-chief hadn't been at liberty to discuss.

○

They were sitting around the desk. Sartout was talking. Jacques only half-listened to the major's account of the events which Jacques himself had put into motion. As his politics had shifted, to the point that he now believed in the urgent necessity of Moroccan independence, he had been aware that owning a local newspaper would provide an outlet for his more progressive views. With Pierre Mas, the rightwing conservative, in control of almost every other paper in town, *Maroc-Presse* had been his best option. He also hoped the paper would help consolidate his influence with the Nationalist political elite, who he now felt certain would soon rise to power. Lesieur Oils could not afford to be left behind again by history, and so he had given shares of the company to Moroccans he had convinced to invest in the paper, consolidating his two poles of influence. Admittedly another consideration had been that shares of *Maroc-Presse* had plummeted as its opinions had become more unpopular among the general French readership, and so he had been able to purchase it with pocket change.

Reveling in his new challenge, he was spending as much time as possible in the newsroom, articulating strategy and reviewing the books. It had been years since he felt central to a revolutionary undertaking, and this time he was convinced he would receive the acclaim he had long deserved. With other liberal Casablanca businessmen, including the paper's investors, he had also formed what he called his Study Group, which met regularly at the Hotel Mansour to discuss the wisest path towards independence. Many of these men were

Moroccan. And while Mazzella's stuttering soldier couldn't possibly understand all that had gone into this, and with those bug eyes and bony torso he unfortunately wasn't too attractive, he did at least appear malleable, and clearly impressed by Monsieur Lemaigre-Dubreuil. He might, Jacques thought, be one of us.

"France can no longer rule Morocco by force." Sartout was still pontificating, as if he held the reins. "And those of us on the Center Left agree that the natives must have a voice in government."

"New Right," Jacques interrupted, turning to address Forestier. "Perhaps we could find some unsatisfying job for you here. Monsieur Mazzella knows more about that than I – and he has been especially complimentary of your pen – but after your extraordinary service, perhaps your talents would make more of an impact elsewhere."

"Something just occurred to me, Albert," Sartout said. "Could you come back tomorrow afternoon? There is someone else I want you to meet."

○

The next day Forestier met Sartout back at *Maroc-Presse*. Also present was a sullen policeman introduced as head of Internal Affairs. "You have shown great bravery on the battlefields of Vietnam," the major said. "And like our enemies there, our enemies here hide their faces. They lurk in the shadows, Albert, but you are courageous, and we would like you to join the police force. I believe you're hiring, aren't you, Lieutenant?" The head of Internal Affairs looked up from the table and nodded. "Are you interested, Albert? If so, you can start today."

Was he interested? He was ecstatic. To be one of the club,

to serve alongside his friends from La Gironde – Congos, the Gypsy, and Méléro, if he was still around. It was almost too good to be true. "What about police academy? Isn't there some kind of entry exam?"

"You have already passed," Sartout said with a wide smile, which Albert reflected back to him, as if the major had just pinned a medal to his chest. Quite an accomplishment, perhaps his greatest until now. "Your mission will be both simple and complex," Sartout continued. "You will be undercover, investigating an armed cell of counter-terrorists." Albert nodded sternly. This just kept getting better. "Your mission will be to integrate yourself into the notorious La Gironde gang and report back to us on the movements of François Avival and his armed associates."

Avival and his armed associates? Surely that was a mistake. Avival the head of a counter-terrorist organization? Impossible, but he just nodded his head.

"We have also come to believe that certain elements of the police may also be involved in this gang, although up until now they have seemed to benefit from the protection of powerful men, and when questioned they have always had perfect alibis, which in itself is suspicious."

Albert squinted slightly, then nodded, hoping he had sufficiently conveyed his own suspicions.

"In the past nine months French counter-terrorists have committed more than eighty murders. In those nine months the police have not made a single arrest. You can change that, Inspector Forestier."

Inspector Forestier. Nice touch.

And so two weeks later Inspector Forestier sat at the bar of La Gironde in his new police uniform, one of the gang now, a notebook tucked in his pocket. When Congos and the Gypsy had asked how he'd earned the badge so fast, Albert had gently reminded them of his service in Indochina. Then when they asked why he wasn't doing traffic like other new recruits, he explained that he had been assigned to an elite counter-terrorism unit, and would appreciate any tips. "We have to keep up the fight for F-F-France," he said, and it was as simple as that. Albert Forestier was undercover.

Now he belonged at the bar with the others. Avival seemed to show him a new respect, sometimes offering drinks or reading him news stories, agitated by the papers as always, and those were the rightwing ones. Albert couldn't imagine his rage if he ever picked up a copy of *Maroc-Presse*, which was Center Left, or New Right. He just listened to Avival's rants while fervently nodding, because honestly Avival made some excellent points. He also chatted with Camille whenever possible, although this somewhat compromised his undercover work, since she steered clear of Avival. Sometimes she brought her daughter and sat with her when business slowed. Shy Micheline had her mother's face, but her hair was blonde and straight. She could draw pictures for hours. Forestier made a point of complimenting her work and had suggested she sign her name like Monet or some famous artist. That was the next step. Hopefully Avival hadn't noticed his interest in Camille, but even if he remained suspicious, Congos and the Gypsy had become outright pals, even inviting Albert to ride along some nights when they collected money from the businesses they protected. These were dangerous times, Congos said, and people depended on the police, as they should. Occasionally they were required to slap a shop owner around a bit to get what they were owed, but for the most part people were happy to contribute. Avival let them borrow his car for these runs, a Peugeot 203 he kept in a garage near the bar. The door to the garage was never locked, because nobody was ever going to mess with Avival or his car.

At the back of the garage a heavy punching bag hung from a chain, and a pair of old leather boxing gloves was hooked over a nail in the wall. The keys to the Peugeot were kept down one glove. In the other was a smaller key that opened a battered steel locker stocked with weapons, including an American Thompson M1 submachine gun and several box-drum magazines holding thirty rounds apiece, some of them already loaded with bullets. Albert detailed things like these in his reports every night before bed.

One evening while collecting money, they stopped off at the Gypsy's mother's place in the mellah. She was a hairdresser for dogs, or something like that, cutting mostly Jewish dogs, but thousands of their owners had fled on the boats to Israel, so business had been slow. The Gypsy talked Spanish with his mother, and Albert understood very little, except everybody knew *amigo*, which was how the Gypsy had introduced him, and the mother had poured out glasses of Fundador that burned the back of his throat.

Another night a shopkeeper in Habbous saw them coming and pulled a gun, shouting "*Freeze!*" like some gangster in an American movie. Albert panicked, admittedly, and drew his pistol, aiming at the spot on the man's forehead calloused by years of praying. Congos and the Gypsy burst out laughing. The gun was just a flare gun, Albert saw then, its barrel as wide as a toilet paper roll. That's how crazy these monkeys were, and they were obliged to smash the shopkeeper's head several times with the butts of their pistols to teach him a lesson about respect. Walking out with his money, Congos aimed the flare gun into the air and pulled the trigger. Turned out the crazy shopkeeper actually kept the thing loaded, and a flare pinged up high into the sky, shedding pink sparks over the neighborhood. "*Merde*, come on," Congos giggled, and they ran for the Peugeot. With those guys you could always count on a good laugh.

One evening Tony Méléro came into La Gironde looking classy. Albert hadn't seen him since returning, but Tony ignored him. Congos and the Gypsy were horsing around at the end of the bar. Tony glared at them and strode the length of the room as Avival called out, "What can I get you, *mon ami?*"

"A Chivas, neat," Méléro said without pausing, "and the check for these two clowns." Avival set down the whiskey next to their two empty glasses. Méléro then slipped a folded bill from a gold money clip and placed it on the bar. Then he slowly sipped the whiskey, rolling it around in his mouth as if he could taste a few dozen flavors imperceptible to others. Then once he was done with that, he led Congos and the Gypsy out onto the street.

"Hey Tony, how are you?" Albert called as they passed.

"We'll catch you later, Albert," Congos said, eyes rolling. Albert grinned. Tony had a stick up his ass. "Can't tie his suede shoes without orders from Rabat," the Gypsy had cracked one night while they made rounds, but Congos had told him to shut his trap. By then Forestier had started playing lookout when they planted a bomb, for example, basic stuff. The way it worked was that Dr. Causse, head of the Presence, the most powerful organization of French settlers, would send over a list of targets. Unfortunately Albert hadn't yet gotten a glimpse of a list, which Avival kept between random pages of his accounting ledger. So Albert spent even more time at La Gironde, increasingly desperate for a chance to steal the list or learn its secrets, while Avival pontificated or grabbed his girlfriend, who had no class, in Albert's opinion, and wasn't older than seventeen.

Albert had thought, at length, about bringing Camille into his elite undercover unit and asking her to get the list, but he wasn't sure what she thought of him, and also she looked so exhausted these days that he wasn't sure he could count on her. "I need a vacation," she said one afternoon, and when he replied that she deserved it, she put her hand on his shoulder with some affection. That evening he found the nerve to ask Avival what the plan was for the night.

"We're feeding the little birds," he said, without looking up from wiping the counter. "A machine-gunning on Rue Pellé, a grenade toss at the Cinema Malika, and a bomb for

Dolbeau, that liberal prick." Albert summoned all his training to keep from gasping aloud. All he'd had to do was ask.

So that night he left La Gironde as early as possible without seeming conspicuous. He no longer wrote in the bar, or anyplace else but home, where he composed long, detailed reports, full of allusion and dark metaphor, which he dropped off at the station in the mornings. The stars in the margins multiplied, private notes of successful masturbations, which of course Sartout would never suspect. Both mind and body burst with excitement, but sleep came with difficulty, and he no longer dreamed. He warded off dreams with remnants of consciousness, because if any dream came, he feared it would feel like a thread slowly being pulled from his brain. Lose control, and he would unravel.

Sometimes it helped to drink a finger of cognac before bed – Camus, the kind his mother had liked. But undercover he was happier than ever before.

o

Congos and the Gypsy walked into the bar late after feeding some birds. Avival had almost finished closing. "Everything all right?"

They nodded and settled on two stools. Avival poured out some whiskey. "I don't trust Forestier," he said, the glass at his lips. "He was nosy tonight."

The Gypsy said he thought the kid was all right.

"There's a way to be sure," Congos said, draining his glass with a toss of his head. "Let's get him to kill a rat."

2

White snails covered clumps of wiry grass at the corners of lawns. The sun had peeled a circle of bare skin the size of a billiard ball from atop Tommy's head. Once the sun set, however, the air cooled as if a switch had been flipped, so he wore Victor's leather coat when he walked the neighborhood at night. It fit too tightly, but it kept him warm and seemed to protect the memories it held. Lucy had made fun the first time she'd seen him in it, but she hadn't mentioned it again. It's not as if their friends were out that time of night.

Off Echo Court, neighborhoods grew ever outward. The houses on India Place at the far end of Center Street, which they jokingly called the suburbs, would be finished within the month. He strolled down the fairway of the golf course's seventh hole, silent skies overhead dotted with a million stars. Now almost every evening before bed, he walked, sometimes sneaking a cigarette, which he cadged at lunch from his construction crews. The evening strolls made him feel like a night guardian, which gave him a sense of quiet benevolence, although he couldn't have said what he was meant to be guarding.

Tonight it was later, almost midnight. They had all gone to bed, and before leaving he'd checked on Jimmy. The boy had been having nightmares. They would hear him screaming, but when they shook him awake, he could never describe the dream, which Tommy imagined was part of the terror. That night Jimmy had been sleeping peacefully. In the gleam of the nightlight, Tommy had seen the brass trumpet on its stand. He had tiptoed over to it and had taken it out into the living room, where into a couch cushion he had played the solo from Copland's *Quiet City*. He wasn't loud, but Lucy had appeared in her nightgown, her face twisted with sleep. "You woke me," she mumbled. He could see her body through the sheer fabric. Still a beauty. "Hollywood," he whispered, guiltily

89

lowering the mouthpiece from his lips. The old nickname. She sighed and went back to bed. And there he was, hunched over a cushion in his own darkened living room. Only after she left did he feel ridiculous.

The neighborhood looked unrecognizable when it slept, and maybe that's why he loved it then. Whoever you met, or spied through a window, would never tell your secret, because it was their secret too. Out beside the riding stables, the Robertson girl, Miss Nouasseur 1954, was smoking alone astride the oil-drum horse, her pleated cheerleader's skirt hiked to the top of her thighs. He wondered why the snails had covered just one of the four poles roped to the oil drum. Perhaps there was some solution. The Robertson girl stared. She seemed to have given herself over to everything, to the stars, the nicotine. He wondered if he should have a word with Robertson, but then he figured she was old enough. He walked on, hearing laughter then, and thinking it was her, he turned around, but she was only smoking, swaying on the oil-drum horse.

In trailer housing, one light shone from a bedroom window. Soon everyone would be moving out of trailer housing into state-of-the-art homes. Johnny Callaghan's two-cylinder scooter lay in the dirt beside his front door. Either he'd come home drunk or had crashed it again, snapping off the kickstand. In the ditch alongside the laundromat lay an errant baseball scuffed with grass. He should fish it out, but he left it there and walked on for another half mile or so. His cigarette had died, and he didn't want another, but neither did he want to go back home.

As he strolled along the salvage yard fence, a streetlamp caught something in the gravel beneath his feet. He stooped and plucked up a one-dollar TCV Rec Club token. Jimmy would get a little bonus if he finally learned his C-scale. The boy could already play the songs Tommy had taught him – simple things like *Hot Cross Buns* – and he seemed to enjoy it, but if he didn't get the scales, he would never learn to improvise, a skill that any moderately serious player needed to master.

Circling aimlessly back around past the Hobby Shop, off South Avenue he heard a radio from an open window at the hospital, which as far as he knew was empty of patients. *This is Radio Nouasseur, signing off at midnight. Turn in for tonight, but tune in tomorrow for* Sunset Jubilee. Some orderly was probably up there catching some shut-eye on a hospital bed. They were infinitely adjustable and had cost a fortune, Tommy knew. Heck, at least one of the darn things was getting some use.

Past the Airmen's Club and the Officers' Club, he came to the old Arab cemetery. Off to the east was the secret birdcage glowing in the night. Many of his late strolls had been spent thinking about the bomb. On different nights it held different meanings for him. Fear, nothingness, freedom, death. The bomb was all of those things, and you could think forever about it, so recently he had tried to stop thinking. The bomb was just something numb that was always there.

Dry grass crackled underfoot, sounding like Texas. The flatness of the landscape was Texas too, Texas exactly, except for some eucalyptus trees. He and Lucy had never been able to recapture the excitement of that year in Corpus Christi. Oh she had been wild, speeding down coastal roads like a fighter pilot, Daddy opposed to everything, especially the fighter pilot to whom she'd given her heart. Then the night she had parked Daddy's car down at the beach, wordlessly climbing into the back seat and lying against the vinyl while unbuttoning her sweater. They hadn't known she was pregnant when he got called up to Norfolk, and when Operation Torch sailed for Casablanca, he hadn't known about war, and probably even less about Texas girls.

Life together after the war had felt like something conquerable. They'd had faith because faith was no struggle, had loved completely because love was easy. But afterwards in Chicago, life had started feeling less extraordinary. Faith faced doubts, love difficulties. And now as hard as he tried to feel that his life had unfurled in some single majestic sweep, the truth was that his past felt entirely disconnected from his present. They had moved into the period of compromises, where you bent yourself to the other or didn't, until no matter whether you gave or you took, the process bent you out of shape, turning you into someone else. Only on these night walks did he still feel purely himself, but even then he could no longer have articulated who exactly that was.

Across runways he walked in the shadows of hulking planes. On the base's south side, more white patches of snails appeared on telephone poles along the perimeter road. Beyond the fence, high up in the branches of a eucalyptus tree, a white plastic bag flapped in the breeze. He felt an urge to climb the fence, then climb the tree and detach the plastic, as if it needed rescuing. Music again played from Little America tonight, an oboe winding through overlapping drums. Past Well 14, he stepped up to the fence, threading his fingers through the links. Somewhere out there was the place he'd crashed his Wildcat a long time ago. He felt for the scar on his forehead, but over the years it had vanished, leaving only a place his fingers wanted to touch. One Saturday a few years earlier, he'd gone out looking for the field where the Spahis had taken him captive, but the city had changed so much that he'd quickly gotten lost. Probably he could have located the spot from the air, but as soon as you were on the ground, Casablanca became immense.

Still, he'd enjoyed the drive. He almost never let himself get lost anymore, but those times when he had were some of his starkest memories. So maybe he should climb the fence and keep walking out past Little America into the night.

That laughter again. Often he heard it around this time, but its source remained a mystery. Maybe the barracks. He wasn't imagining it, in any case. He wasn't going crazy. He wasn't the type. Although tonight they seemed to be laughing at him.

He closed his eyes to listen, but the laughter had stopped, so he tapped the fence with his fingers, accompanying the drums until he was entranced by the syncopated jingling sounds he made, by the vibrations rippling back into his fingertips.

3

Then Saadia's husband came home from Algeria for a visit. "You have to leave the house while he's here," she said to the others. She took the weapons from the secret hiding places and stuck them in a wardrobe in a locked room upstairs. She didn't care about Ahmed or the man from the Sword of God, but seeing Zaïm limp out the front door with his cane almost made her cry. Still, she was a wife. What else could she do?

Her husband stayed for a month. There was nobody he wanted to see, and nothing he wanted to do. He sat around the house all day listening to the radio. Every day after work at the clinic, she cooked a tajine, but he hardly noticed. He filled his stomach. One night she tried her cookies, but they came out inedible. She had never been so bored.

After about two weeks of this, he announced that he was taking her to see a movie at the Cinema Vox. What did she think about that? She would never understand men, how they got these ideas all of a sudden. She laughed in his face and told him Casablanca had changed. Now only French people went to the Vox. What she really wanted to tell him was that she was a resistant, but she held her tongue.

"I've got money," he bragged. "They can't turn us away if we buy a ticket."

"What about curfew?" she asked. Men.

"We'll go this afternoon," he replied, so confident all of a sudden that it made her furious, but then he went upstairs and put on a coat and tie, so she washed her face and polished her good shoes. Sometimes she remembered why she'd liked him in the first place.

At the Vox, the ticket seller let them pass, just as her husband had promised, and they found empty seats in the second balcony. She realized for the first time how enormous the theater was inside. That first time with Ahmed she had moved so quickly down the aisle. She remembered him in the back alley, when her heart nearly exploded. Everything about the Vox reminded her of Ahmed, even all the surrounding Frenchmen in their suits, with women in silk dresses. For a moment she wished she had a silk dress too, something other than what she'd made by hand, but then she didn't care.

She loved the movie, even if she didn't understand anything anybody said. It was a gangster movie with lots of fighting over a girl, but the girl was cracked in the head and only wanted to look at herself in the mirror. Saadia kept shouting at the screen, telling the girl to stop being such a blockhead and go with the one who had wanted to be a singer, but the girl only wanted to look in the mirror. Then a Frenchwoman shushed her, so Saadia held her tongue. Some girls were just blockheads. It was that simple. Through all of this her husband kept trying to hold her hand, which was annoying because then she couldn't concentrate.

Days passed, one like the other, yesterday and today. Occasionally some friend of Zaïm's, someone she knew from the resistance, would knock at the door and call her Farida. "When did you change your name?" her husband asked.

"You don't like the name Farida?" she shouted, and he went off to bed.

She cried every night after he fell asleep. She sewed a new dress for herself while missing the other men, even Ahmed. Her husband was a good husband, but it wasn't the same. The sex was good too, even if she still hurt, but now there was an itch deep inside her belly that he could no longer scratch.

Since the others couldn't visit, she carried the guns herself. Because of her husband, she could no longer use disguises, but she enjoyed devising new ways to smuggle. One of her best tricks was to fill her bicycle lamp with bullets. Nobody would ever think to look there. The problem was that her husband was so lazy and bored that he never left the house, and so she had to keep sneaking into the locked room upstairs where everything was stashed. When one day he asked about the room, she told him to mind his own business.

Every day she went to the clinic, and other times she told him she was going to her mother's, so one day she actually went to her mother's and left a note at the door. The note had been dictated to her friend the secretary at the clinic, and it warned the old woman to stop using French cooking oil and cigarettes or suffer the consequences. This was one of her more satisfying outings.

She always wore the same dress. She had liked trying on new things for Zaïm, but not her husband, who grew more suspicious. "So is this your house now?" he asked.

"Oh, go listen to your radio."

She hid her poison pill and carried it with her everywhere. It gave her peace to know that she could do something terrible. Around this time, in June 1954, Mohamed Zerktouni was finally captured and took his pill in prison before the French could torture him. Suicide was a mortal sin in their religion, but after Zerktouni's death the imams met in a secret conclave and announced that it wasn't actually a sin to take a cyanide capsule if you were a Moroccan patriot captured by the enemy. So she was fine, and the pill stayed on her, like that itch deep inside her belly.

Finally the month passed, and her husband left. The others moved back in. She made cookies, and this time they came out nicely. Zaïm could move around the house now and said that soon he would be going north to fight with the Liberation Army in the hills outside Oujda. Saadia insisted his wounds hadn't healed. He wasn't ready.

"Morocco is ready," he said, "so I am ready too."

For the rest of the day she stayed silent, and then when they sat down to dinner with Touil, she announced that she was ready for her own operation. Ahmed laughed. Zaïm said nothing. Ahmed suggested she put on her golf pants and go over to the Royal Club at Anfa and hit some Nazarene pigs over the head with clubs. "Par Four!" *Boom boom boom!* This was his arm being a golf club on the table.

Zaïm spoke up then. He asked what she had in mind, and her heart fluttered as Touil rolled his eyes. She hadn't thought about it, but she wanted to put a bomb in the Cinema Vox and kill many Nazarenes.

"You're brave, Fadila," Zaïm said. "You'll have to be careful. In the morning I'll make you the bomb and explain it. Touil will help. He's done this before."

Saadia showed her big teeth in a smile. She wanted to throw her arms around Zaïm, but she knew that now she must be serious, and so she made a serious face. Ahmed rolled his eyes again.

The next morning she watched as Zaïm made the bomb. A bomb was such a simple thing, only a few pieces. The work she did on bodies at the clinic was more complex. The wait through that afternoon was long, but she put on her new dress, and after tea served with cookies, she slipped the bomb into her bag and announced that she was ready. Ahmed and the man from the Sword of God had reluctantly agreed to accompany her to the Vox.

Nazarenes crowded the cinema entrance. The movie was about to begin, and the two men refused to approach. They went on discussing the situation until she got so fed up she hissed that if they were chickens, they could at least go ahead and lay some eggs.

They would be recognized, Touil snarled. They were known. The man from the Sword of God kept quiet. He just looked at his shoes like he was worried somebody would steal them. Fat chance with those shoes.

"Oh, go cut cigarettes off faces," Saadia growled. "I'll do it myself."

She huffed off towards the ticket booth, but then she realized she didn't have any money, and turned back. "Give me money for the ticket," she said. Ahmed grudgingly handed over a few coins.

Inside the movie had already started. She stood at the back as her eyes adjusted to the darkness, and then she stared at the backs of the heads of all the filthy Frenchmen. She truly hated them then with the bomb in her bag. She found a seat and placed the bag beneath it, reaching in to start the timer, exactly as Zaïm had demonstrated. She heard his voice saying that from this moment she had five minutes, except that Zaïm wasn't there, and she really had five minutes.

In the next row a man in an overcoat smoked a cigarette, still wearing his hat. Along the row beside her another wore workman's clothes and appeared to be asleep. She was the daring one. She was brave. They were all asleep, their dreams filled with dead Moroccan babies. It was time to get out of there.

The movie was an old one in black and white. A lot of boring men were talking. Nothing happened. But one man wore a white tuxedo. He was the one in charge. He ran the casino, and there was a little man begging him for something, but the police arrived and chased the little man. When they caught him, the one in the white tuxedo said, "*Je ne risquerai ma tête pour personne.*" Although she didn't fully understand the words, she liked the way he spat them out before shooting a commanding look across the casino and striding off.

Then he was talking to some pure white blonde in a pure white dress and diamond earrings, all pretty boring. He smoked cigarettes and nobody cut them off his face. Maybe she still had a minute. Her entire body tingled, every bit of it. Then under her breath she spoke the curse: "Be damned, Nazarenes, sons of dogs, drinkers of alcohol, eaters of pork, and of frogs."[9]

She stood and hurried down the aisle towards the exit, where outside another movie Ahmed Touil had leaned against a wall and had brought her into the resistance. She needed to run, but she waited, wanting to hear the explosion, wanting to

<hr>

9   *The Bottom of the Jar* – Abdellatif Laabi

feel it through her body, and then maybe it would touch the itch deep inside her that nobody else had touched.

And then it came like a wave, and it did.

She heard screams and sirens, but she ran through them all on her strong, short legs. She had done it, she had done it, and her joy felt violent too as she muttered through her clumsy teeth, over and over again, "*Je ne risquerai ma tête pour personne.*"

○

99

The evening's reception had filled the ballroom of the Hotel Lincoln, a few blocks over from the Cinema Vox. At the bar Lucy August had run into Victor Tessier. They were serving only that sugary mint tea, no alcohol. She could have done with a whiskey when Victor said her name. He was polite, however, as if their car chase – that's how she now referred to it in her mind – had never happened. Her eyes escaped out into the room, where a hundred of the city's most prominent Moroccans, and some French, had gathered to raise funds for underprivileged Moroccan girls. These days the two nationalities rarely met peaceably in public, but the power and wealth of those assembled sometimes required them to be better friends than enemies. Lucy was the only American, as far as she knew, and she was proud of having integrated herself into Casablanca society in a way that the insular base wives would have never dared. But she was no longer such a novelty to the Moroccan wives either, and although they were friendly, they did not entirely trust her, perhaps. So the only person who seemed more out of place in that room than she was Victor Tessier.

He had been asked to serve that night as the French military delegation, he explained. Hence the uniform. He said he'd been hoping to run into her and Tommy, having remembered how she had spoken so passionately about her work with the association. He seemed so pleasant and bland that she wondered whether she had misinterpreted the famous car chase. Maybe it hadn't really been a chase, only cars. Maybe they'd simply been heading in the same direction. Then he shot her a crooked smile and glanced out at the room. "They're all dying for a drink or a smoke," he said, "but in public they walk around with frozen grins looking like constipated angels." *Well.* That was more like it. She hadn't imagined a thing. Now she wanted that drink at least as much as Victor's constipated angels.

"That one, for example, Monsieur Berrada." He nodded towards a fat man in a shiny suit accompanied by a wife a head taller in shiny couture. "He and his wife speak French at the dinner table rather than Arabic, desiring to be *chic*. Berrada's also a prominent Nationalist, so you can understand why the lower classes have armed themselves. Then Monsieur Charvet, with the beard, a former economist and one of our leading liberals, although as far as I can tell, his only contribution to the Moroccan economy has been sleeping with Madame Berrada, which has freed her fat husband to invest heavily in the company of young boys. It's so pointless…. I'm sorry.…"

Did she look as horrified as she felt? "Sometimes I think it's pointless too," she said angrily, "but I believe it's a terrible sin for us to give up hope." Yet hadn't she also given up so much hope, exchanging it for a mostly pleasant routine of identical days spent performing the duties of a mother and wife – organizing the lives of others. She had become more or less exactly the woman she had always wished to become, but sometimes alone in the early afternoon she wanted to scream. "Anyway," she said, shaking off her thoughts, "since you're such a gossip, tell me more about the pilot."

Victor followed her eyes out to the middle of the room. She was surprised to see creases appear at the corners of his mouth, troubling his perfect Renaissance face, although with the ding in the forehead and the slight asymmetricality, he'd been done not by Michelangelo but by one of his students. An above-average student. "Touria Chaoui," he said, "and her parents. She's on the board of one of the associations, I believe." He glanced away from the girl in the uniform, his face again sculptural.

Lucy had the sense she'd discovered a crack in his armor, although she wasn't sure why. "I haven't had the opportunity to speak with her yet," she said, her gaze fixed on his face, "but what an amazing young woman! Do you know her?"

Already he regretted speaking. He shouldn't have come. For weeks, months, he had avoided unnecessary evenings, attempting not to slip again into that abyss, but here he was, and here was Lucy. Probably he had hoped she would loathe him.

"I've met her a few times," Victor he said, wondering why he was keeping Touria to himself. She was the one good thing in that room, and he missed seeing her more than he wanted to admit, but he hoped she hadn't spotted him. He wasn't in any state to give her what she deserved. Besides, her parents had always been suspicious. Apart from the hostility she had faced from Directeur Martin, he guessed that at some point she had mentioned that she didn't particularly like Tessier, which was understandable. Yet the sight of her and her parents standing alone, so out of place among these people, made him miserable – with himself. Something needed to change. In this place, but also within himself. Forever had passed since he'd spent time with the stars.

Hajja Aliya Alaoui was now approaching the Chaouis, and although he especially wished he could rescue Touria from that, at least the family's awkwardness would be somewhat relieved. "Oh there's Hajja Aliya," Lucy cried. "And that must be her son."

The young man was handsome and slickly dressed, but his shoulders slumped, and his eyes constantly shifted around the room "Haj Driss," Victor said. "A professional playboy, although now that politics are in fashion and his father has prospects, he's become *engagé*."

"I've never met him," Lucy said, smiling at Victor as if he'd revealed something of himself. "You seem a little tired this evening, Lieutenant Tessier." Her eyes steadied and softened. "Are they working you too hard at the base?" Foolishly he ran a hand through his short hair. He felt her body pulsing, and her beauty was now oppressive. For the first time he clearly saw her desire, and desire was an abyss. He knew absolutely everything about her then, such that even her beauty bored him. "She's quite an attractive girl in her way," Lucy continued, coyly cocking her chin towards Touria while studying his face for a reaction.

"Not as attractive as you," Victor replied. Oh God, he was so bored with women and their talk, the utter transparency of their schemes. Beauty was the promise of happiness, wrote Stendhal. But the promise was invariably broken. Was she aware that this was all a performance, no more than lines spoken by two actors on a screen? Or did she actually think it was real? He shouldn't have come out tonight.

When the explosion came, it sounded no different from thunder, but then the lights flickered and went out. Lucy crashed against him as if she'd lost her balance. In the darkness he snaked an arm around her waist and pulled her firmly towards him, feeling that familiar cold throb in his belly as he heard himself whisper: "We have to get out of here."

Bodies staggered past. A woman wept, somebody babbled in Arabic, but otherwise the room stayed eerily quiet. He guided her through the crowd with his hand flat on her back, insistently murmuring instructions. "Left now. Over there. Look for the service entrance." *Aimed down, you need more power; aimed up, you need less.*

They pushed through the doorway into a stairwell and felt their way down steps, Victor guiding her, feeling her body, she feeling his, the sounds of fear fading above until they could hear only their own deafening heartbeats. "No, this way," he said, pushing through another door. "It's like a maze," she murmured, and perhaps it was, but over the years he had gotten to know too well the back corridors of the Hotel Lincoln.

Nobody else was fleeing, she realized, so she held onto fear, which was all that justified their situation. Wobbling on heels, she kept finding Victor's flat chest. She needed the fear.

A few seconds later the lights flickered on. They were in an empty corridor, industrial white tiles on the walls. She stopped with her back against the wall, so cold her breath caught. *Free me.* They stared past one another, panting, reeling with foolishness.

She put a hand to the bare skin at the plunge of her blouse and turned her head, pressing her cheek to the cold tile, showing him the long line of her neck. *Disappear. She…*

He pounced on her then, grabbing her waist and dipping his head to smash his lips to her collarbone. Kissing her neck, and then her mouth, warm and seeking, her pelvis pressing into his hip. She had no awareness of him undoing the front of her blouse until she felt his hand caress a breast from her bra, and then his tongue traced a quick broken line down her flesh until his teeth were teasing her nipple.

Now she needed to give him every inch of the body he exposed beneath his hands. The threat of exposure only excited her more, and he was rough with her then, grabbing a handful of perfectly coiffed hair to pin to the wall, preventing any resistance when his fingers raked down across her flat belly to dip into her drenched underwear.

"Oh Vic!"

"Never call me that," he snarled, ripping the underwear aside. "It's Victor." She dared to look at him then and pulled him harder into her body as if she wanted the bruises.

○

Once again, he had failed to escape, and now he was just doing tricks in the air, loops and barrel rolls, Immelmanns and chandelles, everything so beautifully executed, leaving pink exhaust trails across the sky which all eventually faded. Look. None of it left a trace.

5

RESIDENCE OF *MAROC-PRESSE* DEPUTY DIRECTOR ATTACKED

CASABLANCA – A pipe bomb exploded last night on the balcony of the apartment inhabited by Mr. Antoine Mazzella, deputy director and editor of the newspaper *Maroc-Presse*. Fortunately, the device caused little damage.

[*Maroc-Presse* – notably via the pen of its director, Henri Sartout – has taken a position in favor of France resuming dialogue with the Moroccan nationalists.][10]

○

The bombing of Mazzella's house changed everything for Albert Forestier. Somebody had spotted Avival and Congos outside. Albert had been stunned by the betrayal and had vowed revenge. He knew Mazzella was brave and could fight his own battles, but his eight-year-old daughter, who had narrowly escaped harm? Forestier had once visited her at the house, her mother too, and they had been kind to him. Tears welled in his eyes. He had not seen the list that day and was furious that Avival had not trusted him with the names. He could not provide any proof for the police to act upon. But he would find something, he swore, because this changed everything.

The next day as he sat with Mazzella in his office at *Maroc-Presse*, a warning arrived with the mail: *That was just the beginning*.

"So where are we, Inspector Forestier?" Sartout asked.

"They keep pushing me to assassinate someone to prove

<hr>

10   *Le Monde* – 10/13/1954

myself," Albert said fiercely, "but don't worry about that. I'm onto something big."

○

Jacques Lemaigre-Dubreuil was incensed by Paris's continued inaction and had said little during the meeting. He had repeatedly warned Mendès France, now prime minister, about the deteriorating situation but had received no response. Now French citizens were targeting French journalists on French territory, with no fear of consequences. It was unimaginable. And unforgiveable.

Sartout insisted that urgent action was required, and he had a plan. They needed proof, so they should stage a fake attack that could be pinned on Avival. "You can plan a fake attack," Mazzella said calmly, "but there are no fake consequences."

Still Jacques said nothing. They needed to beat back the violent tide threatening Morocco, and perhaps Sartout's plan could work, but as owner of the paper, Jacques needed to remain outwardly neutral. Sartout continued, volunteering to be the fake target in the fake attack, assuming his fake assassin was someone in whom they had complete trust. The men turned to Forestier.

○

"You know how to shoot a gun."

"Yes," Albert said, before realizing that it hadn't been a question. Never on the battlefield, perhaps, but there had been extensive training.

107

"You can't use your own," Sartout said. This time Albert nodded seriously. "I'll get you one. Are you a good shot?"

"You had to be a good shot in Indochina. Otherwise I w-w-wouldn't be sitting here."

"Good. Then you'll know how to miss."

That night Forestier glanced around La Gironde before leaning across the bar towards Avival and announcing that he had a plan. Avival groaned. "I liked it better when you sat over there writing poetry in your pretty notebook," he said, making the p in poetry explode. That was the end of that conversation.

Outside on the sidewalk Camille was feeding yesterday's baguettes to the sparrows, talking to them as she always did. Albert watched her through the windows. The conversation seemed serious. Maybe they could really understand her. He didn't know much about birds, but he wished she would talk to him like that sometime. Camille was one good thing amidst all this bad.

Half an hour later, Congos and the Gypsy came in carrying a list. Forestier sidled up next to them. Harraki, Ben Bouazza, Baby Berrada, Zarrouck, Sebti. His hand screamed to take notes. He thought of Mazzella's daughter, and his fear vanished. "I've got someone better," he said. "I've got a plan."

That got a laugh, but he kept talking. In his spare time he had been studying the movements of Major Sartout, the known liberal, director of that newspaper *Maroc-Presse*, where Forestier himself had covered the fights, not politics, when he was a reporter. He knew the man's routine. He knew the path he walked to the police station, where he checked in first each morning, and he knew when he left the house. That's where he would shoot him: right outside the house.

The others were astonished. Ecstatic. Sartout was one of their biggest enemies. They clapped him on the back. Drinks, toasts. Forestier was finally going to get himself a rat.

And two and a half weeks later, on October 29, 1954, Forestier woke early, ate his breakfast, and debated whether to put on a tight black t-shirt, the kind Avival wore. In the bathroom mirror he threw a few punches. He could have gone pro, and there had been so many women. Camille had revealed her body to him, but they had not conceived a child together. The shirt was perfect.

Half an hour later he walked down a quiet residential street near Anfa that was lined with walled villas. A few French schoolchildren skipped past. A maid bustled to work. He attempted to appear casual, sometimes lingering behind trunks of the palm trees that shot up from squares in the sidewalk. The pistol, which Sartout himself had provided, was snug in his pants pocket, and occasionally his hand strayed to touch its cold barrel through the fabric, making him feel invincible. Specks of mica glittered in the sidewalk. A bird warbled from a humid garden beyond a wall. This was Sartout's house. He kneeled behind a car and pretended to tie his shoelace. Still three minutes until the garden door opened. He slowly untied and retied his other shoelace. Then the first shoe felt loose and actually needed tying.

He heard the key in the lock. The major banged at the metal door, the signal. Albert's heart seemed to have exploded, and his blood went cold as it melted through him. The truth was that he had only ever fired a gun at a paper target. He rose from behind the car, sliding the pistol from his pocket and clicking off the safety. He felt outrageously exposed. Sartout emerged from behind the door and locked eyes with him. Albert raised the gun, aiming at a spot on the wall beside the major. As he pulled the trigger, his arm flew into the air as if he'd been hit. As if the major was the one who'd fired the shot. Sartout shouted and fell to the sidewalk, and Albert knew then that he had killed the man.

But Sartout was still glaring at him, furious now, and the bullet had flown much too high, perhaps even over the wall. Albert walked over to the major's body, gripping the gun so tightly that it felt like part of his hand, another few hard bones. He shot two rounds into the sidewalk, nearly rendering both men deaf. That would leave something for ballistics to find.

"Run, you idiot," Sartout growled, and so Albert did, overjoyed by his exploit, his arm still numb from the shots, the pistol flailing wildly in the air, until a block or two later he shoved it into his pocket.

Around lunchtime he showed up at La Gironde, now in uniform. He sat at the bar, where the others had been waiting. "Give me a drink," he said to Avival, looking past him to the newspaper clippings framed over bottles, the photos of the amateur boxer, the cracked gloves pinned to the wall. Perhaps there was a secret key hidden down in those empty hands too. Perhaps the key opened a closet where Avival had kept the bombs planted for Mazzella and his daughter. This bastard's fate was now in Albert Forestier's hands. "Give me a drink," he said again. The fate of all of them was now in his hands, and what he wanted more than anything was to announce that fact. But instead he said: "I did it."

They crowded in closer. Softly he told them about the look on Sartout's face, the three perfectly aimed shots – a tight grouping was the military term – which couldn't have missed. The cool and collected getaway. His face flushed as he told it. He grinned at the memory. They respected him now, all of them, even Camille, who watched from across the room as they whispered. Surely she saw, as everyone else did, that Forestier was now a leader of these men. He was someone to be considered.

"What did you do with the gun?" Congos murmured into his ear, as attentively as a lover.

"I've got it right here," Forestier said brightly, patting his jacket pocket.

"You kept the gun?" Congos's eyes went wide. "Here, give it to me. I'll get rid of it."

Forestier took a napkin from the bar, slipped it into his

pocket, and brought out the pistol, a pointless precaution since the napkin only partly covered the weapon, and probably even drew more attention to it. Shielding the transaction with his body, Congos took the gun and slipped it into his own pocket. So it was done.

And he had even managed to plant the gun.

SHORT CONTROLLED BURSTS
December 1954

Ahmed Touil was parked across the street from a five-floor apartment building at 32 Rue Bergerac, where the Chaoui girl and her family now lived. He sat behind the wheel, trusting nobody else's driving. He'd driven his two men, who had no idea what was so special about that sleepy street, and weren't about to ask. It was time to send a message. Ahmed wasn't going to let Touria Chaoui betray her people anymore.

A week earlier he'd run into her at the Central Post Office. By now her dealings with the French were proven fact. Everybody knew she spread her legs for a French pilot. Moroccans weren't good enough for her anymore. Unless you happened to be the Sultan, of course. Ahmed had it on good authority that before exile she'd been fucking him too.

He'd followed her out of the post office, wanting to say hello, but the bitch was so stuck up now she'd turned up her nose like he was a street bum. Her face was pretty, but they'd screwed up her head. So he'd hissed in her ear – in French: "*Comment ça va, Mademoiselle Chaoui?*" Which got the little whore's attention. She had looked around for somebody to rescue her, not realizing that this was exactly Ahmed's intention. To rescue her from herself. "Come with me to join the resistance, and I'll give you the sacred oath." But she ran off down the sidewalk and shut herself up in the green Morris Minor.

Now the Morris was parked on Rue Bergerac. The car made him furious. Who had bought it for her? Not her father. So who? The French? Never mind, he would forgive her. Lights still burned on the second floor. That was her room. He was almost positive.

Kidnapping was a possibility. That would make a real statement, unlike these toy bombs that killed maybe three people but excited amateurs like Saadia. Also kidnapping would give them a chance to get to know one another, like he'd gotten to know the little nurse they'd been keeping at his house for the past week. His stupid men had mistaken the nurse for the pilot and had snatched her off the sidewalk. But she wasn't Touria Chaoui, as he'd demonstrated by furiously showing them some photographs from his collection. Of course now the little nurse, with her curly hair and dark eyes, couldn't get enough of Ahmed Touil.

The banging from the trunk sounded again. The nurse was getting impatient. They needed to move. The nosy woman in the window upstairs had already been paid off, but you couldn't account for everyone, especially not these days, so he turned the key in the ignition and drove. The message could be delivered some other time when he could make it more personal.

At the end of Rue Camiran, he waved to the water seller, all done up in his Berber costume. Message transmitted. Then on Rond-Point de la Gironde, a few hundred yards from the Chaouis', they passed a pale Frenchman parked in a Peugeot 203. He was just sitting there looking through the foggy windshield, a perfect target, but Ahmed Touil had moved into a new phase. He was being strategic.

o

CARTRIDGES STOLEN FROM U.S. BASE AT NOUASSEUR

CASABLANCA – Previous information had suggested the disappearance of thirty (sixty, according to other rumors) incendiary bombs from the U.S. base at Nouasseur.

Regional security services clarified that they were not bombs, but gun cartridges which were stolen. They were stored in a closely guarded room. U.S. and French authorities are conducting a joint investigation.[11]

115

---

11   *Le Monde* – 01/12/1954

2

Closing time was approaching when Forestier walked in from the cold, his teeth chattering. The date was December 23, 1954. Behind the bar Avival had hung some glittery baubles from the necks of liquor bottles. The plastic snowman had been pulled from storage and sat on the counter, glowing faintly whenever somebody remembered to plug it in. Camille listlessly swept the floor, and a last table of three loud beer drinkers sat near the entrance. They were Moroccans, apparently unaware of the politics of La Gironde. Albert managed to smile at Avival. "Where is everybody?"

He pointed at the glowing snowman. "Don't you have family?" Albert didn't answer. Unbuttoning his coat, he moved towards his old table, wary of sitting too close to Avival. It was possible he knew everything by now.

His teeth wouldn't stop chattering. He had just left Mazzella out on the rocks at Sidi Belyout, where the frigid night had guaranteed privacy. *Maroc-Presse* was under surveillance, and police were stationed at Mazzella's house, allegedly for protection, but also to observe whatever liberals came and went. Icy air had crashed ashore on the waves. Their breaths had fogged their faces, as if they were already ghosts. Mazzella had learned that a police investigator had found the gun used in the Sartout attempt. They also knew the gun was Sartout's. Ballistics had confirmed it.

Mazzella had pulled out a copy of the report, which was about to be released. Not only did it assert that Sartout had faked his own assassination attempt to further the liberal agenda, but it also suggested that the supposed outbreak of attacks by armed French civilians on Moroccans was just another myth he'd invented. In fact, as the unfairly maligned police had been insisting for months, Casablanca had no "counter-terrorism" problem at all. Law and order were being vigilantly maintained.

"What did you do with the gun?" Mazzella had asked, and then Albert had been grateful for the darkness. Had Congos set him up? "I threw it in the ocean." That's what he should have done. That's what they did in the movies. "I'm not some amateur. I know how to d-d-ditch a piece."

"So they're lying? That's what Sartout said. The cops plant false reports all the time. This is nothing new."

"They're lying. It can't be his gun."

Mazzella nodded grimly. "In any case, they're coming after us."

Now Avival loomed over Albert's table. "In uniform tonight, Inspector? You working?"

"You kn-kn-know me, François. I'm always w-w-working."

"What can I get you?"

"A c-c-cognac. C-C-Camus."

Avival strolled back around the bar, poured the cognac, along with a whiskey, and brought the drinks back to the table. "To the victims of the Central Market bombing," he said, raising his glass. "One year ago tomorrow. We will never forget."

"Never forget," Albert murmured, clinking glasses. Even if Avival didn't yet know about the report, he would by tomorrow. Could Albert pretend to have worked with the police to double-cross Sartout? Maybe, but then how would he explain giving the gun to Congos? Too many questions. The gun was a problem. Avival would figure that out if he hadn't already. So the only solution was to get Avival first. Which meant immediately. Tonight.

"Any plans for the holidays?" Albert asked, glancing over at Camille, who was still sweeping. He forced himself to look Avival in the eye. Jab with the left, hook with the right. Put him on the mat.

Avival returned the look. "Naguib, Lazrak, Berrada again, ideally Delanoë…." He went on. Were these even real people?

Had they invented the list to trap him? Across the room the three tipsy Moroccans laughed raucously. Avival rolled his eyes and lit a cigarette. "I've never denied anyone a drink," he explained.

The phone beside the kitchen rang, and Avival rose from the table, taking the whiskey with him. Forestier watched his own heartbeat ripple the surface of his cognac. But Avival casually hung up the phone. It would ring again, however, and the next time or the next, he would know the truth. Albert could not let that happen.

Camille swept over to his table, her smile so faint that it seemed trapped deep inside her. "Where's Micheline tonight?" he asked. "She must be excited about Christmas."

Camille nodded. "She's at the neighbors. They have been kind to us. I hope somebody's taking care of you. Do you have family?"

"My mother's not around anymore, but I'm sure I'll see my father."

"*Encore!*" the Moroccans shouted. "*Encore!*" Camille glanced over at the bar to Avival, who nodded, growling, "But it's their last round."

The words echoed indistinctly in Albert's mind. *It's their last round.*

Then he had to summon all his nonexistent training to avoid leaping from his chair. *Their last round!*

Nobody who knew François Avival could mistake the meaning of those words. Poor Arabs. They had signed their own death warrants the moment they had walked into La Gironde.

Albert now felt a blinding clarity. He walked over to the bar and paid the bill. Outside he buttoned his coat and strode past his Ford Vedette, down the block to Avival's garage. He hoisted the door and circled the Peugeot 203 to the back wall, where in the darkness he patted his bare palms against the cold concrete until he found the hanging boxing gloves. His hands went into the gloves, finding the keys in the fingers of each one. From the locker he took a Thompson M1 and loaded a magazine from another shelf. Opening the passenger-side door of the Peugeot, he placed the machine-gun on the floorboard, then shut the locker and dropped that key back down into the glove. Was there a hat somewhere? He wished he'd worn one. Flipping up his coat collar, he climbed into the car, turned that key in the ignition, and without illuminating the headlights gently reversed onto the street. He would leave the garage door open. If he wasn't back before closing, he was a dead man anyway.

Like a dark phantom he rolled down the street before parking on Boulevard de la Gironde, across the roundabout from the bar. Lowering the sun visor, he sank into his seat. Through the lighted windows he could see Avival, Camille, and the three Moroccans still at their table. The car windows slowly fogged. He wiped a spot clean. The cold no longer touched him. Ten minutes later, at 11:15, the Moroccans rose and walked unsteadily out to the sidewalk, where they piled into a Ford Taunus and rolled off. Forestier started the car, switching on the headlights only after he was turning out of the roundabout to follow them onto Rue de Camiran. He kept his distance.

The Moroccans turned right onto Route de Medouina, then left a hundred meters later onto Rue du Général Humbert, then right onto Boulevard Victor Hugo. Forestier followed as if he had predicted their every turn, occasionally glancing over at the Thompson. The night was quiet, and no other cars passed. Approaching Rue de Constantinople, he accelerated until he drew level with the Taunus. Passing then, he swerved so that the Moroccans were forced to veer towards the gutter. They screeched to a stop. Forestier braked a couple dozen meters later.

Total silence for a moment. The Taunus's headlights picked out the blank façade of the back of an apartment building. Forestier grabbed the machine-gun and wrenched open his door. Out in the cold he ran towards the stunned Moroccan faces on the other side of the windshield. He pointed the machine-gun at the glass and squeezed the trigger.

Bullets sprayed everywhere. The force of the recoil was overpowering, and the gun's barrel waggled like the end of an untended water hose. Albert grasped the gun with both hands, pinning it to his hip. Short controlled bursts. The windshield became spider webs. He kept firing, taking long strides towards the Taunus, around to the side of the car, where through the driver's window he saw that the two in the front were dead.

Leave nothing to chance. This time there could be no oversights. Again he squeezed the trigger, filling the front seat with bullets. Then it was quiet, at least until a bloody palm thumped against the back window. He swiveled and unloaded a stream into the hand. The whole window went red until the stump of an arm burst through the glass. Shoulders followed. He fired until the man's head melted off his body and the gun was just clicking.

How long did he stand there? He didn't know. Eventually he lowered the gun and noticed two other Moroccans in djellabahs watching from against the blank wall, still faintly illuminated by the fading headlights of the Taunus. He ran for Avival's car, holding the Thompson tightly. This time he knew exactly what to do with the gun. Practice makes perfect.

Up Rue de Constantinople and Boulevard de la Marne, across Route de Medouina, all the way to Route des Oulad Ziane, flying around the back way, hardly needing to touch the wheel. The street was empty, the garage silent. He cut the lights and edged in, replacing the gun in the locker, and tossing in the empty magazine as well. Then he lowered the garage door, and out on the street was still alone. This was the most dangerous stretch, the walk back to his Vedette, but he forced himself to move with great slowness. Avival's downfall hung in the air like mist.

Back in his car, he frantically molted his coat onto the seat behind him. 11:35. Then he drove, retracing the exact path from twenty minutes earlier, following an invisible Taunus carrying three laughing Moroccans, all invisible. The lights still burned at La Gironde, but he didn't look. About four minutes later he pulled up to the scene of the crime. The Taunus was slung across the road. Two Moroccans in djellabahs helplessly circled the car, blood on their hands, shouting for help. The driver's side door had been opened, and half a body had spilled out onto the pavement. Forestier parked, took his police-issued pistol from the glove box, and stepped out of the car.

"Hands up," he shouted, moving cautiously towards the men, who instantly obeyed, the loose sleeves of their djellabahs slumping to their shoulders. "What's going on here?"

There had been a shooting. Forestier lowered his gun and spoke very calmly. He knew they hadn't done this thing, he said. He knew they had only tried to help. But had they seen anything? Had they witnessed the crime?

They had. Good. Now this was very important: had they seen the shooter, or shooters? Could they tell him anything that might help with the investigation? Had the shooter or shooters been on foot? Had they said anything? Were they French or Moroccan? "Please. You can lower your hands."

They did, and one finally spoke. There had been one man, probably French, but it had been too dark to be certain, and the lights of the Taunus had been in their eyes. But the car had been a Peugeot 203, and he had even seen its license plate. Forestier whipped out his notebook.

"Please repeat that back to me." His trembling hands struggled to scratch the numbers onto the page. If the numbers were even close to those on Avival's plates, then they finally had their man.

"Can you tell me anything about him at all?" he pressed. "Was he stocky? Short or tall? Was he wearing a hat?" The men briefly discussed this in Arabic. Forestier understood little. Not especially tall, they decided, and definitely not wearing a hat. "Hair cut close to his scalp? Slightly balding? Crooked nose?" The Moroccans conceded that all of these things were possible. And surely he had worn a coat. Was there anything remarkable about the coat? Was it a specific color, for example, or had he worn the collar up? Yes! The shooter's collar had definitely been up. Forestier noted all of this down in his notebook: stocky, close-cropped hair, slightly balding, crooked nose, coat collar up. Which was how Avival wore his coat, a dashing effect that Forestier had always admired.

They gave him their names. He asked for their addresses, and they pointed at the adjacent building. Forestier nodded again. He wanted to hug them, but instead he thanked them on behalf of the Casablanca Police Department, promising that he would do everything in his power to bring to justice the man responsible for this heinous crime.

The next morning at dawn, Christmas Eve, he knocked at the door of Sartout's villa carrying an extensive report written up in the night, of which he was prouder than even his finest boxing pieces. In places, he felt, it attained the psychological insight of Montaigne, or someone of that stature. Sartout answered the door in a robe, his long, pale, skinny legs poking out, mustache uncombed. "You shouldn't be here," he grumbled. "And *mon dieu*, Forestier. It's Christmas Eve."

"I'm sorry if I woke you, but this was too important to wait."

"You didn't wake me," Sartout sighed, waving him in. "I slept badly. Madame Sartout left last night. Temporarily, of course, like all of this."

Forestier hardly heard him. He struggled to concentrate as they sat at the kitchen table waiting for water to boil. Sartout was telling him about the tract that had been distributed around town by his enemies. No, not the damning police report – and they needed to talk about that – but one about his wife, whom the authors of the tract had labeled a "pervert", outing her as the mistress of Thami Ouezzani and several other liberal Moroccans. Everyone in town had seen it. Maybe it was true. She had always been such a passionate supporter of independence. He was…

"Those bastards," Forestier growled, his leg jiggling beneath the table. The water boiled out of the pot and hissed on the burner. Neither man noticed. Sartout continued. The tract had also charged him with falsely accusing innocent French citizens of violent acts. Presumably this was a reference to the list of counter-terrorists Forestier had delivered to Sartout to pass on to higher authorities, which had included Avival and his crew. Or maybe it was all nonsense. Maybe they should all just go back to France.

"Or maybe we should send them to prison for a very long time," Forestier said with a grin, sliding his report across the table. Finally he could tell the story, how he had gone to La Gironde the night before, wanting to find out what Avival knew, foolishly brave perhaps, but then as he'd sat there, Avival had clearly threatened three Moroccan customers. *It's their last round.* A waitress had also heard the threat. Forestier was close to her, no further comment necessary, and she might be willing to testify. In any case, it was all in the report. How he had left a while later without seeing Avival again, and then how he had come upon the Taunus and the three dead Moroccans riddled with bullets. As he spoke, the color returned to Sartout's face, and he drew closer across the table. *Their last round.* Two witnesses at the crime scene had described the shooter, unmistakably Avival. Forestier had taken down their names and addresses. It was all in the report, if he wanted to have a look and….

"We have to get to the station immediately," Sartout cried, springing into action. "I'll get dressed, you do something about coffee."

He rushed off. Forestier rose from the table and walked

over to the stove. The water had all boiled off. He smiled down into the empty pot, and perhaps he would have smiled even wider if he had realized that since the shooting he hadn't stuttered once.

They had called before leaving, and the head of Internal Affairs was waiting glumly in his office. Major Sartout, in full regalia on a Christmas Eve, handed over Inspector Forestier's report. The head of Internal Affairs did not open it. So the major described its contents, leaving out a few of what were – in the opinion of Albert – the more vivid details. But Albert held his tongue.

"We'll look into it," said the head of Internal Affairs, without making eye contact.

"*It's their last round!*" Forestier burst out.

"We'll look into it."

Forestier made two fists in his lap and looked back up at the man. "Then what are your orders, sir?"

"Continue your investigations. But since this is the holiday season, and presumably we all have families, please send any future reports to my office by mail. That will be all."

That's when Albert knew that he was a dead man. He had stood up to power. He had tried to protect innocent lives. And so the powerful would make him a martyr.

o

ELEVEN ATTACKS IN MOROCCO IN TWENTY-FOUR HOURS

THREE DEAD – FIFTEEN INJURED

RABAT – Christmas Day was marked by multiple attacks in Casablanca. In the afternoon at Carrières Centrales, a former moggadem (neighborhood official) was seriously injured by a bullet to the head; in the European quarter...a Moroccan...was found wounded by three bullets.

Three other attacks were reported in the evening. In the first...a locally made bomb killed one Moroccan and injured four, including an eight-year-old girl. A second explosion near a Moorish café wounded the waiter's wife and two neighborhood children, aged seven and six. An hour later a shopkeeper, Allal Ben Ahmed, was killed with a revolver in the new medina.

Shots were fired at a Moroccan police inspector near the Amade roundabout; at two policemen on Rue Moulay Idriss from a van driving without lights; and at a car in which there were two Moroccans. None of these were killed.

Sunday morning...a meat delivery truck was set afire and partially destroyed. Later a device exploded in a European grocery store, causing little damage.

Sunday again, an explosive device detonated in the medina of Fez, in a hair salon near a Moroccan cinema.... The carotid of a twenty-three-year-old Moroccan was cut, instantly killing him, and six others were injured....

In twenty-four hours eleven terrorist attacks have caused three deaths and fifteen injuries.[12]

---

12   *Le Monde* – 12/28/1954

3

She was crazy about him. He wasn't like the others. He respected her and bought her clothes and took her everywhere. They were in love.

After the closing of Bousbir, the prostitutes had migrated to the streets and the *maisons closes*. Suzanne had been working at Chez la Parisienne near Bab Marrakesh. Since the brothel was near the mellah, the *patronne* was always looking for Jewish girls, and although Suzanne had been worried about her dark skin, the *patronne* said it didn't matter in the dark. She had taught Suzanne to dress in European clothes – tight blouses unbuttoned to show off her breasts, but not enough to reveal her tattoo – and how to read the headlines at the newsstands so that she could be cultured. The money wasn't any better than at Bousbir, however, and the living conditions felt worse. Suzanne slept in any available room and was often lonely. Nobody protected her as Zohra once had.

At La Parisienne, the men were mostly Moroccan: neighborhood family men, some teenaged boys, and sometimes rich ones from Rabat. Then there was Haj Driss Alaoui. In his mid-twenties, he came in about once a week, often with an entourage, spending lots of money, sending out for alcohol and collecting several girls to take upstairs. Everybody loved Haj Driss, and although he had never noticed Suzanne, she found herself anticipating his visits.

The night had been quiet. Nobody had wanted her, and so the next morning she was one of the few girls awake. A bang came at the low wooden door that gave onto the narrow medina street. The *patronne* had gone out shopping, so Suzanne tentatively opened it, and Haj Driss came stumbling in, drunk and alone. He wanted her, he said, so she took him to a room, where he clumsily stripped off all his clothes, shocking her with his total nudity. "Let me see you," he said, so she stripped too, blushing so hard that he could probably see the shame

126

even in her dark cheeks.

They spent the whole day in bed, hardly making love, sometimes kissing, mostly just talking. Haj Driss had a lot of problems. His family was rich, of course, but that wasn't always as easy as Suzanne might expect. He wanted to be independent, to do his own thing – something in import-export, maybe luxury cars – but his father insisted he remain in the family business and had threatened to cut off his allowance until he agreed. His mother supported his dreams, and his allowance, let nothing bad be said of her, Allah almighty he respected women, but when you were an Alaoui, there were always family expectations. Suzanne probably couldn't understand something like that, he said, but Suzanne understood completely. His sweet smile made her dizzy, and he liked to look at her body as she awkwardly posed, tracing his nails like a comb across her skin. She had a beautiful body, he said, which astonished her more than anything. The last time she had felt such pride was probably four years earlier under the eyes of the boys at the municipal swimming pool.

Haj Driss started coming more often, and almost always he saw only her. Usually after they had taken off their clothes, he just crawled into bed and rested his cheek on her breasts, talking for hours as she ran her hands through his dark hair. He was so skinny. She could count his ribs without needing to touch them. He talked of the inevitability of independence, and of his role in the new Morocco, which would be so different from his father's Morocco, because it would be run by men like Haj Driss. It made sense. Sometimes her mind drifted, at least until he told her how much he needed her, and then she would come crashing back into him. "*Vive l'amour*," he would mumble, lips locked to her breast. That was one of their little jokes. He brought her expensive gifts, French perfume and jewelry she couldn't imagine anyone affording, but Haj Driss could apparently afford anything. He also knew how to swim in the waves of the sea, as the girls at Bousbir had put it, and with his fingers he gave her the first orgasm of her life. It felt like diving naked into a swimming pool, but there were a million other swimming pools stacked beneath it, and at the bottom of each was a thin membrane through which she burst until she had burst through them all to the fiery center of the earth.

The first time he asked her to go out with him, she almost refused, but then she realized that she was no longer in Bousbir, that Jean Bart was ancient history, and she was free to do as she pleased. But how could a man like Haj Driss let himself be seen with a whore? She was being silly, he said. He loved her, and if she didn't let him take her out and show her off, then she could expect a spanking. She laughed and wiggled her ass, and when he picked her up that night, she had been ready for hours, pacing her room in the short green dress she had bought with some of the money he had given her, not wanting to wrinkle it by sitting.

He drove this beautiful little white car he said was American and called a Corvette. It was a convertible, and although the December night was cold, they rode with the top down. Otherwise there was no point, Haj Driss said. Actually he shouted it, because he liked American music too and played Radio Nouasseur's *Sunset Jubilee* so loud that everybody could hear him coming. *Sh-Boom* by the Crew-Cuts, *I Need You Now* by somebody called Eddie Fisher. She immediately loved the songs and learned to mimic the words. Lie good be a dream. Sha boom, sha boom. Ya la la la la la la la la la.

That first night he took her to a dirty bar in Derb Chorfa-Tolba called Les Nations Unies, where he needed to meet a few people. They sat at the bar, and he ordered a bottle of wine. She tried a glass and didn't like it much, but loved it anyway because it was real wine, and she was with Haj Driss. Even when he went off to a table to talk with a few men who, in her opinion, weren't his type, everybody knew she was with him. Afterwards in the Corvette car, he kissed her hand and apologized for taking her to such a low-class place, promising never to do it again. She was still so amazed that he actually wanted to be seen with her that she couldn't feel the cold as they drove towards Bab Marrakesh, where that crazy man kissed her right out in the open, wrapping her in his arms. Soon one of these nights, she thought, she wouldn't return to La Parisienne. Already she no longer slept with other men. Haj Driss gave her and the *patronne* more than enough money to make it that way. Soon she would no longer be a prostitute. Haj Driss would wash her clean.

"I want you more than anything," he said after they had kissed, "but unfortunately I can't tonight." Later, once she had hung up her green dress and was alone in the room, she touched herself for the first time and experienced another orgasm just thinking about Haj Driss, if you can believe it, just with her hand.

The first time he took her to Paradise, she nearly died. A Bousbir *pass* had told her about Aziza's new shop on Rue Nolly, but she didn't know Casablanca streets anymore. Her city was just a collection of night places where men were allowed to have sex with her. She saw the shop window as Haj Driss parked the Corvette car, her mother's name in the window, because of course she'd named the shop after herself. It was too late, the car was already parked, and she couldn't breathe, but she forced herself to look again while stepping out onto the sidewalk. Beautiful dead dresses hung on headless mannequins. Thankfully at this hour the shop was closed. Aziza probably wouldn't have recognized her anyway, skin lightened by the juice of a thousand lemons, hair shiny and straightened, and on Haj Driss's arm. Thankfully he didn't notice her trembling, or at least he didn't mention it. He said she looked beautiful, in the new dress he'd bought, and led her into the place called Paradise.

Paradise was more like the kind of place she imagined Haj Driss frequenting. The crowd was stylish, with men in elegant suits, beautiful women, some of them even French. There were also American soldiers from the base out at Nouasseur, several in uniform. A Frenchman named Renucci owned the place, Haj Driss said. He was an important figure in import-export and always surrounded by huge bodyguards who never opened their mouths.

At Paradise, Haj Driss seemed to know everyone and was always buying drinks. Sometimes there were other girls too, but she knew he loved her the best. Hardly ever did she leave his side, except sometimes he liked her to flirt with other men, especially Americans, making a game of it. One night she danced on the table and sang in her tight dress as a dozen eyes stripped her naked.

Another time Haj Driss, who wasn't drinking that night, pointed out two Americans at the other end of the bar. They were friends of his, he whispered, stroking the front of her dress. The men laughed, and she waved, wanting to please Haj Driss. He kissed her on the cheek, helped her down off the stool, and led her over, introducing them as his friends Mike and Ron. She said hello in English, sha boom, sha boom, and kissed their cheeks. They were nice. Everybody liked Haj Driss.

"I have to go meet someone," he whispered. "Why don't you stay with our American friends for another drink, and we'll meet up later. Be nice to them." He waved over the bartender and pressed a wad of francs into his hand. Her palms began to sweat. Her dress felt too tight then, her legs too exposed. "That's my girl. Have fun."

Then he left, and the Americans pressed into her from either side. One placed a hand on her hip and left it there. Uncomfortable, she turned to look back across the room, but Haj Driss was gone. He would be back. She would do as he asked.

The American called Mike said something she didn't understand, and the men laughed so loud it hurt her ears, slapping the bar with their hands. She giggled into her glass and bit her lip. Ya la la la la la la la la la.

○

Even Christmas this year was slow. Many of Aziza's best clients had gone back to France. Exhausted from a day spent tending an empty shop, she decided to shut up early. She couldn't remember ever doing that, and hardly knew what to do with herself.

As she turned the key in the lock, a few suspicious-looking Frenchmen were already filing into the nightclub next door. Once she had said hello to the owner, but he had ignored her. Back in the day, men like that would have never dared disrespect Aziza Benayiche, but Morocco had changed, and in their eyes she was just another native. Dusk was falling, the air was cool. She wrapped a woolen scarf around her neck. Across the façade of the Hotel Excelsior, which was opposite, isolated women leaned against balconies of ornate woodwork and stared up at the sky. Aziza looked off down the street. The idea of returning to her rented apartment in Habbous depressed her. Everything temporary in her life had become permanent. Why didn't she just buy a little house for herself, some comfort for her old age? Over the years she had saved up more than enough money. Maybe someday she would even have grandchildren to fill the house with laughter. No. That was a fantasy. Ever since that awful day at Bousbir, Aziza had done her best to put her daughter out of her mind. She had given Suzanne everything, but some girls were just bad. You couldn't explain it, so you had to give up.

○

Intelligence had been watching Tahar Sebti for months. A fabric wholesaler with terrorist ties, his house near the Jardin d'Horticulture had become a meeting point for Nationalist leaders. Sebti was also a member of the subversive Study Group that met regularly at the Hotel Mansour, led by the liberal Jacques Lemaigre-Dubreuil, a self-aggrandizing Arab apologist who had even made Sebti a director of Lesieur-Afrique, installing an enemy of France on the board of one of its biggest companies. What could possibly go wrong? Sebti had studied at the French lycée in Fez and had spent two years in Paris, which was no surprise to Tony. The capital corrupted men, filling their heads with perverted ideas.

On December 30, 1954, the Red Hand prepared to strike. Tony had assembled a crack team: Jean "le Footballeur", refrigeration specialist and former goalie, skilled at wall climbing; Omar "le Sheik", dark like an Arab, possibly part-Arab, driver; Michel "le Juif", Jew; Jean "the Gypsy", gypsy, lunatic, though not as lunatic as Congos, who could no longer be trusted; and Tony Méléro, who needed no nickname, which was what he was planning to say if anybody ever asked. The Sebti house was guarded by French police, but the two cops on duty that afternoon were friendly. Once they disappeared for a stroll around the block, Jean le Footballeur jumped the wall, dropped into the garden, silently scaled the side of the house up to the bedroom balcony, placed the bomb, and moved like a cat back to the car. Tony sat calmly watching this from the passenger seat of the Peugeot 203. He wore one of his older black wool suits, because the new beige one technically shouldn't be worn until spring. His shirt was pale blue, but in a striking touch the collar was white. He fingered the silver bells at his cuffs and glanced down at his new Cordovan leather lace-ups, which had been shined twice that morning by urchins at two separate cafés. The shoes really said it all. Any nickname would have been superfluous.

"Not sure anyone's home," said Jean le Footballeur as

he slid into the back seat. For an instant Tony doubted his planning, but even if Sebti was out, the bomb would send a message. Perfect. At least until the Sheik, who frankly lacked experience, reached to start the car and broke off the key in the ignition. Any second now the bomb would explode. Nobody said a word. They watched the Sheik frantically pinching the broken edge of the key until his fingers bled. Tony practiced a slow-breathing technique he had read about in his self-improvement guide. The Sheik lunged for the glovebox and dug out a pair of pliers. Tony watched placidly, imagining stabbing the Sheik in the heart with the pliers and starting the car himself. Would the blast kill them all? He didn't know much about explosives. You could never tell from looking at a bomb what it might do. Could the wall topple over and crush the Peugeot? Or might it merely send a fizzling signal of their presence to a mob of angry Moroccans and more cops? Carefully, patiently, like some kind of half-Arab brain surgeon, the Sheik clamped the pliers to the slight edge of the key and slowly twisted. The pliers slipped, and he tried again. Again.

Finally the engine roared to life. Despite himself, Tony grinned, and they were already peeling off through the neighborhood when they heard the blast, but then it was only smoke in the rearview mirror. The Sheik! There was no better driver. He was a professional, and as leader of the team, Tony took a moment as they screeched around a corner to congratulate him on his quick thinking in a challenging situation. The Captain would be pleased.

But Jean le Footballeur had been right: the house had been empty. So Tony planned again. The ideas were sound, but God was in the details, and his mind filled with scattered memories of other kills: a chest wound spreading out from a spot on a white shirt, the smell of powder and metal on his fingers, a woman's jagged scream cutting silence like a knife, a dark contorted helpless face, pure images disconnected from any emotion.

The bomb hadn't been a failure. It had merely been the next link in a chain inevitably leading to the terrorist's death – the cocking of the gun before the pulling of the trigger. This was all as obvious to Tony as a shirt that perfectly fit. Now as Tony walked through the streets, he felt strong and purified, an undeniable idea more than anything merely human.

O bell! vibrate yourself with beauty's breath.
So, delirious instrument,
Broken just by touching,
The bell became a lyre,
And to its song I slept.

Returning home to his immaculate apartment, where everything was set at right angles, he would often perch on the edge of the bed and lift the book from its spot on the bedside table. The words were always there, neatly falling one after the other. Sometimes he understood them completely, and other times their meaning escaped him, but it didn't matter. He loved poetry, and after a while he would close the book and set it again in its place on the bedside table, repeating the words aloud, exactly. Too few people took the time to cultivate the life of the mind.

o

The *simsar* had shown her a few places, mostly in Moroccan neighborhoods. Many French families were trying to sell, but even in their desperation they wouldn't sell to her. She refused to engage, refused to be provoked by these monsters who'd killed Tahar Sebti. She would not have lived in their homes even if they had been selling. She would give them nothing of herself. Small-minded settlers from the French countryside, they even dressed like peasants.

Otherwise there were several apartments, and a few houses, but everything looked so dirty and run down, and even if the exterior was well kept, nothing on the inside was ever like the home in which she had imagined living. The morning had passed, and the *simsar* was losing patience. Finally he mentioned a new neighborhood, with new houses, but it would be more expensive. Aziza waved down a taxi.

They rode away from the European neighborhoods towards Habbous, along streets she recognized with growing alarm. *Keep driving,* she thought, but the *simsar* then motioned for the driver to stop, and she blindly passed some money up between the two front seats. Without a word, the *simsar* led her towards the entrance, which was no longer guarded. Was he pretending not to know what she knew? The sun angled down onto freshly painted façades. The main street was silent and swept clean. "Each of these has been converted into a three-story house with all the modern conveniences...." A chill went down her spine. Emptied of its seedy chaos, Bousbir was hardly recognizable, but they had not thought to change the names of the streets: rue de la Marrakshia, de la Oujdia, de la Fassia, de la Doukkalia, de la Chaouia, de la Bidaouia, de la Meknassia, de la Rbatia. All names of the cities once called home by their whores. She couldn't look. She was waiting to be propositioned, or devastated, and was wet beneath her arms. "Is everything all right, Madame Aziza?"

"Show me one of these places," she ordered.

The *simsar* had the keys to a house, and only after they were inside did her eyes begin to see. The main room was clean, large, and like nothing she could remember. The kitchen was bright, and out back there was a little patio for laundry. She followed the *simsar* upstairs, where he raised shutters to let the light stream in. Aziza wandered through the bedrooms. Suddenly she realized that it was a beautiful place.

"There are also several in the neighborhood for rent," the *simsar* murmured, shuffling along behind her. "Some are furnished, which might be advantageous for a, ah, woman on her own...."

"No rentals," she said. "Fix the papers."

4

○

Albert Forestier missed the old crowd, even if they were probably going to kill him. On December 27, the Monday after Christmas, already four days after those three Moroccans had been murdered, he walked into La Gironde and found the gang as pleased to see him as ever.

"*Joyeux Noël!*" he happily replied to their *bonjours*. Congos asked about his Christmas, the family and the presents, and he invented everything. In truth he had eaten breakfast with his father, who had wondered aloud if his mother was still alive and happy, and then he had driven aimlessly through the city. On Sunday he had briefly met with Mazzella, who had spoken to Lemaigre-Dubreuil, in Paris with his family. Concerned for Sartout and Forestier, he had urgently called the Quai d'Orsay but had been unable to reach anyone who mattered. They were on their own.

"Tomorrow we're organizing a spontaneous action," Congos murmured as they drank, apparently still unaware of the problems attached to the gun Forestier had given him. Did Albert want to join? He mentioned two names: Guessous and Chaoui. "And we're getting Mazzella once and for all."

Would it never end? Forestier felt the rage inside, then the panic. Nodding at Congos's invitation, he excused himself to go to the bathroom. Somehow it seemed important to go through the entire routine. He walked back to the toilet, locked the door, took out his prick and held it over the hole, then washed his hands. He hadn't peed, hadn't needed to. Undercover. And now he needed to use the phone. He was already a martyr. What could they still do to a martyr? He walked out to the corridor telephone and dialed Mazzella's number.

"This is the boxer," he whispered. "Vacate the premises. A visitor arrives."

"Who is this?" Mazzella asked.

"Forestier!" he hissed, hunching over the phone. "They're planning to assassinate you tomorrow. It's a *spontaneous action*."

"What does that mean?"

"I don't know. Please. Just get everybody out."

The door to the kitchen banged open. Camille rushed through carrying a tray of glasses and almost ran into him. They both smiled. "So I've got to go," he said coolly into the telephone, as if another dispensable woman had been begging for it again.

"How was your Christmas?" he asked Camille once he'd slotted the phone back into place.

"Oh it was nice," she said. "Only me and Micheline."

"Such a beautiful name."

"It was my mother's. How about yours?"

"Claudette. She doesn't live with us anymore."

Camille nodded blankly. "I'm sorry," she said. "I meant your Christmas."

Perhaps Albert blushed a bit. So Camille cared about him at least a little. "Oh, I was working." And then he had an idea.

He nodded at the phone. "Actually I just found out that I have to go up to Ifrane for some police work. I figured I'd make it a long weekend for New Year's and stay in this wonderful hotel I used to visit with my parents." Ifrane had just popped into his head, but he longed for the mountains, or escape. "Have you ever been to Ifrane?"

"I haven't left Casablanca since I arrived at eighteen."

"There's skiing," he said. "Ifrane was built on the model of an Alpine village. Pitched roofs. Designed for snow." He could hardly remember the place, except that they had been happy.

"It sounds wonderful."

"Could you get off work?" The words had left his mouth before he'd considered them, but they were the ones he had deeply wanted to say, and so he continued: "I leave Friday morning…. We could celebrate the New Year together."

Several seconds later she still hadn't refused, which was extraordinary, and his heart soared: "Do you want to come?"

"Well, the bar is closing, so it is a long weekend for me."

"You could bring Micheline," he said uncomfortably. "There are monkeys." He needed to get out of town anyway, at least until Internal Affairs decided to act. And then maybe everything would work itself out.

"No," she said, furrowing her brow, so cute, looking a decade younger. "I can find someone to keep her."

"Okay!" he cried, and then she left him there, carrying off her clinking glasses. He took a deep breath and crept back out to the bar. Nobody paid him any attention.

The next morning at Cazès airport, he met Mazzella, his daughter and wife. Across the tarmac a propeller roared, and so they shouted. The daughter looked stricken, captive, and paid no attention to the flying machine, which still peripherally fascinated Forestier. He realized that he had forgotten the girl's name. Mélanie? Elodie?

They were going to Paris for a while, several months if required, but Mazzella, at least, would return once it was safe.

The Morocco he loved could not be held hostage much longer by desperate thugs. Forestier embraced his old friend and handed over a heavy notebook. "Everything is in there. All of my reports, specific incidents, lists, every name." Mazzella thanked him, and they embraced one last time before the editor-in-chief led his family up the rolling staircase into the cabin.

Albert stood on the tarmac looking along the row of oval windows and wondering which was his friend's. Only briefly was he crippled by panic, and then it was fine.

On Friday morning he drove to Ifrane with Camille in the Ford Vedette. Her three suitcases were so large that they occupied the whole trunk. She hadn't known what she might need. He didn't mind. The more of her she brought along, the better he liked it.

The drive took six hours, through Khemisset and up into the Middle Atlas. He stopped sometimes to consult a map, and she pretended to be anxious about where he was taking her, but he had always been good with directions, often leading his battalion to safety through the jungles of Indochina without the aid of a compass. He was so pleased to be with her that for long stretches of road he forgot everything else. This was the man he had always wanted to become. Right now.

She was thirty-one, she said, and he pretended not to believe it, but she was also too tired to insist. It had been years since she'd gotten even three days off from work, and she had never taken a vacation. He watched the dusty landscape shifting past and thought about how an older woman would have more experience, at least in that department.

Mostly he talked about himself, because she seemed so interested, and he told her that once upon a time he had almost become a professional boxer. She didn't know anything about boxing, she said, but had once seen Marcel Cerdan, rest in peace, fight some American at the Stade Philippe.

"Was his name Sampson?" Albert cried. "I was there too!

What did you think of the fight?"

"There wasn't enough time to like anything. It was over in a few seconds."

Albert nodded, the joy of the memory fading from his face. He had run off that day, wanting to be closer to the ring and the great Casablanca Clouter, but surrounded by all those drunken soldiers and their shouts, he had become terrified, and one of the Americans had mocked his tears. Later that night his mother had beat him as his father helplessly watched. He had never forgiven either of them, he realized, and he never would, which came as an immense relief. He was his own man now, and here was this beautiful Camille, with whom he felt a connection stronger than anything he had ever felt for his own family.

Ifrane was a colonial resort city built by the French in the 1930s between the Park of Dark Shadows and the Park of the Island of Love. Designed on the model of Alpine resorts, with dramatically pitched roofs and tree-lined streets, in summer it was popular with functionaries escaping the heat of the coastal capitals to hike, fish, and hunt. In winter, when the red tiles of the roofs covered themselves with snow, there were natural spas bubbling with healing waters, and skiing up on the mountain. The town was also home to the French national police academy, whose requirements Albert had fulfilled remotely.

He had booked a room at the Grand Hotel. The lobby was crowded with families and couples up for the holiday. At the front desk the receptionist asked if they would like a double bed or two singles. The porter waited behind them, rocking his cart, the wheels creaking under the weight of Camille's luggage. Albert glanced sidelong at her, but she had retreated into herself, her shoulders hunched forward like a child's, her lips murmuring silent words. "A double, I think," he mumbled. The receptionist passed him a key and wished them a pleasant stay. A special New Year's Eve dinner would be served from seven, and room service was available.

"I'm happy to sleep on the couch, if you like," he said once the porter had left them in the room. Camille didn't answer. She was humming to herself and unpacking mountains of clothes, suitcases spread across the bed. The room was large, which pleased him, since he'd spent perhaps too much of his policeman's salary. He sat on the couch and watched her work, a truly odd creature, more beautiful than he remembered from when he had glanced at her a minute earlier. He could not believe his luck, but then he didn't believe in luck: destiny was made by a man, not thrust upon him.

"I think I'll take a shower before dinner," she said, turning to look at him. She gathered up a few mysterious things and scampered off to the bathroom, leaving a remarkable mess on the bed, tornados of silk and lace. Once the bathroom door shut, he suppressed an urge to dive headlong into her soft miscellanea. Instead he sat on the couch, wondering if he should order room service, maybe at least a drink – champagne, or was that too obvious? – then just listening to her belt out some song he'd never heard against an accompaniment of hissing water. She seemed happy, and he was glad he'd offered her the chance to get out of town.

Twenty minutes later she was still showering, still singing. He stood from the couch and paced, weaving around the half-dozen scattered pairs of shoes she'd brought. What would he do when this shower was finally completed? Had she brought clothes into the bathroom? He didn't think so, and pictured a wet, white towel molded to her body, a coy look, the twist of a hand, the towel collapsing to the floor. Where would they do it? There wasn't any room on the bed. The couch then. "I'll wait downstairs at the bar," he shouted at the bathroom door. She just kept singing. He didn't think she'd heard. He called out again, thought of knocking, but didn't want to make her nervous. She'd figure it out.

The bar was full of policemen, some in uniform, others

in civilian dress, but he recognized the look. Did they also make him for a cop? He sat at the bar and thought of Congos and the Gypsy back at La Gironde. He raised his glass, toasting the fraternity. Then he looked around at the cops again, wondering if they were also watching him. On his second drink Camille showed up in a short red dress, and the room fell silent for a moment, which felt like an eternity as he watched her approach with a smile sketched across her face. Her skin was luminescent, her dark curls wet against her head.

"You have a beautiful voice," he said, as she hitched herself up onto the next stool. After a brief hesitation, she ordered a Scotch whisky, just as Avival would have done.

"I used to dance a bit too," she said. "At a club called the Don Quichotte. But they didn't appreciate artists. What I really liked was the *bal musette*. Like those old Django Reinhardt songs."

"The guitarist with the missing fingers?"

"They weren't missing. They were just paralyzed. But he played something more beautiful than the jazz they play today, which only makes me nervous."

Albert smiled. "Don't be nervous."

She put her head on her shoulder and made a frown. "He died last year."

"Don't be sad either, Camille. It's almost 1955." She smiled, seeming utterly transformed by her shower. She was no longer a sweeper of littered bar floors. She was something much rarer and smelled of soap.

At dinner he ordered the *pastilla*, a traditional Moroccan dish, he explained, appreciated by connoisseurs and made with nuts and spices and the finest baby pigeon flesh. Camille burst into tears, and for several moments she was inconsolable. She would not say why, wouldn't speak at all. The waiter brought water. Albert figured she missed little Micheline. They had never been so far apart, and the maternal instinct, he'd been told, was powerful. His mother had been an exception.

Then she drank a lot, first champagne, which had in fact been the right choice, and then red wine. She spoke little, concentrating on her food, arranging and rearranging it on her plate before snapping up tiny bites with her fork, which she gripped in a fist. She did say, when Albert asked, that the father of Micheline was no longer around, and that Avival had been horrible – not in so many words, but that was the sense he got. He was eager to hear more, but she just ate.

After dinner she ran up to the room for a coat – surely there were many, but this one was pink, and matched nicely with the dress – and they took a stroll down the main boulevard through the snow. At one point he put his arm around her and pointed off towards the dark mountain and the skiing, or at least where he remembered it being. He had never skied himself. Rowdy young police officers roamed everywhere in packs, and Camille asked if he'd been to the academy there. No, he said, he'd been on a special track, and he couldn't talk about it further, or else he'd have to kill her.

She giggled. "I'm serious," he said, and she giggled some more.

Back at the hotel parking lot, more young policemen milled about, several against the hood of the Vedette. They glared at Camille, and also at him, as he guided her into the lobby. Then in the room they silently spent several minutes arranging their belongings until outside everybody roared. "Happy New Year, I guess," he said.

"I'm just going to use the toilet," she said, ducking around him. Unsure of what to do, he quickly changed into his pajamas and sat down on the bed. She ran out from the bathroom then, still in the red dress, and without looking at him rummaged through the chaos of her clothing, now strewn across the floor, cursing beneath her breath until she found what she needed and ran back off to the bathroom in her bare feet, slamming the door behind her. He continued sitting on the bed in his pajamas.

Hours could have passed. Every moment was as electric as the last, until finally she emerged in a sheer yellow slip with lacy shoulder straps, the most thrilling sight of Albert's twenty-five years. "You're so beautiful," he coughed, truly astonished. The breasts squeezed by transparent fabric. All he could see.

"Oh, it's just an old thing," she said, looking up at the ceiling, swaying back and forth on the balls of her feet. She stepped over to him then, into the angle made by his legs. He reached up and pulled down one of her shoulder straps, baring a breast that swelled to him, and slowly, as if bending to accept a priest's wafer, he took her nipple into his mouth. He kissed it until she said, "Let's get under the covers," and although her body felt strange once he finally had it in his hands, he was happy, and it was fine.

o

In the morning after breakfast, they decided to take a long walk through the woods. Neither talked of what had happened the night before, and there was no physical contact as they negotiated up the narrow path, not even a brushing of hands. They hardly talked, and she concentrated on the trees, on the birds puffed up on their branches against the cold. The air was still, crystalizing, the woods eerily silent. Nature's only sounds that day were the ones they made against it, the crack of a twig underfoot, a faint breathing sound.

At first Camille had thought the trip would be miserable, especially after Albert had reminded her of that boxing match. All she remembered of that day was afterwards, when she had given Mag the pigeon called Henri, and Henri had never come home. Mag must not have made it through the war, not that it mattered now. For years she had actually wished for his death, because that would have made it easier, but she was ashamed of wishing for that now, and she hoped he was alive and thought of her sometimes. Maybe that was all she could hope for, to be some occasional dream in the head of a man whom she would never see again.

She didn't regret sleeping with Albert. It hadn't disturbed her one way or the other, and she was as ambivalent about him now as she had been before, but she wished she didn't have to go back to Casablanca so soon. She was like a pigeon, she thought, staring up at a black bird she couldn't name. She was always coming straight back home, as if she'd been trained that way and had no choice in the matter. She wondered what message she would send back to herself now if she could tie a rolled slip of paper to her leg. She giggled at that, and Albert smiled. He thought she was happy.

Dear Camille, she started, but that was all she could think to say. She was tired then, and he led her back to the hotel, where he left her for an hour or two to nap, and then late in the afternoon they went ice skating on the lake.

She let him have her again that night. He was sure of her now and finished quickly. She slept immediately and didn't dream. Then late on the morning of January 2, she woke to the sound of the radio. Albert wore a striped bathrobe and was pacing at the foot of the bed. The Nationalist Tahar Sebti had been assassinated, he said, and mourners were massing in the streets of Casablanca, thousands of them. Sebti had been a family man, on the boards of Lesieur Oils and *Maroc-Presse*, which meant nothing to her. Albert's apparent grief seemed odd, and she wondered if he was reacting to something she'd done, or hadn't. "These people must be stopped," he said, but she had no idea which people he meant.

After lunch in the dining room, their bags packed upstairs, he asked if she wanted to take the long way home, the scenic route through the mountains. She beamed at the suggestion, suffused with the only real joy she'd felt since they'd left home.

"It's been a good weekend," he said, taking her hand.

○

On the winding road from Azrou to Khenifra, the spectacular Middle Atlas rose starkly on all sides. Occasionally one of them would comment on something beautiful, and the other would agree that it was beautiful. Was that the same car again in his rearview mirror? He couldn't speed up here. The road was too dangerous, the mountain on one side, a deep ravine on the other. Tiny snow-flecked pine trees dotted the valley below. The car behind them edged closer.

Around the next bend a truck in the opposite lane bore down upon them. Suddenly the steering wheel felt disconnected from the road. All the panic he'd been fighting for weeks was compressed into an instant. He ripped the wheel back and forth, but it spun uselessly, and the Vedette careened towards the guardrail, which snapped as easily as a ribbon. The wheels left the pavement, and the air seemed endless as the car arched down into the valley, towards the pine trees flecked with snow. And then Albert knew.

IV. FREEDOM
1955–1956
JOSH SHOEMAKE
F-AIUL
THE CASABLANCA QUARTET

THE CASABLANCA QUARTET

IV. FREEDOM

1955–1956

Based on true stories

JOSH SHOEMAKE

Opium Books

WAR
LANDING
1942
Victor Tessier
Franklin Sydney Felton
Mike "Mag" Magursky
Tommy August
Lucy August
Franklin Sydney Felton
Jacques Lemaigre-Dubreuil
Camille Morin
Tommy August
Mike "Mag" Magursky
Tommy August
Victor Tessier
YELLOW MAGIC
1943
Mike "Mag" Magursky
Camille Morin
Franklin Sydney Felton
Abdelwahed Chaoui
Touria Chaoui
Mike "Mag" Magursky
Ahmed Touil
Aziza Benayiche
Mike "Mag" Magursky
GENTLEMEN CALLERS
Fadila
Camille Morin
Mike "Mag" Magursky
Victor Tessier
Tommy August
Fadila
ANIMAL KINGDOM
1944
Mike "Mag" Magursky
Ahmed Touil
Jacques Lemaigre-Dubreuil
Camille Morin
Franklin Sydney Felton
Tony Méléro
Victor Tessier
Mike "Mag" Magursky
Camille Morin
Mike "Mag" Magursky
Albert Forestier
Ahmed Touil
Abdelwahed Chaoui
Aziza Benayiche
Suzanne Benayiche
1945
Touria Chaoui
Mike "Mag" Magursky
Aziza Benayiche
Camille Morin
PEACE
THE ANGLE OF ATTACK
1948
Abdelwahed Chaoui
Touria Chaoui
Zina Chaoui
Salah Chaoui
Tony Méléro
Abdelwahed Chaoui
Albert Forestier
1949
Touria Chaoui
Franklin Sydney Felton
Camille Morin
Jacques Lemaigre-Dubreuil
Fadila
Suzanne Benayiche
Touria Chaoui
Tony Méléro
BLUESHIFT
1950
1951
Abdelwahed Chaoui
Touria Chaoui
Victor Tessier
Victor Tessier
Abdelwahed Chaoui
Suzanne Benayiche
Victor Tessier
Touria Chaoui
Fadila
Suzanne Benayiche
Touria Chaoui
Abdelwahed Chaoui
HANDS
Tony Méléro
1952
Aziza Benayiche
Touria Chaoui
Hajja Aliya Alaoui
Tony Méléro
Camille Morin
Tommy August
Albert Forestier
Lucy August
Suzanne Benayiche
Victor Tessier
Aziza Benayiche
Albert Forestier
Suzanne Benayiche
Abdelwahed Chaoui
Albert Forestier
Hajja Aliya Alaoui
Touria Chaoui

RESISTANCE
EXILE
1953
Jacques Lemaigre-Dubreuil
Fadila
Tommy August
Victor Tessier
Lucy August
Tony Méléro
Touria Chaoui
Jacques Lemaigre-Dubreuil
Saadia Taibi
Abdelwahed Chaoui
Jacques Lemaigre-Dubreuil
1954
CIGARETTES
Saadia Taibi
Ahmed Touil
Victor Tessier
Lucy August
Franklin Sydney Felton
Ahmed Touil
Saadia Taibi
Abdelwahed Chaoui
Saadia Taibi
Albert Forestier
THE BIG SCREEN
Camille Morin
Jacques Lemaigre-Dubreuil
Tommy August
Saadia Taibi
Ahmed Touil
Victor Tessier
Lucy August
SHORT CONTROLLED BURSTS
Touria Chaoui
Aziza Benayiche
Suzanne Benayiche
Camille Morin
Albert Forestier
1955
Ahmed Touil
Albert Forestier
FREEDOM
Albert Forestier
DJINNS
Lucy August
Tommy August
Victor Tessier
Suzanne Benayiche
Victor Tessier
Touria Chaoui
Hajja Aliya Alaoui
Touria Chaoui
Tony Méléro
Jacques Lemaigre-Dubreuil
INVISIBLE LINES
Touria Chaoui
Aziza Benayiche
Tony Méléro
Saadia Taibi
Hajja Aliya Alaoui
Victor Tessier
Mike "Mag" Magursky
Aziza Benayiche
Ahmed Touil
Touria Chaoui
Mike "Mag" Magursky
Fadila
Tony Méléro
1956
THE BIRDCAGE
Ahmed Touil
Mike "Mag" Magursky
Touria Chaoui
Fadila
Suzanne Benayiche
Suzanne Benayiche
Aziza Benayiche
Hajja Aliya Alaoui
Touria Chaoui
Tommy August
DEPENDENCE DAY
Lucy August
Salah Chaoui
Tony Méléro
Tony Méléro
Saadia Taibi
Tommy August
a Benayiche
Abdelwahed Chaoui
dila
Victor Tessier
Mike "Mag" Magursky

DJINNS
1955

WHY WE NEED AN OPEN FORUM

by Jacques Lemaigre-Dubreuil

Is it still possible to conceive of a reconciliation between a policy of force that only fills prisons and a policy of trust that spreads hope? This is a question that, with the support of our new team at *Maroc-Presse*, I have been asking those responsible for France's policy.

This is because I have been assured that our government has finally decided – with understandable prudence given the current international situation – to support a policy in Morocco of freedom of expression and freedom of the press. This is also because I have received, from the most powerful members of our government, the encouragement to persevere along this path...which is why I decided to entrust this newspaper to a team of independent, far-sighted men who have not limited themselves to a narrow nationalism....

France's greatest achievements here...will devolve into terrible chaos if, having conquered Morocco's body, we fail to marry its soul.

Readers, friends, loyal adversaries, French and Moroccan youth...help us, write to us.[13]

o

Lucy still hadn't returned from her dinner at the Alaouis'. Malaria or the orphans, Tommy had forgotten. Mrs. Alaoui

---

13   *Maroc-Presse* – 04/25/1955

155

hadn't been well, and Lucy had left early to have some time alone with her friend. Now it was late, and the June night was chilly. He wandered along Arnold Boulevard. Headlights appeared on the main road beyond the perimeter fence of the base, and he wondered if that was the Cadillac. No, it was the 10:30 bus, the last from town. At the gate the bus's interior lights shone for inspection, and then a dozen drunk soldiers staggered out. There weren't many of them tonight, although a couple whooped as they stumbled towards their barracks, likely celebrating a sordid evening in the *maisons closes*, which at least weren't quite as sordid as old Bousbir had been. He shifted the garbage bag to his left hand and struggled to free the pack of Luckys from his coat pocket. Vic's leather pea coat had gotten even tighter, although of course it wasn't the coat that had changed. Lucy wanted to get him on a diet.

Recently she had been almost girlish, like the Lucy he remembered, flirting as she had back in Texas. Although startlingly less prudish, often wearing nothing more than a light wrap around the house, which showed off her body. She complained about the climate and said it was just too unbearably humid all the time for clothes.

That afternoon, for example, he'd arrived home to find her tanning on their little back lawn. Spread out on a towel, she had even tossed her bikini top off onto the brown grass, unconcerned that the Pickerings could have seen her naked if they'd only glanced through the fence. "I'm home," Tommy had said.

"Oh, you scared me," she drawled without opening her eyes. He knew she'd felt him standing there, and that he hadn't scared her at all. The kids were still over at the Cedar Loop pool, she said. Could he pick them up?

"And Fatima?"

"I sent her home." Lazily she had stretched one arm into the air with her fingers splayed like flower petals. Lucy's battles with the maid had been constant, and increasingly she had found excuses to send her away. Fatima believed that djinns, or evil spirits, came into the house through the drains. You were tempting the devil if you walked shoeless into the kitchen or bathroom, because the djinns lurked in stagnant water and possessed you through your feet. Lucy goaded Fatima by refusing to wear shoes in the kitchen. Once he had even seen her kick them off in the dining room before stepping onto the linoleum. "It's my house," she had said. Now Fatima dreaded his wife, certain that the blonde infidel was possessed by spirits intent on bringing evil into their house.

"Does this bother you?" she had asked from the grass, running a hand over her bare chest. Still she hadn't turned to look at him.

"Of course not, Lucy. You're free to do whatever you like." Only then did she turn, frowning slightly.

And now there were still no headlights in sight. She had been drinking beforehand, although at the Alaouis' she wasn't likely to have gotten wine.

He cut past the barbershop and the dining hall over to West Avenue, hearing voices in the night, somebody pleading with somebody else, or with the stars. In the distance *Strange Cargo* loomed on the parking apron. The famous B-29 Superfortress had now been converted into a maintenance plane, but in the summer of 1945, it had taken off from the Mariana Islands along with *Enola Gay* to drop "pumpkin bombs", non-nuclear replicas of Fat Man, on targets in various Japanese cities. Forty-nine bombs were dropped on fourteen targets from thirty thousand feet. Tommy had talked with some of the men on those missions, and although they had been confident of their ability to hit their targets, what had always been unclear was whether they would survive an atomic blast. Those long-range Superfortresses moved slowly, and the explosions would likely burn up through the air until they vaporized the winged metal from which they'd come. Nobody had ever dropped a bomb like that before, so all you could do was practice turning sharply after the release to avoid the blast as best you could.

Tommy wondered if he would have had the nerve to fly those missions over Japan. Maybe when he'd still been green, like that first day over Casablanca, but by the time his squadron had launched airstrikes on Okinawa in early 1945, he had already crashed twice and knew that the cockpit's vacuum was an illusion, and that in an instant a single shrieking bullet could bring the world rushing in. Maybe isolated in the desert you could still find that vacuum. Maybe only there. If he kept walking, how long would it take?

He passed the nuclear storage depot with its locked birdcage inside, the secret atomic heart beating at the center of Nouasseur. But his walks every night had been leading him past there to the perimeter fence, which was where he stopped and opened the mouth of the garbage bag.

o

"Am I your captive now?" Lucy's ankles were lashed together with her silk scarf. Her wrists were tied behind her back just above her ass, which was mottled with handprints. Utterly naked, she had dutifully remained on her knees.

Night pressed through the open window of Victor's bedroom. The villa was quiet, as if the air itself was still recovering from the sharp sounds that had filled the room. There were ornate dressers and side tables covered with books, candles and silver boxes. Paintings covered the walls. The bed, stripped of its covers, was larger than any she had ever seen, much less been in. Her shoulders supported her weight, and her head was turned, cheek pressed to the mattress. She watched him by the window, smoking a cigarette on his wooden chair, body hard and pale. Her ass ached, her nipples throbbed. Surely from where he sat he could see everything between her legs. She wanted him to keep looking. With Tommy they had always made love in the dark, except in those early days, when they had been too timid to look. Over time she had forgotten that love was not shameful. But with Victor she wanted to expose everything.

Not once had she been horrified by his strange desires. Even if her heart had beat in fear, she had never been afraid of him. Any horror she felt was of what she might be doing to her family, but some horrors could be made to wait, and now she wanted him again. Maybe Fatima had been right about her damned djinns. One of them had possessed her through her bare feet. It had taken her over, and it needed more.

Victor smoked and watched with no expression as she writhed on the bed. He whistled one of those little tunes he always whistled when he did these things to her. "Back on your knees," he commanded, stubbing out the cigarette in the gold ashtray. She gratefully obeyed. She had not lost him, she wouldn't. She would do everything, and she was capable of even more than everything. He walked slowly over to the bed, some jungle cat, his flat belly, the thrust of his ass. His hand reared back smoothly and spanked her hard. She cried out, wanting the whole city to hear, then sunk forward and whimpered into a pillow, as if she was miserable, but her ass rose ever so slightly to meet the next blow, and this time his hand remained, caressing down between her legs. She groaned, rocking back against him, rocking until there was a sea inside her, and she became a Gulf Coast hurricane, crashing through levees and streaming down highways, sweeping off whole towns. Even then it didn't stop. The ocean waterfalled through the top of her head, and she rubbed clouds against her breasts.

o

"Do you still have those postcards Tommy sent during the war?"

"I doubt it. They were not very interesting, I promise." He sat in the chair again smoking, disturbed by how eager Lucy appeared to throw away her life. Foolishly he had imagined that she might be sufficiently self-possessed to return him to a more human place, but the patterns had emerged as quickly as ever, and again he was trapped.

After she had told him about this lustful djinn which had possessed her, in which she seriously appeared to believe, he had beaten her with real anger. He would not let her blame her lust on some external magic. Lust was the only real honesty between two people, and if you didn't assume it, then the sex was a lie. Now he shut his eyes. He wanted to get into bed and sleep, but then she would soften with romantic victory. So he would have to remain sitting on his wooden chair. There was no place else to go. He had played the game with her, winning as always, or losing, one move after the other leading to the inevitable conclusion.

He shifted slightly on the chair, and she stirred. "I think I might be falling for you, Lieutenant Tessier," she said.

○

○

From the garbage bag Tommy took the gimbri, the simple three-stringed lute, camel skin stretched over a wooden box. The instrument anchored the gnawa music he'd heard for months coming from the slums of Little America. He had bought it one Saturday morning at the Little America flea market from a thin old man sitting cross-legged on the dirt with odds and ends spread across

161

the hem of his djellabah. Tommy had sensed that if he bought all the thin man's odds and ends – a transistor, a light bulb, three drill bits – the man himself might float away. The gimbri had been in the man's lap, and Tommy had half-heartedly haggled. After bringing it home, he had hidden it at the back of his closet beside some dusty shoes, like a boy with a secret treasure. He wasn't exactly sure why he had hidden it, but since that day he had been sneaking the gimbri out at night, learning to play it at the perimeter fence. Now he could accompany the distant music – softly, so that he wouldn't be discovered. He was even composing songs again, Fanfares for Little America, maybe, inspired by the pulsing magic of that shabby place, by thin old men who anchored themselves to the earth with drill bits. These works would never premiere before audiences in Chicago or New York, but he hadn't been so happy in years. The rest of his life receded. His night walks became music.

That night as he played, all his frustration flowed out through his fingers, until he heard another sound behind him and stopped. Lowering the instrument, he turned and found himself facing a beautiful dark-skinned Moroccan girl in a short shiny dress ripped open at the back. Tears ran down her face, rivulets through thick makeup, and she shivered, although maybe not from the cold. Perplexed, but more disturbed by her misery, he peeled off Victor's leather coat and held it out. She stepped over and quickly put it on, her lips trembling, her eyes unfocused as if she wasn't quite yet seeing him.

"Where did you come from? What happened? Are you hurt?" The girl shook her head. He couldn't tell whether she had understood or not. She was forbidden on the base at this time of night, of course. "Cigarette?"

She drew herself into the coat as if she wanted to hide, mistrustful of everything, including Tommy.

"Are you from Little America? *Little America?*"

She shook her head.

"Who are you with?" But she just went on crying and shivering. "Let's get you some help," he said, putting his hand on her elbow. She snatched it away. He inhaled the overwhelming scent of cheap perfume. She needed to come with him, he knew, but that didn't seem likely, so he told her to wait there by the fence. He would go find help. There were a couple of Moroccan orderlies who worked the night shift at the hospital, and one of them could look her over, and then maybe they could figure out how she'd wound up on base. Now in the distance frogs were croaking, and the music had stopped.

"Wait right here," he said, and started walking.

"No.... Play gimbri."

He smiled and turned to face her again. "So you do speak English."

"A little."

"You want me to play a little?" he said, stepping back towards her, the gimbri humming in his hand.

"Yes. You play good."

He should take her to the guards. But first he would play. Something terrible had happened, and it wasn't as if she could escape from this place.

So he strummed the instrument with his index finger and thumb, a technique he'd learned from watching the natives, slapping a rhythm into its neck with the knuckles of his other hand, creating that syncopated drone. The girl's eyes grew wide with pleasure, until she actually smiled, and then she sang in a beautiful voice as surprising to him as his playing had been to her. He wasn't playing a song, really, or anything she might have known. It was just one of his odd compositions, more like accompaniment for the night. And yet she sang as if she knew the words, guttural Arabic like roots ripped from dirt, modulating to soft trills where surely she sang of love. Effortlessly she invented a song, and he would have given anything then to understand her language.

She sang softly, as if she understood the risk he was taking, and when they had finished the song together, he asked for her name.

2

At nine o'clock one evening in early September, Touria was driving home from a meeting of The Future of the Moroccan Girl. She always wore her pilot's uniform to these meetings, as Madame Alaoui had requested, Touria's accomplishments being such an inspiration to the general membership. Touria, however, had begun to wonder whether her presence on the board was ornamental. She strongly believed in the association's mission but was never asked to do anything except appear and smile, especially at fundraising events. She had met few actual Moroccan girls, and wasn't involved in their futures. These concerns she had not yet mentioned to Madame Alaoui, because the association president had been struck by an inexplicable illness that had partially paralyzed her face, which she was attempting to hide by adopting the headscarf.

Touria angrily wondered again whether she was being used. If the Sultan had not been exiled, she could have gone to him for counsel. But she was alone, and loneliness wasn't a feeling she often indulged, so she immediately buried it. If only she could find more time to fly.

Was she being followed? That car was too close, not even attempting to hide. Her hands clenched the wheel as her mind fogged with the familiar dread. As she turned through Rond-Point de la Gironde, three hundred yards from the family's apartment on Rue Bergerac, the car flashed its lights. She groaned as the panic spread. From the roundabout she sped out onto Rue de Camiran, and the car followed, still flashing its lights. If only she could make it home. He wouldn't attack her there. Her father would see, neighbors would gather. Faster.

The car followed her all the way to the curb in front of the apartment building. As she parked, it pulled up behind her, and in the rearview mirror she watched as a man in a uniform stepped out. Once he had risen to his full height, she saw that it was Lieutenant Tessier and laughed uncontrollably, touching her forehead to the wheel.

Tessier strolled over to her window, which she lowered to flash him a smile. "I hope I didn't scare you," he said.

"How could *you* ever scare me, Lieutenant Tessier?" She was still grinning.

The lieutenant's face remained a mask. He hadn't changed a bit. It had been months, maybe even a year, since she had seen him or Noguera. As president of the Tit Mellil Pilots Club, which she had founded, she spent time at the airfield, but they were military, and she had never been welcome among them, although the airfield administrators had learned to tolerate her presence. "I have some news that I wanted to deliver in person," he said.

"Do you want to come in?"

"I shouldn't. Although please do say hello to your parents." He seemed nervous. She had never seen him like this, although perhaps she was only seeing her own nervousness reflected in him. "Should I get in the car?" he asked, glancing up and down the street.

She looked through the windshield. The neighborhood was deserted. "If you like," she said, "but if you would move, maybe I could get out."

He moved, and she stepped out onto the sidewalk. He paced back and forth. "Your uniform," he muttered, and she nodded. What a strange man.

Finally he stopped pacing and fixed her with his pale blue eyes. "I was flying with Noguera today, practicing some crossing maneuvers, and he lost control. There was no time to eject…." He cleared his throat, looked away. "His plane was obliterated."

Even before her smile had completely melted, tears were flowing down her face. She looked at the gutter. Tears dripped to the pavement. A flattened disk of bubble gum.

"I know how you loved him," she heard him say. "There were the men out at the airfield, but otherwise I didn't know who else to tell." She turned then and passionately threw her arms around him.

Victor felt her hot tears through his shirt. He hadn't admitted it to himself, but in coming here he had hoped to find something honest. Touria Chaoui was the only person who had never disappointed him.

"I'm so sorry, Lieutenant," she whispered.

"He clipped my stabilizer," he murmured to the top of her head. "I should have gone down."

"I'm glad you didn't," she said, and then he pushed her away, clearing his throat again. "I thought you should hear it from me."

"Thank you, Lieutenant." She leaned against the hood of the Morris Minor and arched her thin neck to look up at the stars. Her hair was long now, and not quite as curly. She was eighteen, a woman. He hesitated for a moment, and then went around to the front of the car to sit beside her.

"I saw you at that reception at the Hotel Lincoln a few months ago," she said after a while. "I guess you didn't see me."

"I don't do too well at those soirées, as you can imagine," he said, not exactly responding to the question.

She smiled slightly into the darkness, her cheeks still gleaming. "Neither do I. They're only using me, those women. I help them get donations. Nobody knows where the donations go."

"Be careful." He had heard that reckless tone in her voice before, which he both loved and feared. She was so stubborn. "Most people only want you to be what they need you to be.

Those people become dangerous when you're something else too."

"I have nightmares," she said, "but I never remember them, so I never really know what's frightening me. I just wake up screaming."

For several minutes they remained silent. Eventually he looked up and scanned the sky before pointing out the Great Bear. She nodded. "I know it. My father used to show me the stars."

"When I was young, much younger than you, I used to draw them differently. I would find other stars and draw the bear as a rhinoceros, or a jackal. Who was it that first looked up and saw a bear, and then how did he convince others to see it too?"

"I did that too," she said. "Everything's like that."

"What do you mean?"

"I'm like that. I picked out a few stars, became a pilot, and now that's me. I'm proud of it, but occasionally I might like to be drawn differently."

Tessier nodded. He missed the nights on the roof at Tit Mellil, and the days flying with Touria. He could have brought out his telescope again, but he hadn't. Perhaps he had wanted to see her and tell her the news, because he had known that he would feel something again.

"Goodnight, Touria. I'll call you about the funeral if you and your father want to come."

○

"Thank you, Lieutenant Tessier." She saw his steely face one last time through his windshield before he drove away. Then she stayed for a moment longer, drying the last of her tears on the sleeve of her uniform. Nosy old Hajar from across the street watched from her window. Touria waved and forced a smile. Then she went inside. She hadn't decided whether to tell her parents about Noguera or not, but she knew now that at the next association meeting she would confront Madame Alaoui. She was not the Great Bear. She was a rhinoceros, or a jackal, or something else entirely. A woman.

Over the next month as Salah slept across the room, she pored over pages of association records by the light of a single lamp, propped on pillows in her narrow bed. Madame Alaoui had delayed handing over the records, but Touria's insistence had eventually left her no choice. Touria was a board member, after all, and had a right to review the accounts. Madame Alaoui and the other officers had obviously not considered this when granting her the honorary title. They had underestimated her. And the last time she'd been underestimated, she'd learned to fly.

She had told her father about her suspicions. He worried, she knew, and creases had filled his forehead, but his advice had been the same as always. Follow your instincts. Stand up for yourself. Follow the truth. The truth was that the board's accounting didn't add up. Donations came in, lots since Touria had joined, with great sums from the palace, but they were allocated to nonexistent projects or administrative costs. Some of the money simply disappeared. Touria continued taking notes. For many nights she had been taking notes until long after the house had gone quiet.

A week later, the general membership of The Future of the Moroccan Girl met to discuss their plans for the fall of 1955. Touria took her seat at the front of the room with the other board members. She was not wearing her uniform. She wore a white shirt under her favorite overalls, and boots. Madame Alaoui opened the meeting, speaking more deliberately than usual, because of her half-paralyzed face, but dressed as elegantly as always. Her headscarf was printed with the name of a French fashion house.

When the time came for general business, Touria asked to speak. To the podium she took her pages of notes. She was not nervous. She was as well prepared as she had been the day of her pilot's test. She knew her speech by heart, and the truth would be its own explanation. The membership would be as outraged as she had been, and the money would be recovered, and put to use actually improving the future of Moroccan girls.

She stated the facts, without embellishment, although her anger was evident. The board had embezzled money, and their president, Madame Alaoui, was complicit. She watched as the faces of her audience slowly turned to stone. They shared her anger now, it seemed, but once she returned to her seat, there was no further discussion, and the meeting was quickly adjourned. Nobody came up to speak to her afterwards, and she realized, with a mixture of astonishment and alarm, that nobody cared. As she walked out of the room, she heard Madame Alaoui hissing through the side of her mouth to a circle of distraught admirers. "We'll show that bitch!"

3

June 9, 1955. *Green light for Lemaigre-Dubreuil.* The order had come from Captain Fillette. The target was travelling on a flight from Paris to Cazès, arriving at 11:45am on Saturday, June 11. You never got this sort of precision on a homo op. Clearly somebody high up in Paris finally understood the menace posed by men like Lemaigre-Dubreuil. Taking another man's life should always be the last resort, Tony believed, but Lemaigre-Dubreuil was the worst kind of traitor and deserved to die. Thanks to his editorials condemning what he claimed were a series of police murders and cover-ups, the Casablanca chief of police had been sacked. National security had been handed from the cops to the military. Congos and the Gypsy, and Tony sometimes too, had been spending their days windmilling at traffic while France lost control of its protectorate.

Tony took a quick glance around his apartment before leaving. Everything was in its place. *Souvenirs poétiques de l'école romantique, 1825 à 1840* was shut on the bedside table.

Poor innocents,
You long to stand atop high towers,
Among the mists and clouds
Like a nest of vultures.
Poetry. He was always ready.

○

Jacques Lemaigre-Dubreuil landed at Cazès before noon carrying only his leather briefcase. Traveling under a pseudonym, he had told no one in Morocco of his trip, except the driver and Simon, who hadn't bothered to show up at the airport. "I stopped by his house and knocked," Ahmed mumbled, leading his boss out to the Studebaker. "Probably he is still sleeping." The sun shone, and despite Jacques's annoyance, and Ahmed's rumpled suit, which the driver had been told a thousand times to press, he smiled. He was home, and since the authorities had not been informed of his arrival, for once they drove freely through the city without a police escort.

At home the maid fixed him a simple lunch, which he ate quickly before making a few phone calls. On a beautiful summer Saturday almost nobody answered, but he went through the motions, ignoring a thought he acknowledged but wasn't yet willing to admit. The thought was like the lines on his face, which he had also learned to ignore in the mirror, until one day he had been shocked by a photograph of himself. He had no particular reason to be in Casablanca, at least not today. The trip had been capricious. He had simply missed Simon so intensely that he hadn't wanted to stand it anymore. The foolishness of this alarmed him, but it was also thrilling. Something had changed inside him. He hardly recognized himself anymore, but he was happy. He was hoping to bring the boy into the business too – Lesieur, but also maybe the paper over time. Sometimes Simon could be extraordinarily clever about current events. No official announcement had been made, of course, and for the moment he had asked Simon to keep it quiet, but from now on they would be working together closely.

By three o'clock Simon had still not appeared. Repressing an urge to drive over to his apartment, Jacques decided instead to stop by the offices of *Maroc-Presse* and chat with a few people, even just copywriters or secretaries, to get a better sense of the place. But now Ahmed was nowhere to be found. Annoyed, Jacques drove himself, rolling down the Studebaker windows as he crawled north through the neighborhood of La Gironde, winding along quiet streets he had never explored, and thinking of poor Albert. Still they had not caught whoever had sabotaged his car, but in tribute *Maroc-Presse* had published the list of presumed counter-terrorists Albert had provided before his death, including Avival, Congos, and Méléro.

Mazzella was in his office and surprised to see him. Albert's death had brought them closer, even if the paper's dwindling circulation had forced Lemaigre-Dubreuil to cut his editor's salary in half. Everyone would have to make sacrifices, at least for the time being. Mazzella understood this.

"I am going to Rabat tomorrow to meet the new Resident General," Jacques said over coffee, and that's exactly what he would do, he decided then. The Resident General was floundering and needed firmer guidance if independence was to be achieved. Lemaigre-Dubreuil would have a big role in the new Morocco. Perhaps not initially governing, but as a seasoned advisor and proven friend of the nation. This could only give him an advantage over Lesieur's competitors, and he would be well placed to compete with the steadily advancing Americans. Time was of the essence. This would be his message to the Resident General.

At five o'clock he arrived back at the Liberty Building. There was still no sign of Simon, and the maid had left. He could smell the bitter mint from her afternoon tea. Opening the windows, he poured himself a cognac, rolling it around in the tumbler as he moved along the mantelpiece, picking up each porcelain figurine until he was lost in memories of his youth on the green hills of Limousin. He thought of the poor children of Tahar Sebti, whom he had visited several times since their father's death. They were so young, and had looked so helpless, prisoners of a tragedy that for them would never end. All their father could offer them now was his legacy.

A sound at the door startled him from these thoughts. He turned, and finally there was Simon, haggard, sheepish, avoiding eye contact as if he expected a fight. Jacques smiled and walked over to him, put his hand on the boy's neck, and kissed him deeply. Simon pulled away, but it had been a kiss, and Jacques was pleased. He knew how much Simon disliked such intimacy. Then he led Simon into the bedroom, where they undressed and wrestled each other to the mattress. Jacques felt like a fresh-faced soldier then, lithe and dominant, at least twenty years younger. The feeling remained once they had exhausted themselves and lay next to one another, basking in the breeze that drifted through the windows.

"What are you doing here anyway?" the boy mumbled after a while.

Because I missed you? No, that wouldn't do. "I have a meeting with a man from Dakar."

Their old excuse. Jacques chuckled to himself.

o

At eight o'clock that evening the sky turned pink. Tony Méléro, Rémy, André "El Negro", and a driver sent by Fillette named François rolled down Rue Franchet d'Esperey in a black Citroën 15 CV with fake plates. They parked before reaching Rond-Point de la Révolution Française. The car was one of several identical ones kept by the SDECE in a nearby garage. Congos and the Gypsy knew nothing of Tony's whereabouts. This operation was restricted to the experienced core of the Action Service.

Across the roundabout, the Liberty Building soared, lights in the windows up its seventeen stories flicking on against the dusk. The top floor penthouse remained dark. The green Studebaker was parked on the street, however, angled into the sidewalk with the driver's door facing the Action team. He was up there. They would wait. This had been the plan. You never knew which way a man might turn when leaving his car, but heading towards it he was predictable.

Tony and El Negro sat in the back with MAT-49 submachine guns at their feet. They had rolled down the windows, but the air in the Citroën was still hot and heavy. They cooked in dull professional silence, watching the traffic, the Moroccans hurrying home through the roundabout before curfew. Once the light had faded, Rémy got out and walked across to the building's entrance. This had also been part of the plan. Beside the entrance he stood casually smoking one cigarette after another, watching to see if one of the building's two elevators moved, and to which floor. When some resident occasionally exited the building, he would then step inside to call the elevator back down to the lobby. This would give them exactly one minute and thirty seconds before the elevator went up the seventeenth floor and back down again. They had timed it.

○

Jacques woke from a deep sleep. Naps were a waste of time, he had always believed. Fundamentally they sapped one's strength. He hadn't taken one in years and was surprised that night had fallen. He stepped out of bed and shut the windows. Pulling on a robe, he saw that Simon was still sleeping.

In the living room Ahmed sat in the darkness in Jacques's armchair, looking out at the city. "What are you doing?" Jacques chuckled. Crazy Moroccans. You never knew what they were thinking.

"I am waiting for you, monsieur," Ahmed said without moving.

"Well you could turn on the lights, at least," Jacques said, stepping over to the switch on the wall. "Is there something to eat?"

"There are some eggs."

"Then I'll have an omelet. Simon likes his over-easy now."

Ahmed huffed and rocked up out of the chair. Jacques went back into the bedroom and whipped the sheets off the boy. A Greek statue came to life, yawning loudly as he rubbed his eyes. "We'll go up to Bouregreg and spend the weekend in the country together. Tomorrow I can go into Rabat and see the Resident General." Simon groaned and sat up.

They dressed beside each other in the bathroom mirror. Like this Jacques could dare to observe the boy closer, and again he couldn't believe his luck. Dior had understandably hired him on the spot, but modeling was one of the doubtful privileges of youth, and not worthy of a man. Now alongside Lemaigre-Dubreuil, Simon Castet was destined for greatness.

Out in the dining room they sat and poured wine. Ahmed eventually emerged with two omelets. As soon as the plate rattled to the table, Simon growled and pushed it away. "What is this shit? Jacques, do you see how he is?"

"Monsieur said two omelets," Ahmed purred. The force of Jacques's anger surprised even Jacques. "You know exactly what I said, idiot! Simon is my right hand! Over-easy, as ordered!"

Ahmed stormed off, slamming the apartment door behind him, and they heard the whirr of the elevator through the walls. Jacques had lost his appetite. He was so tired of the fighting, every day, on every street corner, even in his own home. They couldn't have built the Liberty Building high enough, but he imagined it anyway, a tower built so high that at its top you could only love.

Across the table Simon sat scowling at his eggs.

o

The lights on the seventeenth floor had flicked on. Yet they waited another hour until 10:55, when Rémy gave the signal. Ninety seconds. Tony and El Negro brought the MAT-49s to their laps. If all went as planned, El Negro, on the passenger side, would be the shooter as they swept through the roundabout. Hopefully a quick drive-by would be enough, so that they wouldn't have to get out of the car. François released the parking brake, and the Citroën silently rolled forward. Their timing was already slightly off, Tony knew, but they couldn't afford to start the engine and startle the target. Then Rémy waved them off. François hit the brakes and edged over to the sidewalk again. The elevator doors had opened, and it was only the Moroccan driver, ignoring the Studebaker to rush off into the night.

This was a stroke of luck. Now the target would be driving, placing himself directly in their line of fire, and at 11:05 Rémy again gave the signal. The Citroën rolled down the hill, and then the target burst out of the lobby, shouting into the night, trailed by the man called Simon Castet, a male model according to Intelligence. Where were they going at this time of night? It didn't matter. Both were too agitated to notice the silently approaching car.

The target strode around the Studebaker and wrenched open the driver's door. François flicked on the headlights, pinning Lemaigre-Dubreuil with its beams. El Negro's torso was already out of the Citroën, and he took aim with his MAT-49. Before you could blink, he had put ten bullets in the target's back. The rattle of the submachine gun sounded like an exhaust pipe dragging on asphalt, and Tony watched as the male model ducked for safety behind the car, screaming "Jacques! Jacques!" But Jacques was already sliding down the side of the green Studebaker. Dozens of bullet holes punctured the steel as François sped through the roundabout onto Boulevard de la Liberté, the wrong way on a one-way street, but he flew, and within a hundred meters he slammed right onto Rue du General Lapperine, and then they were home free.

○

Sirens echoed through the city that night, along the Boulevard de Londres and through the dark palms of Parc Murdoch. Jacques Lemaigre-Dubreuil died in the ambulance on the way to the Hôpital Jules Colombani.

That same night police investigated the scene at the Liberty Building. Simon Castet was questioned and quickly released. Mad with grief, he could only repeat that Monsieur Lemaigre-Dubreuil had been scheduled to meet with a man from Dakar. That was all he knew. A man from Dakar. Castet immediately returned to France. Several months later he was found hanged at the Côte d'Azur villa of a right-wing French politician.

Then on Tuesday, June 14, Lemaigre-Dubreuil's funeral was held at the Sacré Coeur cathedral. An estimated 2500 mourners showed up, mostly Moroccans – Nationalist leaders, middle-class merchants, and the poor who streamed out of the medina to show their respects to the one Frenchman who had been brave enough to articulate the injustice of French rule in Morocco.

DJINNS
1955

After Jacques Lemaigre-Dubreuil's death, France lost any remaining will to maintain the Moroccan protectorate.

On November 16, 1955, the Sultan returned from exile, and Moroccans flowed into the streets, ignoring the massive French police presence. Whether the cops liked it or not, Morocco would be free.

Touria rejoiced. She had corresponded with the Sultan during his exile, and after her resignation from The Future of the Moroccan Girl, he had helped sponsor an association of her own, named after the Sultan's daughter born in exile. The Institution Lalla Amina was located in a house on Rue de Lisbonne, a quiet street south of Parc Murdoch. A dozen girls came every day from nearby Derb Sultan and Habbous, working-class Moroccan neighborhoods. The youngest were ten, and mostly uneducated, while others had finished their junior high studies. Touria remembered her own aimless frustration at that age, when it had been presumed that marriage, childbirth, and death were her only remaining milestones, and she was determined to give these girls the chance she'd had. Along with several volunteers she worked to improve their reading and writing, while also helping them develop employable skills like typing and sewing. The Sultan was returning, she told them, and independence was coming, even for girls.

The Fête du Trône, the holiday marking the Sultan's accession, traditionally fell on November 18. In 1955, the day was set to be the biggest celebration in Morocco's history. As Touria woke at dawn, neighbors were already out down on Rue Bergerac. She crept out of bed so as not to wake Salah, bathed, and solemnly put on her pilot's uniform. Downstairs she kissed her mother and went out to the Morris Minor.

The airfield at Tit Mellil was manned by a skeleton staff that day. The French military was focused on what were sure to be chaotic Casablanca streets, not on its placid skies. Only two cars were parked outside the office, and Touria drove past them towards a familiar Cessna, stopping at the edge of the tarmac. She cut the engine and stepped out of the Morris, glancing anxiously back towards the office. Check-in would have to be done at the last possible instant, she had decided. The sun was bright, the crisp autumn air cool on her face. The risk was great. She opened the trunk.

Working quickly, she hoisted a stack of paper fliers and carried them to the plane, where she heaved them up onto the co-pilot's seat. There were thousands of fliers, and after several trips a low-level secretary stepped out of the office and blinked in the sun. Slowly he walked towards the Cessna, eventually calling out, "Hey! Miss Chaoui?" The man – just a boy, really, scrawny in his uniform, pimpled face – continued to creep forward, his body angled back away from her as if she might lunge and sink fangs into his leg. She ignored the man, or the boy, and kept moving between car and plane. When the bewildered secretary crept even closer, she paused to take from the glove compartment a different sheet of paper, which she defiantly thrust towards him like a magic charm. "This is from the palace," she said. "The Sultan himself has given me permission to fly today."

"Okay. I need to make a phone call." He scampered back to the office, appearing relieved to have hit upon a secretarial solution to the problem. She laughed to herself, amazed it had been that easy. Not that a palatial decree couldn't simply be ignored by a French commander with more power than the secretary. Not that she was any less nervous, or that her heart beat any less quickly....

With the last stack loaded, she drove the Minor over into the hangar, hurried back to the plane, and climbed into the cockpit, fitting the headset over her ears. On the radio somebody was shouting. She took off the headset. Bravery was her responsibility. This had always been an instinct rather than any conscious idea she'd had. The Sultan had returned, so you shouted it, you showed the world what it could be. This was your responsibility.

The secretary came running out of the office again. Across

the tarmac he was a mirage, a flicker of color, a trick of the sun. As the propeller jerked to life, she ran through her checklist. Okay. Wind from the west, too weak to maintain the telltale horizontal. Taxi towards the runway. You pause. You feel the emptiness in front of you and above. At first your flesh in its metal envelope always feels too fragile against that void. The propeller whirrs towards invisibility, you release the brake, and the plane jolts forward, rushing towards the horizon.

In the air she never doubted herself. Fear could be squelched with mechanical adjustments. You tweaked the rudder or a flap. All you needed was the knowledge and the practice, and then you could control yourself, trim the blind nightmares that made you scream into darkness. Down below the secretary was pinned to the tarmac, his arm thrust up against the weight of the sun. Lieutenant Tessier might have smiled if he had been her co-pilot that day.

She flew west towards the city over Carrières Centrales. The slums were black smoke against rough texture like a dirty fabric she could have run her fingers across. She banked left in a tight circle for a better view, the sea glittering to the north. The Atlantic she had seen from above, one day when Noguera had let her stray from the pattern, but permission had never been granted to fly over the city, which from the sky now looked nothing like her Casablanca, or like anything connected to her life. But then, banking south away from the ocean, she spotted the train station, and in the distance, the Liberty Tower. Then from above she began recognizing certain pieces of herself. The palace approached fast as she let herself lose altitude, but first, just a few blocks over, was Rue Bergerac. Her heart skipped, as if she had unexpectedly caught sight of herself in a mirror. Was her father still at home, or had he left for the celebrations? Her mother and Salah? The sidewalks were crowded and traffic crawled, especially on the boulevards around the palace. Almost everyone she loved could be spotted from this place in the sky, if only she knew where to look.

Steadying the plane, she reached over and grabbed a handful of fliers. With her left hand, she turned the clasp at the base of the rectangular window beside her. This was the part she hadn't been able to rehearse. You couldn't rehearse what you were forbidden to do. When the stakes were high, it was always real. Just as when she and her father had once pretended to enroll her in flight school. They hadn't really been pretending. This had always been her life.

Now, keep a grip on the window clasp as you push it out against the slipstream, praying the wind won't snap off your fingers. She was moving faster than anything on the earth or in the air, and speed was noise, static on a radio with the knobs turned up. The noise snatched the fliers out, first whipping about in her grasp like a tangled bird, then ripped from her fingers to scatter, a white explosion in her wake that hovered gently like a cloud, expanding, until a hundred distinct rectangles rocked silently towards the earth.

This was no love letter or proclamation. Not a warning or a demand. Touria Chaoui had wanted nothing but to rejoice, to welcome the Sultan home to this beautiful white city furled out beneath her, because his courage, and that of others, was about to make Casablanca theirs again. Two thousand feet in the air, it never occurred to her that she might be one of the courageous ones. Beneath the portrait of the Sultan on every page stacked beside her was this welcome she had composed, celebrating the return of this great man, along with the royal family, and the independence they had won. Grinning, she flung handfuls of fliers out the window, covering the city, swooping down over the medina, up again, down along the quays of the port, up again, down low over the trees in Parc Lyautey, up again, scraping the roofs of the riads in Habbous, hands waving up at her, up again.

One last pass over the apartment building on Rue Bergerac, and more fliers for Salah, and then on to the palace, where she tossed out the last of the pages, letting her fingers bend against the wind before gripping the controls again, diving to gather speed. Then over the palace gardens, vaster than she ever could have imagined, she went into a barrel roll, twice, three times, her body like a cloud of fliers scattering. Then up again, at the edge of stalling, edging up into the endless blue to gather her capacity for speed again. Poor Noguera would have killed her. Probably Tessier too. She smiled, imagining their disapproval. Close your eyes, *messieurs*. You won't like what's coming next.

Again she went down, hard this time, falling straighter than the rain, streaking fast towards the palace roof, going for maximum speed before easing up towards horizontal, and then further up again, up again and over, upside-down, a perfect loop over Casablanca, the force upon her so powerful that she felt as if she had been compressed into a single beating heart.

○

Aziza Benayiche had slept late. The shop was closed for the holiday, and she had looked forward to spending the day relaxing in her new house. This would be her celebration. Ideally she would have avoided the madness of the streets. That excitement seemed so distant from her life. But no food remained in the kitchen, so she had stepped outside, hearing almost immediately the buzz of the airplane. She glanced up just in time to see it zip across a sky bracketed by the façades of Bousbir. The noise faded, then roared back, and she watched the blue until the plane appeared again, this time leaving in its wake the fliers that floated down towards her outstretched hand.

She knew it was Touria then, and her pride was

bittersweet. Years had passed since she had seen Abdelwahed, and she regretted that. Her friend had raised an extraordinary girl. And that was bittersweet.

○

How had they let this happen? Or *who* had let it happen? As if street parades weren't enough. Now they were dropping fliers celebrating the return of their dictator. What was next? Fireworks? Tony Méléro was disgusted. He closed his shutters against the day and looked around the empty room, the bed made hours ago, the poetry at right angles on the bedside table.

He paced at the foot of the bed. On Bastille Day that year – *Bastille Day!* – a month after the Lemaigre-Dubreuil job, with the party in full swing on Place Mers-Sultan, an orchestra playing, innocent people dancing everywhere, a terrorist had set off a bomb killing seven. On Bastille Day. And now these people had been given permission to celebrate their treachery in public. It was a total disgrace.

○

Saadia Taibi rode her bike the wrong way through blocked traffic, grinning up at all the paper falling from the sky like the snow that sometimes fell in the movies. Weaving down a sidewalk through a crowd, she heard people saying that the strange sight was the work of spirits, but Saadia knew better. It was Touria Chaoui, the girl pilot, the one Ahmed hated, but Saadia didn't. Whenever she'd seen her up there, she'd always said hello. *Labas Touria?* She rode faster, grinning up at the falling paper. The resistance had won, and she no longer needed to wear her golf pants for smuggling things, but she just liked the way they felt on her, always had, and they were much better than skirts for riding a bike.

○

Hajja Aliya Alaoui rolled her wheelchair away from the bedroom window. So the little tramp was making another spectacle.

She rolled into the Moroccan reception room, low couches around the perimeter, and clattered into a copper table. She cursed again at the wheeled contraption. First one side of her face, and now her legs were paralyzed. The doctors had no diagnosis, and a few days earlier she had watched as her sister had gone through her drawers picking out favorites from Hajja Aliya's beloved collection of silk stockings. Hajja Aliya had silently watched as her sister rolled these stockings up her fine, firm legs. Skirts, too. Slim Parisian dresses. But the stockings, the endless stockings. Furious, she had wanted to rip them to shreds, to shove them into somebody's mouth, the mouth of the world to keep it from talking. But no, she had smiled sweetly as her sister slid one after another up her legs. Hajja Aliya had sacrificed her own feelings for her sister's pleasure.

That was the past. Now Allah guided Hajja Aliya, and she had put on the headscarf once and for all. She would wear plain kaftans and retire from this crass new Morocco, where thugs took power and upstarts were admired for scattering litter on the heads of pedestrians.

○

Victor Tessier stood at the window, sheet wrapped around his waist, thinking of the night of November 7, 1942, of losing his virginity as American fliers rained from the sky. *We have come only to destroy your enemies – we do not wish to harm you.* The night after those fliers, he had met Tommy and had resolved to become a pilot. And now it was Touria, whom he had taught to fly. The fliers were falling again, the sky specked with his own memories, as if he'd lifted a snow globe from a box stored in a cellar and had shaken it to life.

A woman called out from bed, but he kept his eyes on Touria's plane. He was thirty years old, and there was no longer any time to lose.

2

THE PRESS: CASABLANCA CRUSADE

'You've got to be a hero to work here.' For *Maroc-Presse's* 20 reporters and editors, courage is another requirement of the job; theirs is the most utterly hated newspaper in the world. Reporters are regularly beaten up, death threats come into the city desk almost daily. Editor Antoine Mazzella had his apartment bombed, Publisher Jacques Lemaigre-Dubreuil was machine-gunned to death on the street (*TIME*, June 27). Three weeks ago, a mob of Europeans swarmed into the paper's plant, smashed printing equipment....

Even the French police make no bones about their hatred of the paper. Two of them recently beat a British photographer because they thought he worked for *Maroc-Presse*; a top police official warned the U.S. Air Force public-information officer in the area not to associate with the paper's editors. Why do Editor Mazzella and his staff refuse to give in to the terrorists? Says Editor Mazzella: 'I'm fulfilling a human obligation I just can't run away from. I'm attached to *Maroc-Presse*. It's the only newspaper that's ever given me the means to defend an ideal.'[14]

o

In a suite at the Hotel Lincoln on Boulevard de la Gare, a large, unshaven American in a plush bathrobe was reading a *Time* magazine he had bought at the airport. A knock sounded at the door. The American rose with a huff and padded across

---

14   *Time* – 08/08/1955

the carpet. Two Moroccans in white gloves ushered in a cart set with several covered breakfast platters.

"Will that be all, Mister Magoor…?"

"Just Mag's fine," the American interrupted, slipping a thick wallet from the front pocket of his bathrobe and pulling out two bills, then another.

After breakfast he took a hot bath and pulled on an expensive suit stained with food and drink from the long trip across the Atlantic. Then went down into the Boulevard, glancing into the Central Market, where her bird man no longer kept his stall, and then along the arcades towards the Place de France. Casablanca was even dirtier than he remembered it, with reeking piles of refuse, hundreds of crumpled scraps of paper printed with the Sultan's portrait. Approaching Rue Nolly, he walked with his eyes cast up to the sky, hoping to spot a pigeon. "The cows have come home to roost," he murmured, stopping to light a cigarette. Fuggin' Stec and his dumb codes. Often he wished he could disentangle his memories and remember those days differently. Back there at the end, it had all gone to shit.

Would she recognize him? He was convinced that he would recognize her. He had been seeing her in his mind almost every night for the past nine years. But hell, she could be married, probably was. With all this crazy killing around, she could even be back in France. He looked up again. Pure blue sky. Maybe it was morning naptime for the birds.

Mag! Among the street's cacophony he heard his name. Surely he had just imagined it. Still, his heart clenched, and he looked around uncertainly, overjoyed by the possibility of seeing her, but also terrified.

"Mag!" There it was again, a woman's voice from across the street. He spotted her now, but it wasn't Camille. Amazingly it was Aziza. She'd aged even more than he had. And had put on almost as much weight. She wore a wide flowery kaftan and waved him over, kissing him on both cheeks, which he awkwardly reciprocated. Even after his time in Europe, he'd never gotten used to kissing hellos. She invited him into the shop. Her shop, she said. He had never doubted that Aziza would be all right. He wondered if she'd taken the money he'd left behind to move herself into Frenchtown. Probably, but it didn't matter anymore.

"I would get you a drink," she said once the door had clinked shut behind them, "but I do not keep it here anymore." He nodded once and looked around the shop, full of fine things, far finer than the things they'd once hustled. If life had taught him one thing, it was how to recognize quality women's clothing, especially undergarments, and he moved around the shop assessing her stock.

"You see what you helped build, Mag. I never forgot it. You look like you had good business too. I am happy to see you."

"Me too," he said, too nervous to meet her eyes. So she'd used the money. Good. Hopefully Camille had gotten some of it too. "How's Ahmed? You still see him?"

"He is a bad man now," Aziza said, although Mag was hardly listening. "A police detective in the seventh arrondissement. Nobody can touch him."

"Remember the last time we saw each other?" he interrupted.

"*Naam.*" She smiled as her eyes clouded with the past.

"I asked you to look out for that girl Camille. She lives upstairs. Or at least she used to."

Aziza's face fell, and her eyes came into hard focus. "I did," she said, quickly lighting a cigarette from the pack on the counter. "I did for a while. I got her an acting job, a dancing job…. Like you asked. But she left this place when her mother died."

This wasn't how he had imagined it. He should have gone directly up to Camille's apartment as he had in the past. Then she would have been waiting, just as he had planned.

"*Ouili ouili ouili*," Aziza murmured miserably, crumpling a swatch of fabric in her fist as Mag grew increasingly alarmed, moving over towards her to support himself against the counter. And then, once they were close, Aziza told him the story of Camille, or at least the parts of it she knew. Camille had been pregnant when he left. She had given birth to a daughter. And then the accident. Aziza didn't know what had happened to the girl.

Mag felt as if he had been ripped open, eviscerated. As she spoke, he slumped lower onto the counter, heavy on his spreading elbows, lessened. There had always remained the hope that leaving Casablanca had not been a mistake, but a digression, something they could eventually laugh about. But now he knew. Leaving Casablanca had been the biggest mistake of his life.

He crashed out of the shop. The streets heaved up around him. He wanted to disappear. He stumbled into the cool entrance of the apartment building, memories screaming in his head. That sign was still by the elevator. *L'ascenseur est interdit aux chiens et aux domestiques.* Now he could read it after those months in France at the end of the war. The elevator is forbidden to dogs and servants. Fuggin' French bastards. He remembered the days when the most exciting moment in his life had been pushing that elevator button. In the years since, he'd dreamed of the button, he'd dreamed of the number four. Now he stepped into the elevator and stretched out the severed index finger of his left hand to push number five. The box lurched upwards through the shaft. As he exited, he did not let his eyes wander towards the staircase to the floor below. He huffed up to the roof.

The metal door gave way with a firm nudge of his shoulder. Then the sun exploded. Heat rose in waves from the tar paper slathered underfoot. Slowly his eyes adjusted as he stepped over to the center of the roof, towards Camille's cages. They were still there, all empty. Some of their bars were bent or broken. Several of their doors hung off from rusty hinges. Soot and dried pigeon shit coated their bottoms. The sky was blank.

Sometime later he found himself down on the street, then inside a taxi. The police station of the seventh arrondissement was far south in an unfamiliar neighborhood called Derb Baladia. Casablanca had spread such that it was mostly unrecognizable to him. The taxi let him off in front of the station, and he lit a cigarette beneath a tree, sweat coating his back from the ride in the tin can. Should he just walk in and announce himself? Probably he shouldn't have come at all, but then he hadn't known what else to do. Eventually, after a second cigarette, Ahmed Touil appeared, just as he'd always eventually tended to do.

He strode out of the station flanked by two gorillas. Mag watched from the shade of the tree as the three men approached a large Citroën. One of the gorillas held open the passenger door for Ahmed. Mag stepped down off the curb and crossed the street. When the gorillas registered him, they reached for their waists, but Mag held out a palm and shouted: "You got your own car!"

Ahmed turned, confused by the English, and possibly by the oversized stranger. Then his gray face broke into a yellow grin, and he flung out his arms to embrace Mag. "My friend! My American friend!"

Mag stepped over to return the embrace. Ahmed smelled of smoke and acid, and on his wrist was a Gallet Flying Officer. "Got a nice watch too," he said.

"I even have my own driver now," Ahmed cackled, and Mag glanced again at the two bruisers. If they spoke English, they weren't showing it. He also noticed that their knuckles were covered with scabs.

"We have done good," Ahmed said, holding Mag at arm's length to look him over. "I am so happy to see you, my friend. You have heard about the opportunities here? Everything is changing in Morocco, and we can do big business together.

Now I make the laws."

Mag nodded as they stepped up onto the sidewalk together. "I'm not interested in business, Ahmed. My business days are done. I came here to find someone. It's good to see you, but you're not the someone. Remember that French girl I used to know?" Ahmed did, and so Mag briefly told him the story. "So I have a daughter," he said, "and I'd like to find her. I don't know anything more than that. I'd just like to see her for myself, maybe even talk to her if that's possible."

"Anything for you, my friend," Ahmed said brightly, which only made Mag's agony feel more acute. "They call me the magician, and women are my special trick." He leered and elbowed Mag in the ribs, but Mag felt nothing.

"This is my daughter, Ahmed."

"Hey, anything for you my friend. My oldest friend…." He showed his yellow teeth again and shot his hand into his breast pocket, wiggling his thickened torso about, his eyes narrowed to concentrate on whatever he expected to find. The suit wasn't bad, Mag noticed, although it was cut so wide that even he would have fit in it. Wool, likely Super 100. Eventually Ahmed fished out what looked like a gray gob of dried gum and held it out between two fingers.

"What's that?" Mag growled.

"It is you, man. The finger of my oldest friend. I carry it for good luck. The finger of my brother Mag who helped me get my start."

Mag looked at him bleakly while feeling the nub of his index finger with his thumb. That wasn't him, but Ahmed wasn't Ahmed either, Casablanca wasn't Casablanca, nothing was nothing. How long did the silence last? Touil shifted uneasily on his feet until finally he said, "We will need a few francs – friend price, nothing for me, just for my men – to get the investigation started." Mag nodded, pulled out his wallet, and emptied its contents into Ahmed's hand. It wasn't until he got back to the Hotel Lincoln, ordered a bottle of whiskey, and chained the door, that he let his tears escape.

○

TEN EUROPEANS ARRESTED, INCLUDING SIX POLICEMEN AND OWNER OF LA GIRONDE CAFÉ

Mr. Edgar Faure stressed that Inspector Forestier, who died accidentally on January 3, 'was no ordinary policeman,' and it should be noted that he had made known as early as November 1954 the role played by François Avival, the owner of La Gironde café. ...In a note delivered two months before his death to the prime minister, Mr. Lemaigre-Dubreuil included information given him by Forestier...:

'The team of Avival was, strictly speaking, a team of killers with a machine gun; they orchestrated drive-by shootings of Moroccans found at night in the street....

'...Inspector Forestier continued gathering information until the evening of December 22, 1954... when he found himself at La Gironde, on the boulevard of the same name, owned by Avival. Three Moroccans were there drinking. It was about 10pm. The Moroccans ordered more drinks, which Madame Avival, wanting to close shop, refused to serve them. Avival intervened with an expression that struck Forestier: "Serve them, but this is their 'last round'."

'... The next day he learned from the police that around 10:30pm on Boulevard Victor Hugo, not far from La Gironde, three Moroccans in a car had been chased by a 203, run into the sidewalk, and forced to stop. The occupants of the 203 had then shot the Moroccans with a machine gun, killing two and seriously wounding the third. He visited the victims and recognized them from the night before.'

[This version has been questioned by police. Forestier would not have gone to the morgue to identify victims....][15]

15   *Le Monde* – 06/23/1955

Many of the girls were orphans, and more appeared every day. Some came for the hot lunch, others for the opportunity to draw with paper and colored pencils. Sometimes they fought, sometimes they stole, still caught up in the battles they brought in from the streets, but over time the Institution Lalla Amina was becoming the place where they could be free of those battles, and so they tended to keep coming back. Touria taught reading and writing in the mornings, then maybe sewing in the afternoons to the older girls, although she was clumsy at sewing, and the more practiced girls often had to demonstrate the stitches. She was the girl who flew airplanes, they knew, even if she rarely talked about it. Their admiration sometimes made her feel alone among them, or at least apart. This was a new feeling to her. Sometimes she wondered if she might even be bored, but she didn't let the thought linger, because these girls needed her. She was a sort of mother to them, she had realized, and then she had tried to imagine motherhood, and the years her own mother had spent raising her and Salah. For the first time Touria saw how growing up might limit her freedoms.

Shaking this thought from her head, she focused her attention on little nine-year-old Micheline, who sat alone on a low chair in the corner. She wore one of her oddly beautiful dresses – sky blue with ruffles at the shoulders and neck – and sat primly with a book in her lap, watching Touria intently out the corner of her eye. Her hair was long and pale blonde, almost white in the sunlight on the days they went to the park, with bangs cut in a sharp straight line across her forehead. Micheline was their only French girl, and the others hated her for it. She had appeared one day with an old French woman who lived in the neighborhood. The woman had said only that the girl was another orphan. This was still a mystery to Touria and her fellow volunteers, as there were hardly any French orphans anymore, and when there had been a few during the war, they had all been taken by the church. But Touria had seen a desperate loneliness in Micheline, as well as a certain intelligence.

"Come read me a story," she called out in French. A smile momentarily cracked Micheline's solemn face, and she stood to walk shyly to the table with her book clasped in both hands. Touria maintained awareness of the scrutiny her favors drew, but reading with Micheline was one of her real pleasures, and the girls needed to see that Nazarenes were also worth befriending, especially if they could read. Even in Arabic, Micheline read well, stories that sometimes led Touria to tell her flying stories, which excited Micheline to the point that she sometimes forgot to be shy and peppered Touria with questions about the clouds and the birds as the other girls tentatively gathered round. Micheline wanted to fly too, she had announced one day, to the great derision of the others, but that confession seemed as brave to Touria as flying seemed to the girls. She felt less lonely after Micheline's arrival, and rediscovered her commitment to the association's work, even if she might no longer be so free as she had imagined she would always be.

4

○

The truck dropped her off in the outskirts of town. She had not forgotten the promises that had been made to her. She walked all the way into the center, through Parc Lyautey to Boulevard Jean-Courtin and the offices of the Spectacles and Morality police. The BMC medal she had received before shipping out from Saigon was pinned to the front of her shirt – a man's shirt, rolled at the sleeves, revealing tattoos, which she no longer wished to hide. The skirt that fell to her sandals was slit down one side, occasionally revealing the angel's wing extended across a thigh. A collection of dog tags hung from a chain around her neck. Men's names were on the tags, names they had never spoken to her, but which she had collected from the ones who slept. Her eyes were shielded by dark sunglasses once belonging to a French soldier, another gift, of sorts. Apart from the canvas duffel bag slung over her shoulder and filled with what remained of her clothing, these things were all she possessed. She had spent all her money on the boat trip home, in the ports of tropical cities whose names

200

she had not known, places she could have stayed but never did, always making her way back to the boat before departure, moving closer towards Casablanca. Now the time had come to claim her reward.

She would never again return to Bousbir. The policeman had promised that after serving her country she would have the right to live in the bordello of her choice. Deep in the Vietnamese jungle, in the sodden tents where she had serviced the men, she had thought often of bordellos, of a room of her own with a lock on the door and a desk where she would draw on stacks of thick paper. Of men who would not hurt her, or would pay well if they did. Of the respect she would be shown by other girls with the medal pinned to her chest. She had gone to the war in Indochina on a boat. She had heard monkeys screaming in the night. She had played baseball one Sunday with some Americans on a beach near Da Nang. She had seen a dead Viet Minh infantryman with eyes eaten by maggots. She had been away for two years, but she remembered the policeman's name and asked for him at the front desk. "Tell him that Fadila has returned from Vietnam."

The policeman refused to see her. She raged in the lobby, screaming at the secretary, spitting and scratching at the air, until two policemen did appear, lifted her up, and dumped her outside on the sidewalk. Crushed, she lay there forever as pedestrians wove around her. It didn't matter what you did. It didn't matter if you went on a filthy boat to Indochina and heard jungle monkeys scream. Nothing ever changed. Nothing ever changed. Whispering these words, she pulled herself to her feet and walked mechanically towards Bousbir.

She would not speak to Suzanne. She would offer herself to another *patronne*, never Jean Bart again. She had been to the war in Indochina in the service of her country, and she had the medal to prove it. She would never again allow their disrespect.

When she arrived at the gates, Bousbir had disappeared.

For a moment she assumed she had made a wrong turn. Casablanca had changed even in two years, and along her walk many places had been unrecognizable. But as she walked up the central street, now disconcertingly quiet, she knew that she was not mistaken. This was Bousbir, but the girls were gone, the brothels transformed into houses, birds chirping in the trees. Nobody paid her any attention. A woman in a headscarf moved past. Nobody tried to press his hand between her thighs. Again she lowered herself to the sidewalk, but even then she wasn't lonely. How could she be lonely when she didn't even exist?

Then she wandered for hours. Wandering was the same as lying on the sidewalk. They both felt like nothing. She wandered into Frenchtown, letting them all stare or not, wandered through Place de France to the big Galeries Lafayette department store, which she had never even dared walk past, much less enter. But she didn't exist, and the menacing Moroccan guard at the door didn't matter, and she wanted to defy him, anyone, so she walked right past the guard and into the store.

Inside were endless rows of food cans with labels in thousands of colors, all perfectly aligned on the shelves as if they were not meant to be touched. Stacks of clothes, identical sweaters piled up. She could see her reflection in the floors, and guards roamed everywhere. Whole dining rooms and bedrooms without walls laid out one after another. Never had she seen anything so extraordinary, even in all the places she had visited on her journey around the world.

Eventually she found her way back to the grocery section, eyes wide behind sunglasses. The choice was overwhelming, and never in her life had she shopped for food before. Food had always been given, or found. So she took some green tea, a small yellow bottle of Lesieur cooking oil, and three eggs from a carton she lifted open. These she slipped into her canvas sack before walking towards the exit.

○

Mag sat on a café terrace beneath an arcade on a corner across from Galeries Lafayette. The street was muddy, the air patchy with humidity. On the sidewalk a Moroccan Santa Claus in a ratty red suit whipped a dull tin bell and shouted in Arabic. His palm cupped only a few drops of rain.

There had been no news from Ahmed Touil, which wasn't surprising. So Mag had done his best to find his daughter on his own. The American Consulate had been friendly enough, especially when he mentioned his war service in Casa, but they could do nothing to locate a nine-year-old French girl without a name. The French Consulate had been equally unhelpful, but unfriendly. Weeks had passed. He had gotten to know the room service attendants at the Lincoln. Then one day, still hoping his military past might help his cause, he had hailed a taxi out to Cazès. As the city crawled past, he had braced himself for unpleasant memories, only to discover that there was no longer a base at Cazès. The Americans had moved out to Nouasseur, he was told at the airfield, and so he had ordered the driver to continue on to wherever that was.

Nouasseur was massive. At the front gate they hadn't even let him in. Who was he there to see? *My daughter* was the answer, and she didn't live at Nouasseur. Other cars, Buicks and Fords, whipped past with their drivers casually waving as he sat there dumbly attempting to negotiate some other hopeless outcome. His frustration mounting, he had attempted to slip the guard a couple of bills, but the guard had just looked sick before retreating towards the booth and his telephone.

"Hotel Lincoln," Mag had grumbled to the driver. "Better make it quick." *Hell*, he had thought as they drove back along the endless base fence towards town, hulking bombers in the distance. *Back in the old days, Spanky would have done anything for a measly pack of Chesterfields.* Times had changed.

Everything started at a human scale, but then the system got bigger and bigger until it had nothing to do with you, and you could do nothing about it. The system had gotten a whole lot bigger than Mag. A handshake and a pack of Chesterfields were no longer worth a damn. Maybe he'd always been more Moroccan than American, he realized – bartering, trading, finding the smallest of angles. Looking out the taxi window at the endless base still rolling past, smelling the eucalyptus trees as the wind batted his face, it seemed that if he'd managed to make it past that prissy guard into the base that surely resembled America, he might simply have disappeared. But he couldn't disappear. At least not yet.

Now Ahmed the waiter was bringing him another coffee. There were so many Ahmeds. At least this one always knew when to bring the next coffee. Also he didn't carry your severed finger around in his pocket. What had he been thinking to amputate himself? Well, he'd been drinking, for one. Also just plain dumb. And in puppy love with Camille. Now he tried to think about Camille as little as possible.

The odd-looking Moroccan girl he had watched entering Galeries Lafayette came out just five minutes later. She was tattooed like the Berber women who came down from the mountains to sell their vegetables from blankets under the arcades beside the Central Market. Sometimes early in the morning he would watch them from his window at the Hotel Lincoln. The tattoos appeared to cover the girl's entire body, and she was dressed like a cross between a soldier, a drug addict, and a French farmer's daughter. She wore dark sunglasses and was possibly beautiful. She didn't fit any category he knew, which Mag found intriguing enough to keep watching, but he wasn't alone. He watched as the guard at the department store entrance stepped into her path, put a hand on her shoulder, and snatched her sack away. The girl fought back, snarling, beating a fist against the guard's chest while tugging violently at the sack. Still, the guard was being rougher than she deserved.

Mag motioned to Ahmed the waiter, rose from his table, and strode across the street, stopping traffic from both directions.

"Leave her alone, fella. Back off. You're three times her size. She ain't going nowhere." The guard was big, although not as big as Mag. He pulled a tea tin from the sack and shoved it at Mag's face, a broken egg dripping through his fingers. He shouted in Arabic as the girl stood pouting.

"Take it easy, pal," Mag said, raising his fleshy hands. "Give her the sack, and she'll give back the merchandise." The guard didn't appear to understand English. Again he opened the mouth of the sack, but the girl lunged and ripped it from his hands. Furious, she pulled out a bottle of oil and threw it at him, then an egg, then another egg. Both eggs missed and splatted on the sidewalk. Then the girl slung the sack back onto her shoulder. Tattoos dotted even her cheeks, her chin. They covered her bare arms too. Mag shook his head as he reached into his pocket, pulling out a bill and passing it to the guard, who broke into such a pleasant smile that Mag briefly wondered if the two Moroccans had conspired to swindle him.

The girl then turned and plodded off down the sidewalk. Mag hesitated. Why was he looking for trouble? He hustled after her. "Come have a coffee with me." She stopped and turned but otherwise made no response. He couldn't see her eyes behind the dark glasses and wasn't sure she had understood. But then, like a wounded animal, keeping her distance, she followed him back across the street to his table on the terrace.

For several minutes she remained too angry to acknowledge his presence. Muttering to herself, she furiously pulled items of clothing from the sack, wiping the egg from them with paper napkins. Mag chuckled. What did she want to drink? No response. Waving Ahmed over, he asked him to bring the young lady a coffee. She reached out and took a cigarette from his pack on the table.

"You're welcome to it," he said, "but I wouldn't light up

here. I don't guess you're from Casablanca, but these days, they see someone like you smoking, they cut that cigarette right off your face."

She hesitated for a moment, then shoved the cigarette into her sack, snarling, "Leave me alone."

"She speaks. English too. How'd you learn that, soldier?"

"Vietnam. Serving my country. Da Nang, Kaoba, Haiphong. American military people."

Mag stared in disbelief. "You Moroccan?"

She nodded and then appeared to want to hide, squirming down into her seat as Ahmed set down her coffee. She raised the little cup to her mouth with both hands and slurped it down, surely burning her beautiful lips.

"I didn't know the Americans were over there," Mag said, "but I guess we can't let the French have all the fun. What were you doing?"

"Fighting," she said defiantly, staring right at him, or at least he assumed she was. He wished she would take off the sunglasses so that he could see her eyes, but he left it at that, motioning for Ahmed to bring her another coffee. Pastry too. They sat in silence until the next round, and then she gobbled the pastry, shredding it to dip into her coffee until both were gone. Mag had never been much on table manners either.

"You want some advice?" he said, craving a cigarette, but not wanting her even more irritable.

"No."

"My advice is that if you gonna pilfer, you gotta be smarter about it. All that for some measly tea and a cracked egg? Cooking oil? You gotta be kidding. They're always gonna catch you for that piddling stuff, and even if they don't, it's not worth it. You're doing the exact thing they're set up to catch. You're just what they expect."

"You don't know me," the girl said. But she didn't appear to be in any hurry to leave.

"I mean there are better ways to do it. What you gotta

understand is that once any product is packaged, it's too late. Once the package sits on the shelf, the stores are set up to defend themselves against people like us, and even if you get lucky, you're never gonna get enough to make it interesting." Finally she had set the sunglasses on the table. Her eyes were large and dark and brimming. *People like us.*

"What you want is to boost the product somewhere between where it's made and where it's sold. There's this whole system at work that most people don't even suspect exists. I always had a knack for seeing the invisible lines between shipping containers, truck routes, purchasing departments, warehouses. That's where the value is. Everything happens along those invisible lines. Because once the thing is packaged, you're the sucker. And you don't look like a sucker, lady. But hell, that's just my advice. You can keep stealing bottled cooking oil if you like."

She said nothing, but no longer seemed so angry. "What's that on your leg, by the way?" he asked.

"A drawing."

"Yeah, I can see that. It's nice." He reached into his pocket and passed a wad of bills across the table. "It's gonna start getting cold at night. Buy yourself a proper coat."

She looked scared. "Take it or don't," he said, leaving the money on the table. After a moment she reached out and shoved it into her sack.

"Good," he said. "And I'm here most mornings for when you get into your next mess."

5

Tony had not been expecting another call from Rabat. The terrorists were now operating unchecked, settling scores without fear of retribution, which everyone but the craven politicians in Paris could have foreseen. A grenade had been tossed through the window of La Gironde, killing a few patrons. Avival had taped up the windows, refusing to close. Then he had been arrested. The Red Hand in Morocco had been dormant ever since Paris had shifted its focus to Algeria, which might still be saved. So Tony had been pleasantly surprised to receive the summons from Captain Fillette, although not as surprised as he was to walk into the office that morning and find the captain with another man.

They rose from their chairs, and Fillette introduced Major Zubov, his counterpart in the Soviet secret service. Was this what it had come to? The communists? Tony shook the man's hand. "Méléro is one of our best men," the captain said, which Tony acknowledged with a nod as he seated himself, ramrod straight. Zubov's uniform was worn threadbare at the cuffs. He looked to be in his forties…and still a major. Since when did France reveal the secrets of the Red Hand to the midlevel functionaries of sworn enemies?

Fillette nodded at Zubov, who asked in perfect French, "Have you heard of Haj Driss Alaoui?" Tony clicked his nails on the desktop and spoke quickly: "Rich kid, mid-twenties, good-looking, likes a party, possibly a drunk, hangs around with Americans in Paradise on Rue Nolly, drives a white convertible Chevrolet Corvette. Links to the Sultan via his father, whose political network includes French liberals."

Fillette shot him a warning look before casually remarking to the ceiling: "Lieutenant Méléro's police work keeps him apprised of local characters. Up until now we have not judged Alaoui to be a particular threat."

Local characters. As if Tony were on the vice squad.

Captain Fillette knew a few local characters himself, Tony had discovered. He'd heard that the SDECE had asked Jo Renucci, Paradise's gangster owner, to execute Lemaigre-Dubreuil. When Renucci had refused, the job had gone to Tony and his team. Fillette's betrayal still stung.

Now the strange little Soviet cleared his throat. "Haj Driss Alaoui wants to follow his father into politics," he murmured, "but the leaders of the resistance want nothing to do with a playboy. He came to me looking for an ally, and I must confess that I became his case officer. Quickly it became clear that his intelligence could not be relied upon. His principal talent remains wasting time. So he is frustrated and increasingly megalomaniacal. Unfortunately he also now has a plan by which he hopes to be taken seriously. Next week he will rob the ordnance depot at the American base at Nouasseur."

"Good luck," Tony said wryly, but the captain again cut him off with a glance. What did this have to do with them anyway?

"That was my reaction," Zubov said. "What is perhaps more worrisome is his backup plan: if he does not succeed at robbing the ordnance depot, he will blow it up. Either way, he feels he will have gained the respect he has been denied, assuring a position of power once the protectorate has been dismantled."

Now interested, Tony leaned forward. "How is he going to do this?"

"He has contacts within the base military police."

"Close contacts?"

"He gets them drunk and provides them with young Moroccan women," Zubov said stiffly.

Tony glanced over at Fillette, who revealed nothing, then back at Zubov.

"So I find myself in this ridiculous situation." The Russian smiled sadly. "I can't go to the Americans with my information. They will assume I am lying. But you, they will have to trust. And we must do something. If the boy manages to execute even part of his plan, it will be bad for all of us. So I am humbly requesting your help."

"Thank you, Major Zubov," Fillette said crisply. "We'll take it from here." So Zubov rose uncertainly and shuffled out the door, murmuring *mercis*.

As soon as the door shut, Fillette said, "I don't trust the communists any more than you, but if he's coming to us, there's a good reason. The head of U.S. Air Force Office of Special Investigations has agreed to meet you for dinner next Monday at Nouasseur. I know I don't have to say it, but you'll go alone."

Tony was pleased to have regained the Captain's confidence, but he could hardly see the point. Was France now nothing more than a go-between? Again it had capitulated, and capitulation had always been the surest path to servitude. Who had said that? He would have to check the compilation so that next time he could cite the source.

THE BIRDCAGE
1956

○

Mag spent his mornings at the corner café across from
Galeries Lafayette. He drank coffee and read the papers. He

watched Ahmed the waiter fight with another waiter named Ahmed over the choice of radio station on the portable receiver with the blown-out speaker at the bar. Ahmed liked the Moroccan music that sounded like strangled chickens, while Ahmed's new favorite was Elvis Presley. The two Ahmeds hated one another. Extended shouting matches emanated from the cavernous room. Patrons sat abandoned on the terrace. Orders were forgotten.

But mostly Mag just waited. He didn't mind it so much, and he wondered if he was getting old. For the first time in his life, he didn't need to know what he was doing or where he was going. The afternoons, however, were more difficult and seemed to stretch on endlessly. He would stroll around the city center or return to the hotel for a nap. The winter was cold, and the Casablanca humidity could work its way into your bones. Sometimes he was lonely, but it wasn't too bad, at least not as bad as it was for that Elvis Presley, who lived in a hotel on Lonely Street, so lonely he could die. Ahmed knew all the lyrics. Yet often Mag did feel disconnected from anything that mattered, which was a feeling he tried not to indulge.

One afternoon when he got back to the hotel, there was a message for him at the desk. It was from Ahmed Touil, in whom he'd long since given up hope. The message instructed him to meet the next day at noon on the central promenade of Parc Murdoch. He probably wanted more money, Mag thought, trudging towards the elevator. But that evening he ordered his suit pressed, and the next morning he left the café early to flag down a taxi.

Why hadn't he visited the park before? He hadn't imagined that Casablanca could contain something so lush and cool, planted with carefully tended bushes and trees of all sorts, none of which he could have named, except for two rows of towering palms lining a long strip of grass. In the thin black shadow of each trunk was a wooden bench. At the opposite end of the grass, he spotted Ahmed, a silhouette flanked by two larger silhouettes. Mag approached, the sound of his shoes on the gravel scattering birdsongs.

Ahmed grinned and hugged him but didn't say a word. He led them to a nearby bench not far from a sandy play area where a group of girls were climbing over a jungle gym shaped like a giant egg. The two men sat. The two gorillas sat on the next bench. Mag watched the girls play until he couldn't stand it anymore: "Well?"

Touil still said nothing, which would have been miraculous back in the old days, but then what the hell did he know about Ahmed Touil anymore? He stared at the Moroccan's face in profile, gray and blank, dark hollows beneath the eyes, searching for some further clue, no longer daring to look at the girls. This couldn't be it. She couldn't be here. Ahmed wasn't watching the jungle gym, however. An older Moroccan girl transfixed him, sort of tomboyish, looking after the others as if she were in charge. "Well?" Mag insisted.

Touil turned irritably. "My American friend wanted me to find a girl," he said, "so I found the girl. Count on Ahmed Touil."

Nauseous, Mag forced himself to look back at the jungle gym. He had already seen her. He already knew. She was the only possibility, as strange in this setting as Mag himself. She was beautiful, she really was, her blonde hair cropped straight across her forehead, seeming like part of the sunlight. Camille hadn't been blonde, but he had been as a child. The frilly dress reminded him of Camille, however, and the feminine way her fingers curled into the air, as if she'd touched something sticky. Did the girl have friends? The others were all Moroccan, and she played alone, her pale face so serious, brow furrowed in concentration.

"You know her name?" he mumbled, his mouth so dry that the words stuck to his tongue like flecks of tobacco.

"Not yet," Ahmed said.

"Never mind. What is this? A school? Who are those

other girls?"

Ahmed briefly described the institute, which was a few blocks south on Rue de Lisbonne.

"Does she live there?" So many questions.

Ahmed shook his head. "Some old French lady in the neighborhood. But in the daytime she goes to the institute. They come over here around lunch to play."

"How did you find her?"

"I am a police detective," Ahmed said vaguely, glancing back towards the tomboyish Moroccan and whispering something to himself. The shadow of a palm trunk had shifted up into Mag's lap. He could ask questions for hours, and Ahmed might even answer a few, but Touil was never going to be able to tell him what to do next, which was what mattered now. He reached for his wallet.

"Not here," Ahmed said. "Some other time." He seemed sad, or angry. From the moment they had met, his emotions had always run together, such that Mag couldn't tell one from the other. He wouldn't have been surprised if Ahmed had burst into laughter, or wept, but he stood and walked off down the gravel path, his gorillas falling in beside him, leaving Mag on the bench with no idea what to do with the next minute, or the next day, or the next week. So he sat and watched his daughter climb the bars to the top of a metal egg.

o

In the mornings then he sat at the café, read the papers, and watched the world while listening to the Ahmeds' Elvis Presley war. Then he would arrive in a taxi at the gates of Parc Murdoch at precisely noon and sit for an hour on his bench.

Her name was Micheline, like the tire. He had heard other girls calling her that. At first he had wondered if it was a joke. She was the dreamy type, tending to keep to herself, and maybe wasn't particularly well liked. She would find objects in the sand – dead flowers or pinecones – and stare at them for ages just talking to herself. But then he had heard the attendants – sometimes the tomboy, who usually wore overalls, sometimes others – calling her Micheline too, so he figured it was actually her name. Crazy Camille. So in his head he called her Mitch.

He so often wanted to go over and keep her company, maybe show her a magic trick, but he didn't dare. How could you begin that conversation? Did she speak English? Probably not. Had her mother ever told her about Mag the American? And then he wondered, especially in the evenings after a couple of drinks, whether he wanted a daughter at all, whether he was cut out for that kind of life, or simply kidding himself, bored. Maybe what he really needed was a new business venture. This was probably crazy.

This routine went on for weeks. The weather turned warmer, and flowers bloomed in neat square beds cut into the grass. Old men sat on benches reading the papers, cleaning their glasses with the hems of their sweaters. Others exercised, high-stepping around the perimeter path, pausing occasionally to bounce on their feet and deliver combinations of fists at invisible adversaries, hissing like air being let out of a tire. Nurses in white uniforms rolled wheelchairs down wide paths, carrying pale patients from the clinic at the gate. Babies crawled across blankets on the grass in the shade of more trees Mag couldn't name. More flowers blossomed, bright red ones with black centers. Maybe he was getting used to Mitch's habits, or even starting to understand her a bit, but she now seemed to fit in better with the other girls. She smiled more often, missing a front tooth, and occasionally she would join a group to push sand up into mounds, making lumpy cities out there. She could be downright chatty with the friendly tomboy, who was obviously fond of Mitch, or Micheline.

One morning at the café the girl with the tattoos turned up and slumped down into the opposite chair. She carried her sack, which she placed beneath the table, and wore an enormous blue coat that fell to her ankles, gold epaulets on the shoulders. He ordered her a coffee and waited to hear what she wanted, or what she'd stolen, but the girl said nothing. She actually appeared to be in a good mood.

"You okay?" he asked.

"Yes you okay?" He nodded and looked at his watch – no longer the Gallet Flying Officer, but at least he now knew he hadn't lost it, and Ahmed had repaid the theft. It was already twenty minutes till noon. "Could you help me with something?" he asked. "I'll pay for your time."

Either she wasn't in such a good mood after all, or this hadn't been the right thing to say. Take the combined rage of the dueling Ahmeds, add in a bottle of that hot harissa sauce the Moroccans put in their couscous, and still you wouldn't have approached this girl's sudden heat.

"You can't afford me, mister!" she shouted, repeatedly banging her palms on the table so that their coffee cups rattled in their saucers.

"Come on," he growled, glancing at his watch again. "The name's Mag, by the way, and it's nothing like that. I just need you to go to a park with me and sit on a bench in the sun."

She narrowed her eyes and puffed out her lips, still dubious but willing. Then in the taxi she announced that her name was Fadila, which he pointed out sounded a lot like Fedala, which was where he'd first landed in Morocco in 1942 after having narrowly avoided being feasted on by a pig. But then he really didn't want to get into it, and she probably wouldn't have been interested anyway.

Fadila smiled.

At the park they sat on the bench together and watched Mitch play. "Her name's Micheline," Mag said softly, "but I call her Mitch."

"She's pretty," Fadila said. He nodded.

"I can't go talk to her. I don't speak French or Arabic. And look at me. They'll call the cops." He glanced over at Fadila and smiled, realizing the flaw in his hastily devised plan: Fadila wouldn't inspire much confidence either.

"You know she's your daughter?"

He sighed. He hadn't wanted to get into the whole Camille story, but he had told her a bit about his time in Casablanca, how he'd loved this crazy French girl who'd loved pigeons, how he'd once taken her to see the great Marcel Cerdan fight at the Stade Philippe, how they'd had some good times, but then he'd been given orders and had packed off to Europe. "So I guess that's why I came back. They said it was a car crash. Then I heard about Mitch."

Fadila had listened intently to the story, her black eyes boring into him. Had she lost her sunglasses? Her eyes contained the whole of Casablanca, all the beauty and the filth, and he cursed himself for struggling to meet their intensity.

When he had finished speaking, she nodded once and walked over to the jungle gym.

○

Fadila had refused to tell him where she was staying, but every morning she would turn up at the café before noon. The first couple of days he had wanted to take his usual taxi, but she had insisted they walk. He needed the exercise, she said, and started arriving even earlier so that they could walk together. The trip was about a mile and a half, past the clock tower of the Hotel de Ville and through Mers Sultan, and he grew to like even the walking. There was so much of the city he hadn't discovered. There was the kid they passed every few days on his bike, his legs so short that he could only pump the pedals at the top of their circle. There were the men on the side streets who tied strings to electricity poles and with wooden dowels spun the strings into yarn.

He had made a small donation to the Institution Lalla Amina, which hadn't actually been necessary, because like magic Fadila had taken care of everything. She would translate between him and Mitch in the hour they spent together, and the girl seemed to enjoy the game. She didn't yet call him *Father*, or *Dad*, but she taught him French and Arabic words in her tiny, precise voice, making him repeat them until she was satisfied, or threw her arms in the air with an exasperated shake of her head. In the mornings he tried out his new words on the Ahmeds, who finally united in greeting each with ecstatic praise. Unfortunately he couldn't yet understand whatever they said next.

Then somehow Fadila worked it out so that some afternoons they could walk Mitch back to the institute, taking their time. Mitch was learning English fast. She was talented at languages and would point out places she knew and wanted Mag and Fadila to see. Most days they stopped for ice cream. They were an odd trio and got some looks, but none of them minded, at least until one day when a man in a white djellabah walked past and called Fadila a *pute*, one word Mag didn't need to be taught. It was the word every soldier had needed to know during the war in Morocco and France. Furious, he wheeled on the man and pushed up into his face. "What did you say? Say it! Say it again!" But Fadila had grabbed his arm and pulled him off. "Never mind, Mag. Never mind men like that." And not wanting to embarrass her any further, he had let Fadila drag him down the sidewalk.

After they dropped off Mitch, he would take Fadila to lunch someplace in the neighborhood. There wasn't always much to discuss, but it didn't seem to matter, and Fadila was constantly surprising him. When he wondered about the trees in Parc Murdoch, she came back the next day with their names. Cypress, ficus, banana. She couldn't read or write, so he didn't know how she did it. Sometimes after lunch they would return to their café, always on foot, until it seemed he knew the city better than his face in the mirror, although maybe not as well as he knew Fadila's. He was reading a book about Morocco that he'd found in English at one of the stalls along the Boulevard de la Gare, learning what he could, the pashas and the Almoravids and all that. Fadila would sit quietly drawing her angels in the notebooks he offered her, pictures she mostly gave to Mitch, who loved them, because Mitch wanted to fly. She talked about it often. One of her best friends knew how to fly, she said, and one day she would too. The other girls made fun of her for this, but Mag admired the girl's imagination. He'd known some people who could fly, he told her, and figured one day she would get the hang of it.

Pickering of the U.S. Air Force OSI was a fat man with a wild mustache. His accent was Canadian, but his French was floridly perfect. As head of the Nouasseur counter-espionage unit, he existed outside the chain of command, a fact he obviously relished, wearing an ostentatious double-breasted sharkskin suit. His pudgy fingers wormed through the air as he savored another French turn of phrase, gallantly suggesting, for instance, that the two men dispense with formalities and *se tutoyer*. Beneath this surface, however, Tony sensed a sharp intelligence, and Madame Pickering, after presenting the roast, had left them to eat and to discuss what she called in a flat American accent "business".

It was mid-January, but the house was still full of garish Christmas decorations, colored lights hung outside from the eaves, which cast the dining room in repeating shades of green, red, yellow, and blue. After dinner two MPs were summoned by telephone to accompany them on a stroll around the base, and Pickering once again repeated a phrase he had been uttering since Tony's arrival: "Not a word to anyone. *Même pas le moindre petit mot.*" By this point Tony, who felt that he had remained cool and professional throughout the bewildering feast, was convinced that they would find nothing incriminating on the base, and his opinion of Captain Fillette had fallen even further. The Russians had set them on a merry-go-round, and Tony was now required to ride his plastic horse, spurred by a fat Canadian who wanted to be French, and yet had probably never even heard of the poet Henri de Lacretelle.

Every munitions bunker was guarded by two soldiers day and night, Pickering had explained. While one kept watch, the other rested in a little guard room. The two MPs followed them through the night, down American streets towards the bunkers. Tony felt as if he had been dropped down on another planet, one he recognized only from movies. There was a soda shop and even a bowling alley. He discreetly felt his cufflinks, the bells. Here he was.

Pickering took base security seriously. If there had been a breach, he was intent on finding it, and bunker by bunker they barged in for inspections. The first whore, dark and pulpy, they found in bed in the guard room of Bunker Two. The second, a dead-eyed Berber from the mountains, they found hiding in Bunker Nine. Those four soldiers were immediately arrested. Then Pickering had all the other guards arrested for good measure, casually turning to Tony and saying, "Perhaps you could have a little word with the ladies, *mon bonhomme*."

They took the girls to the stockade, where Pickering left Tony alone with them in a brightly lit office. "I'm afraid my Arabic is rather unaccomplished," the Canadian said, gently shutting the door behind him. The girls slumped into two chairs. Tony stood behind the desk glaring at their painted faces, then decided the best technique would to be keep his prisoners off balance by moving around the room. First, however, he removed his tie, taking his time to neatly fold it on the desk. Let the little whores sweat a bit, see what kind of man he was. Then he circled, circled like a shark.

"These Americans don't fool around," he said in Arabic to the backs of their heads. "You'll go to prison. For life." The girls burst into tears and promised to tell him everything. He snickered. With his thumb he wiped a tear from the cheek of the vapid little Berber. "I can set you free," he whispered into her ear. "Tell me who brought you here and how you did it, and I'll put in a good word with the Americans." Of course the little *putes* said nothing. They just pushed out more tears, batting their eyelashes, heaving up their chests. The air reeked of cheap perfume.

Circling, seeming disinterested, then spinning back again: "Tell me, have you ever met a man called Haj Driss Alaoui?"

The dark one, who wore a leather coat, then sobbed for real. "Is he in trouble?" she burbled through thick lips.

"Not yet," Tony said, hitching himself up on the desk, stroking her plump arm. He could have had her then, he knew, but he didn't go for whores.

"He didn't do anything," she moaned, eyes darting over his face. "You should talk to those American soldiers. They are the ones who brought us here." Tony drew back his arm and slapped her hard. This gave him no pleasure. Women should be respected, but these were no ordinary women, and he had an obligation. The dark girl took the blow admirably, merely wiping her nose with the back of her hand, then sobbing some more, so he slapped her again. She was pretty. "Remind me of your name, angel."

"Suzanne," she sobbed as Tony nodded slowly, as if for the first time since their fortuitous meeting, she'd actually made some sense. The Berber girl just sat there looking terrified. She wouldn't be good for much. So grabbing the dark one by the arm and twisting, he asked her again to tell him everything, and after another quick slap she finally understood.

The girls had been driven to the base a few nights a week by an MP, she said, in his personal car, and then back into town the next morning. For Haj Driss Alaoui, the girls had noted down the movements and the names of guards. Tony stroked her hair and thanked her for her honesty, for doing the right thing.

Then Pickering brought in the arrested American guards and paraded them in front of the girls, who pointed out the ones they knew, and – after more persistent questioning from Tony – exactly what they had done with each. In the end, nine men were sent back to the United States and court-martialed.

"Can we go now?" Suzanne asked as dawn pushed into the office windows. "Are we free?"

Tony laughed. Sleep was weakness. "We're just getting started, Suzanne. So why don't you tell me about that leather coat. Some soldier give it to you?"

○

Four B-47 Stratojets had left MacDill Air Force Base in Florida for a non-stop flight to Morocco. Their first aerial refueling had been routine, but when it had come time to drop from the clouds for a second refueling over the sea, one of the B-47s had failed to make contact with the tanker. That had been two days ago, and there had been no sign of the aircraft since. The base was in a state of alert, and Tommy kept finding himself staring up at the sky, as if he could conjure the missing plane and its men from the clouds over Nouasseur.

Lucy hadn't come home that night. He hadn't seen her since their fight, the day the plane had gone missing. Although he guessed it hadn't really been a fight. It had started with the sound of breaking glass from the kitchen. He had run in to find her holding only the handle of the Waring Blendor in her trembling hands. The blender had been her birthday present. He'd had it sent from the States, smuggling it into the house and leaving it on the kitchen counter as a surprise. The jar of the blender had been smashed, and thick shards of glass covered the floor, glinting in the sunlight that streamed through the open kitchen door. Lucy was wearing her red bikini. Suntanning in January. On a clear day, in the afternoon, you could just about stand it without freezing to death. Any excuse to scandalize the neighbors. Her feet were bare, of course, and she had risen on her toes, looking across the floor around her, trapped by the glass with her face twisted in agony. Fatima would have felt darkly vindicated by the sight if Fatima still worked for them. Lucy had fired her. While Tommy had found himself increasingly sympathetic to their former maid's suspicions of black magic. And now here they were, a thousand sharp demons nipping at Lucy's feet. She had squeezed angry tears from her eyes and had groaned from somewhere deep inside her chest, although Tommy could hardly hear it over the radio. She'd been blasting Radio Nouasseur, that song by the kid called Elvis, which they played morning, noon and night. *Heartbreak Hotel*, one of the strangest songs Tommy had ever heard, this Elvis moaning and groaning and muttering to himself, as if he, too, had been possessed by a djinn. Lucy reached towards the radio, but it was further than her fingers stretched, his beautiful, strange wife in her tiny, fading bikini, trapped in the middle of her own kitchen. Tommy moved towards the counter, but realized his feet were also bare. So he stopped, and they stared at each other, and Elvis was so lonely he could die.

When the song ended, she'd cried, "How did we get this way?" Tommy went back to their bedroom to grab the first pair of shoes he came upon, pink heels, which he carried back to the kitchen and tossed to Lucy, like feeding an alligator. She deftly raised each of her long, tanned legs, reaching down to slip her feet into the heels, and then she strode past him out of the kitchen, glass crunching beneath her toes. "Please don't feel the need to respond," she said.

He sighed and followed her out into the living room. "Respond to what?"

"How did we *get* this way, Tommy?" She turned to look at him then, her eyes narrow and pleading, arms rigid by her sides. In heels she was half an inch taller than him. "*Say something.*"

"Little by little," he said off towards the wall. Wallpaper just wasn't suitable in this climate. Theirs was peeling again. "Just like that," he said. "We didn't know we were doing it."

"Oh, *damn* you, Tommy August," she cried. "You used to *be* something. You knew everything about music, you were cultured and had principles and I *admired* you, but you…. I didn't even see it happening. I just woke up one day, and this was us. What was I supposed to do? What, Tommy? *Say something, please!*"

He had looked down at the carpet, dug his toes into it.

He didn't know what to say. He looked at her body, beautiful and so familiar. He felt no desire. Her flesh was like his own flesh, heavy and humid at the end of a day. "I'd better go clean up that glass before the children get home," he said, and later, when he came back out into the living room, she was gone. So that had been their fight, or whatever you wanted to call it. And then she hadn't come home that night, but he hadn't missed her. It felt as if she was still there. They had been in rooms together for years.

Now after breakfast, after the children had gone off to school, there came a knock at the door. Lucy wouldn't knock. Tommy rose from the couch, where he sat absently drinking another cup of coffee, and plodded across the carpet to the door. Two MPs stood on his front porch. "Good morning, Mister August."

Tommy blinked in the light. "Is it Lucy? Is she all right?"

"Excuse me, sir?"

"My wife. Lucy."

"We will inform her. We're also informing the school."

The school? Why would they inform the school? Had they found the missing pilots?

"We're not going to cuff you, Mister August. Please just follow us out to the car."

Cuff me? Tommy grinned. "Snodgrass put you up to this, didn't he?"

"Please come with us now, Mister August," the MP said, fastening a hand to Tommy's elbow. *Captain August,* he wanted to say, but those Air Force boys would take it as a provocation. Obviously there had been some misunderstanding. Everyone would see that soon enough. In the meantime, however, there didn't appear to be much choice but to follow these two out to their car.

They rode past a windowless bunker with walls several meters thick, where locked behind bars in a birdcage was Africa's lone atomic bomb.

○

The night after his interview with the two whores, Tony waited for Haj Driss Alaoui on the sidewalk outside Paradise. It was better to get him there and avoid making a scene. Also he wasn't too eager to run into Jo Renucci. Did the gangster know that it had been he who had eliminated Lemaigre-Dubreuil? Better not find out. You didn't want a man like Renucci knowing your secrets. So Tony waited in the cold shadows.

Just before midnight, he heard a roar up Rue Nolly, and the white Corvette, top opened to the frigid night, came speeding up and lurched onto the sidewalk. The engine died. Tony nodded to the undercover Buick parked down the block and swiftly moved out from the wall, keeping his gun holstered. With a punk like this, fists would be more than enough. "Police," he shouted.

Haj Driss's hands were already flailing in the air, a woman, a jellyfish. He was stinking drunk and terrified. "I demand a phone call!" Two hulking cops materialized on either side of Tony. They snatched open the door of the Corvette and actually lifted Haj Driss, still flailing, from the front seat. Then they carried him down the block and threw him into the back of the Buick. Tony got into the passenger seat and turned to watch the spectacle.

"My name is Haj Driss Alaoui, and I demand to speak to the police commissioner! You're making a big mistake. I will speak with the commissioner immediately!"

Tony laughed. Haj Driss reeked of wine, and a pink stain decorated the front of his shirt. He went limp for a moment, then bolted upright with another idea: "I demand a translator! This is my right as a Moroccan citizen!"

Tony sighed. "My name is not important," he said in perfect Arabic, a smile traced across his lips. "Nobody knows you're here. You're drunk. Somebody at some bar will attest to that. Maybe you were too drunk to see straight. Maybe you crashed your Corvette into a tree. I am your translator this evening, Haj Driss, and yes, we know exactly who you are."

That shut him up. They drove to a warehouse Tony sometimes used, a dark place with gray walls and no windows. The only words Haj Driss said during the entire trip were, "Can you at least turn on Radio Nouasseur, please please?" Which was funny, because the radio was as close as the kid would ever get to Nouasseur again. The request was wordlessly denied.

In the warehouse they tied him to a chair, but Haj Driss had fallen apart before they needed to beat him. "Then give us names," Tony said as the boy frantically nodded. "Tell us who's protecting you and who knows about your plan. Then you'll be free to go." Which wasn't exactly true, but the kid yapped for an hour, fingering the greater part of Casablanca, detailing how he had intended to move the American ordnance to a network of armed cells he controlled, although perhaps it would be more accurate to say these were cells he *advised*, although perhaps that was overstating it too. Could he get a glass of whiskey? They found a bottle, and he signed a confession, crying out "My poor mother!" as he set down the pen. "Can you send me someplace else? Can you hide me in Tangier? I have family there. Please! In Casablanca I'm a dead man."

The next day they organized the paperwork, and Haj Driss Alaoui was driven to Tangier, where his passport was revoked. For weeks detectives attempted to track down his network which, it soon became clear, existed only in the mind of Haj Driss.

o

Lucy didn't come, but in his heart he knew, and so he didn't think about her. Thinking was just like not thinking now, and so he didn't have to think anymore. The cell was not uncomfortable. The cot was padded, and the window let in a good deal of light. He knew. He'd built the place.

It was something about the girl, he suspected, the one he had met that night at the fence, although they hadn't told him anything yet. Probably he should have turned her in, but it hadn't felt right. They wouldn't hold him long, they couldn't, but this was the military, and they had their ironclad procedures. He had minded at first, had thought about how it would look, but now he didn't mind so much anymore.

There had been no food or water, no more coffee. But the building seemed to play music. Or he was the musical instrument and the building played him. Pipes burbled unseen through the ceiling, but he had studied the plans and could see through the concrete. Distant footsteps echoed, collapsing into one another. Outside a truck crept over gravel, the pop of compacted stones. Closer there were birds, sparrows probably, staccato. If he could sit very still on his cot, his ears grew even sharper. A fly now, bouncing against the wall within a little blip of silence. The ripping sound as a toilet began to flush, then the rush of water, making the pipes overhead burble again. His heart beating, the pulse quicker than he remembered. And maybe, just maybe, the syncopated sound of a gimbri being strummed way beyond the fence in Little America.

"Guard!" he shouted, rushing to the bars, banging his palms against them, feeling them vibrate, then silencing them with his grasp. Eventually a guard appeared, and Tommy begged for pencil and paper, which were brought.

He was happy then, maybe happier than he'd been since flying with the Red Rippers over Casablanca. For hours he listened, scribbling furiously, the notes appearing as if they had spilled from his fingers, page after page, front and back, calling for more, music finally flowing from him again, as if he was flying again. All he had to do was reach out into the slipstream and grab whole symphonies.

Later he heard a metal door creak open down the corridor, slightly scraping the floor, but they weren't coming for him, at least not yet. There was still time.

○

Aziza was in the concrete corridor outside the cell. Suzanne felt her presence even before she saw her. There had been nobody else to call. When Haj Driss had fallen out with the *patronne* of La Parisienne, Suzanne had fallen out with her too. Since then she had been living with other girls, a couch one night, a floor the next, and sometimes a guard's bed at the American base – every man, she had hoped, a pathway to Haj Driss's heart. So her mother's shop had been the only place where somebody she knew had been sure to be found.

It was only then that she had really started crying, once her mother was coming. They would not tell her anything more about Haj Driss. So she had been crying silently to herself, still wearing the same dress. The guards had exchanged the coat for a thin blanket, which was wrapped around her shoulders.

When her mother appeared through the bars, she looked old and tired and pale. Suzanne stopped crying. The door of the cell swung open. The guard nodded and her mother stepped in, handing over a kaftan so that Suzanne could cover herself.

○

Anger had always come easier to Hajja Aliya than grief. That was the way it was. The phone had rung that morning, and she was still berating her husband. "You let this happen to your only son! You let them take him from us! You did this!" But her husband was as devastated as she, and stunned by his failure. So her anger roamed, deep into her bones, as if seeking its own source to hate, and there was a place inside, a place that still made her blind with pain when touched, calling immediately to mind the one who had put it there, the traitorous Touria Chaoui.

Everything had turned rotten once her reputation had been slandered by that girl. This was no coincidence. Evil had come into her body, called forth by that girl, and evil had not been content merely to destroy her health. Evil was greedy and had needed to destroy her family too. This was how the djinns worked. Haj Driss now exiled, and still the little pilot posed for pictures, glorifying her own association under the patronage of a Sultan who would now be king. Hadn't Hajja Aliya given her whole life, her very body, to Morocco? Who had done more for the poor? Whose name was synonymous with charity throughout Casablanca and beyond?

The next morning an article appeared in the paper – no photograph this time, Allah be praised, but a glowing account of Miss Chaoui's work at the Institution Lalla Amina. "She has destroyed us," Hajja Aliya said to her husband through gritted teeth. "Do something for once."

○

Aziza watched Suzanne's face as the taxi approached Bousbir. She wasn't a girl anymore. Aziza had to do the math, because until then she had needed to forget: twenty-two, and even more beautiful than she would have guessed. The taxi

232

stopped. Suzanne scowled but did not yet dare speak. Aziza forgave her. She understood, more than Suzanne realized, and in time maybe they could discuss the past.

Suzanne still said nothing as Aziza guided her through the front door. *See these beautiful things, Suzanne. They were not made to be enjoyed alone.* "Let me show you your room." Now she was too nervous to look at her daughter's face.

Everything had been prepared. She had only needed to make the bed quickly before hailing the taxi to Nouasseur. She opened the wardrobe, which was filled with her shop's finest clothes. "These are for you." Suzanne merely glanced at the clothes before stepping over to the window and opening it. Aziza followed her gaze out to the patio and the laundry hanging below. There wasn't much else to see. "Better close it so you don't catch cold. Why don't you wash up, and I'll make us tea."

Suzanne spun from the open window and finally spoke, "I hate tea!" Aziza nodded, managing to hold her tongue. The girl was spoiled. It wasn't her fault. Aziza had been a bad mother. The truth of this pained her, but it wasn't too late. She would work less. For years she had been planning to work less. They could be a family, and then who knew....

In the kitchen she boiled the water. She put a handful of mint into the pot, several spoonfuls of green tea, and a block of sugar. She filled the pot with hot water from the kettle and waited, finding satisfaction in the ritual that she hadn't felt in years. She sung to herself as she waited, and when the tea had brewed, she set the pot with glasses on a silver platter, along with a plate of almond cookies dusted with white sugar. When everything looked perfect, she went to the bottom of the staircase and called up to Suzanne. When Suzanne didn't come, she called up again. Still nothing.

So Aziza went up to the room. The window was still open, and nothing had been touched. Nothing had changed. Suzanne was gone.

3

Salah came running out of the school playground towards the green Morris Minor, his partially unzipped backpack slung over one shoulder, notebooks hanging out of the gap. Touria smiled at her brother. A barrage of firecrackers went off down the street. It was Thursday, March 1, 1956. A Moroccan government had been formed, and the next day the French would hand over the country. Touria had celebrated that afternoon with the girls at the institute, so elated that she had given them a speech before sending them off for the long weekend. The rest of their lives would be lived in a free country. Now they could become anything they wanted to be. Everything had changed. Tomorrow was Independence Day.

She thought of Micheline as Salah dawdled, saying goodbye to a couple of friends. The French girl had been especially inspired by Touria's talk of freedom, and why not? Morocco was as much hers as the other girls', and she had learned to dream. *Come on, Salah.* She didn't want to be late to the airfield, where she had called a meeting of the pilots club to discuss future plans. Maybe afterwards she would fly and see if this new Morocco looked any different from the air. But first she had to get Salah home.

He struggled to open the door, and she leaned over to help push it open. "How was your day, little brother?"

Traffic crawled up Rue du Général Humbert. Horns blared in a deafening chorus of frustration and joy. The sidewalks were packed, and boys scampered through the crowd setting off firecrackers. She shifted lanes once, and then again, pressing forward. Briefly she noticed a Citroën following her from lane to lane. Everyone was in a hurry.

Salah had pulled a drawing from his bag and held it out for her to see. Only eleven, he was already developing into an exceptional artist. She paused to look intently at the scene he had drawn, a landscape with a remarkably accurate Fez in the distance, remembered from his early childhood. "You are a true artist, brother," she said, rubbing the back of his neck with her palm.

But today that's how she felt about everything. Morocco was theirs to create. Maybe she should get into politics. The Sultan had already spoken to her about an advisory position to the cabinet, focused on women's rights. Maybe she would even become prime minister one day. There would be opportunities for women now. It was possible.

The Citroën followed as she turned right onto Route de Medouina, but then it pulled over to the side of the road and receded in the rearview mirror. How long would it take before she wasn't so paranoid all the time? Weeks? Months? Years?

Driving down Rue de Bergerac, she smiled and waved to Hajar, the old gossip, at her usual post in her window. The side streets were less crowded, but firecrackers still went off everywhere – *snap snap!* Across from their apartment building at number 32, she braked and let the car idle without cutting the engine. Salah struggled to get his notebooks and papers crammed back into his bag. Her mother stepped out onto the second-floor balcony, and they happily waved to one another.

A shape appeared, a shadow. Touria saw him only for an instant, once it was already done, a thin Moroccan with slicked-back hair. He blocked out the light and offered something with his hand. A gun.

Two firecrackers went off, and she saw her own head slump to the wheel, Salah spattered in blood. Her mother still waved from the balcony, but then she was screaming, her beautiful mother.

The green Morris Minor got smaller and smaller. Soon Rue de Bergerac looked like any other tiny city street, and all of Casablanca was spread out beneath her, until it was gone.

o

INDEPENDENCE DAY
1956

Men brought her in from the street. His father had not yet arrived home. Salah stood atop the staircase looking down into the light streaming through the front door. The men were black shapes, his sister's body a black shape slung between them. He heard nothing, not even the wailing of his mother, whose hands flew in the air as if they had been lit on fire. They brought her up. Tomorrow they would bury her, they said, on Independence Day.

o

The Gypsy, of all people, had decided he was a hero. He had actually attempted to assassinate Pierre Mendès France, the prime minister who had overseen the French withdrawal from Morocco. Mendès France had been visiting the Residence in Rabat, and so the Gypsy, who didn't know the first thing about homo ops, had decided to climb the wall of the Residence and assassinate him. Before he could even begin to figure out how to get up the wall, however, the Residence guards had shot him. Tony was furious. He had been obliged to break the idiot out of his hospital room, where he was guarded round the clock by the Brigade Spéciale of the Moroccan police, now actually armed. Otherwise the Gypsy might have spilled everything – not just the assassinations plotted by the Avival gang, but also the operations of the Red Hand, from Tony all the way up to Captain Fillette. Fillette would stick up for him, Tony felt certain, but he couldn't take the chance.

So at a supply shop he'd found a nurse's uniform, which he'd worn into the hospital's service entrance while the Sheik, who was as angry as Tony but could presumably be trusted, had waited outside in the car. Tony had disarmed the guard without too much fuss and had rolled an ecstatic Gypsy out through the formaldehyde fog of the morgue, counting on the childish Muslim fear of dead bodies to give him a clear path back out to the Sheik. Now the Gypsy was in a safe house in Mers Sultan, convalescing while waiting on a boat to smuggle him back to France, where he could disappear into the countryside.

Tony should have never mentioned the Red Hand to his friends. Those guys hadn't progressed beyond the old days. They hadn't evolved. Maybe their hearts had been in the right place, but they had lacked the intellectual capacity to understand the stakes, and now it was too late. A bomb would have been the way to do it. Sometimes Tony felt as if he was the only person in the whole city who was holding it together.

A few weeks passed. They kept their distance from the safe house. The Gypsy got lonely and missed his mother. He started going down to the corner bistro to drink in the afternoons, and then one day he called her and gave her the address. He wanted a paella. Within minutes the Moroccan police had descended upon the place. They had been given a tip about a European with a bullet wound living upstairs from the bistro and had tapped the phone. The police arrested the Gypsy, and now the boat was meant for Tony, because everybody knew the Gypsy would rat on him in a flash.

The boat was called the *Lyautey*. He didn't see much of it. They smuggled him into the port in the back of a truck, and then they loaded him straight down into the hold, where for three days he stayed, surviving on a canister of water until they arrived in Marseilles. It was the first time Tony had ever set foot in the France he loved. He was met by a police lieutenant who knew his name and was put on a train for Paris, where he would receive further orders.

In Paris, he went directly to the central police station. There would be a decoration, he felt certain, perhaps a Legion of Honor, an appropriate acknowledgement of his service to his country, and then some cushy job near the top, likely with the secret service. Captain Fillette had promised to put in a good word.

But the officer responsible for his case was oddly hostile and claimed that his dossier was still in Rabat. Until Paris received it, nothing could be done. In the meantime there was no post for Tony. Perhaps he could check back in a week or two, preferably by telephone.

The dossier never appeared. They claimed it was lost. So Tony called Captain Fillette, but his secretary in Rabat said he was travelling and couldn't be reached. So he wandered the streets of Paris, up the hill to Montmartre and back down again, past the nightclubs of Pigalle, across the river to the Eiffel Tower, seeing it all but missing Morocco more with each passing day. The Parisians looked at him with such disdain that he could have been an Arab, and on his long, frustrated walks through this city which he had always assumed would feel like paradise, he found himself increasingly drawn to the outer arrondissements of the Right Bank, where an influx of North African immigrants had their own vegetable markets and served tagines from narrow shops.

One afternoon when he felt he couldn't stand it anymore, he went down to Rue Rivoli and bought himself two shirts of Egyptian cotton and a pair of gold cufflinks. This somewhat restored his spirits, and that evening he decided to splurge on an elegant dinner. First he went back to his hotel, chose one of the new shirts, and fastened the cufflinks. Then he took a taxi to a glittering restaurant on the Champs-Élysées, where the waiters wore black ties and the duck was famous, although in his opinion not quite as good as at the Petit Poucet back in Casablanca on the Boulevard de la Gare. For dessert he ordered a plate of grapes.

The waiter was another pretentious Parisian, whom Tony had felt looking down his nose at him from the moment he had arrived, so when he set down the grapes, Tony frowned. Was there a problem, monsieur? Indeed there was. Tony preferred his grapes peeled. How could a reputable restaurant serve them in the skins?

"I will have the chef peel them immediately, monsieur," the waiter said.

"No," Tony replied. "I prefer that you do it in front of me so that I can be certain it is done correctly."

Glowering, the waiter went to the service station and brought back a sharp knife, then laboriously cut the skin off each grape before setting it down on the plate again. The whole process seemed to take an eternity, but Tony enjoyed every second of it, and once the grapes were peeled and as slick as eyeballs, he popped one after another into his mouth, cufflinks glinting in the candlelight. Other diners were now watching him, but he took his time. Of course they were watching. He was that sort of man.

o

Saadia Taibi stood over the kitchen table furiously attempting to prepare couscous. The neighborhood women did it so easily, but nothing exhausted her more. The only cooking she'd ever enjoyed were the cookies she'd made for Zaïm. But Zaïm was dead, shot by three French policemen on the train to Oujda, and her husband had returned home from Algeria to live with her again. He cared nothing about the resistance. He just wanted his couscous topped with caramelized onions.

Really she was furious because she had wanted to go to the funeral of the pilot Touria Chaoui, but her husband had refused to let her go out alone. He said he had no interest in some girl who wasn't family. Now he just sat there listening to his radio. He had learned about the role she had played in the resistance, running guns and setting off bombs to kill the Nazarenes – what had he done? – but that was the past, and the world had returned to the way he assumed it was meant to be.

"You proved yourself capable of all that," he had said. "Now it's time for you to stay home." Then he had sold her bicycle and insisted she put on the scarf. She had obliged, because he was her husband, but she never forgot what she could have been, and caramelized his onions until they were as thick and as black as tar.

○

The funeral cortege left the house early that morning so as not to interfere with celebrations of Independence Day. Dozens of people were already waiting outside on Rue de Bergerac when they descended from the apartment with the coffin, which was light enough to be carried by four men. Abdelwahed was not one of those who carried his daughter. He was broken, bowed. Even his clothes looked like an afterthought. He should have been carried himself, and although he was only forty-five, he wouldn't live much longer. Touria had been his masterpiece, and the artist in him had died.

They walked past the spot where two bullets had killed her. The Morris Minor had been moved. Already the crowd murmured rumors. She had been killed by a corrupt cop named Ahmed Touil, who had been jealous over Touria's French lover. The French had ordered it as their final revenge. No, her lover had been the Sultan, and powerful Moroccan political factions had settled a score.

Several weeks later Touil's car would be shot to pieces in a police ambush beside the gas station on Boulevard Guerrero. Chief Zaoui would appear at the house and ask Abdelwahed to accompany him to the scene. He would show him the body of the suspected murderer, and Abdelwahed would thank him before trudging back home, unable to believe that a dead Touil explained anything. Nothing could be that simple, especially not the death of his daughter.

Dozens more joined them as they moved up Route de Medouina, across town to the Ahl Fass cemetery, five hundred meters from the sea, where the tops of some tombstones were still chipped from the bullets American planes had rained down fifteen years before. As they walked, they picked up mourners until hundreds trailed behind the tiny coffin, then thousands, stretching for almost a mile.

At the cemetery the grave had been dug, and at noon the coffin was placed onto two ropes and lowered into the hole. Abdelwahed stepped up onto a makeshift wooden platform. Accustomed to performing before packed theaters, he could hardly raise his voice above a whisper. There was nothing to say, or everything. He spoke for about a minute. At the end, however, he raised his voice to speak the only phrase he had been able to prepare during that endless night: "Today we bury colonialism." The words rang hollow, and he collapsed into the arms of those who had been attending him. He would never accept that what they had buried was his daughter.

Aziza Benayiche watched from near the front of the crowd. That morning she had walked all the way from Bousbir before joining up with the funeral cortege, dressed in her finest black kaftan and clutching a white lily. When Abdelwahed collapsed, wild grief overcame her and she rushed forward to drop the lily into the grave. *Ouili ouili ouili!* She wailed for Touria, whom she had followed as closely as if she had been her own daughter. She wailed for Suzanne and for herself.

At least one other mourner that day was notable, a

Frenchman standing alone at the back of the cemetery. Those who remarked him assumed from his bearing that he was military, although he did not wear a uniform. Later they would say that he had been Touria's lover, because the tears had rolled down his cheeks as steady as March rain.

○

○

The crowds danced in the Place de France, shouting to the skies. Whole extended families had trundled out onto the sidewalks to gape at the celebrations. Morocco was free.

The streets had been closed to traffic, and firecrackers popped outside the packed café. Mag, Fadila, and Mitch sat pressed together at their table, marveling at the chaos. With the institute closed for the holiday, they were spending the weekend together. Mag had never seen Fadila happier, although he wondered if she fully understood what it all meant. She had softened over the past months, becoming more beautiful. Even her tempestuous outbursts had become rarer, but these he also enjoyed and accepted with tranquility. He knew nothing about art, but she was working more intently than ever on her drawings, and occasionally gave him one. They hung on the walls of his hotel room.

Mitch's eyes were wide and full of wonder. She had never seen so many people in one place and kept turning to one or the other of them to make some observation in Arabic, French, or English, which she now spoke with ease. She and Fadila had their little secrets, and hardly needed to talk to communicate. Mag liked to watch them together and wonder what they were up to.

Another firecracker went off. Mitch jumped and grabbed her father's arm before exploding into giggles. He reached beneath the table and took Fadila's hand. She smiled crookedly and looked off into the distance. Casablanca was dancing, and he would never let her go.

SELECTED BIBLIOGRAPHY

Michel Abitbol, *Histoire du Maroc*, Perrin, 2009.

Michel Abitbol, *Les Juifs d'Afrique du Nord sous Vichy*, Riveneuve Éditions, 2008.

Charles-Robert Ageron, *La décolonisation française*, Armand Colin, 1994.

Rick Atkinson, *An Army at Dawn: The War in North Africa, 1942–1943, Volume One of the Liberation Trilogy*, Henry Holt and Co., 2002.

Alison Baker, *Voices of Resistance: Oral Histories of Moroccan Women*, State University of New York Press, 1998.

Jean-Claude Baker, *Josephine: The Hungry Heart*, Random House, 2003.

Leon Borden Blair, *Western Window of the Arab world*, University of Texas Press, 1970.

Nadir Bouzar, *L'Armée de Libération Nationale Marocaine: Retour sans visa (journal d'un résistant maghrébin)*, Publisud, 2002.

Tim Brady, *Twelve Desperate Miles: The Epic World War II Voyage of the SS Contessa*, Crown, 2012.

François Broche, *L'assassinat de Lemaigre-Dubreuil: Casablanca, le 11 juin 1955*, Balland, 1977.

Paul Brown, *The Whorehouse of the World: Tales of Wartime Italy – Casablanca, Algiers and Sicily*, AuthorHouse, 2004.

Jean-Louis Cohen and Monique Eleb, *Casablanca, mythes et figures d'une aventure urbaine*, Hazan, 2004.

Carleton Stevens Coon, *A North Africa Story: The Anthropologist as OSS Agent 1941–1943*, Gambit Publications, 1980.

Guy Delanoë, *Le retour du Roi et l'indépendance retrouvée, Tome 3*, L'Harmattan, 1991.

Guy Delanoë, *Lyautey, Juin, Mohamed V, Fin d'un protectorat, Tome 1*, L'Harmattan, 1988.

Carlo d'Este, *Patton, A Genius for War*, Harper-Collins, 1995.

Gilbert Grandval, *Ma mission au Maroc*, Plon, 1956.

Luella Jemima Hall, *The United States and Morocco, 1776–1956*, Scarecrow, 1971.

James J. Heaphey, *Legerdemain: The President's Secret Plan, the Bomb, And What the French Never Knew*, History Publishing Co., 2007.

William A. Hoisington, Jr., *The Assassination of Jacques Lemaigre-Dubreuil: A Frenchman between France and North Africa*, Routledge, 2011.

Abdellatif Laabi, *The Bottom of the Jar*, Archipelago, 2013.

John W. Lambert, *Wildcats over Casablanca*, Phalanx, 1992.

Rom Landau, *Moroccan Drama*, Robert Hale, 1956.

Christine Lévisse-Touzé, *L'Afrique du Nord dans la guerre, 1939–1945*, Albin Michel, 1998.

Jean Mathieu and P.H. Maury, *Bousbir: La prostitution à Casablanca*, Paris Méditerranée, 2003.

Antoine Méléro, *La main rouge: L'armée secrète de la République*, Éditions du Rocher, 1997.

Marc Méraud, *Histoire des A.I.: Le service des Affaires indigènes*, Public-réalisations, 1990.

Susan Gilson Miller, *A History of Modern Morocco*, Cambridge University Press, 2013.

Jacques Mordal, *La bataille de Casablanca*, Plon, 1952.

Robert Murphy, *Diplomat Among Warriors*, Doubleday, 1964.

Kenneth M. Pendar, *Adventures in Diplomacy: Our French Dilemma*, Simon Publications, 2003.

C.R. Pennell, *Morocco since 1830: A History*, NYU Press, 2001.

Douglas Porch, *The French Secret Service*, Farrar-Straus-Giroux, 1995.

Elliott Roosevelt, *As He Saw It*, Greenwood Press, 1974.

Beatrice Russell, *Living in State*, D. McKay, 1959.

Richard Harris Smith, *OSS: The Secret History of America's First Central Intelligence Agency*, University of California Press, 1972.

Georges Spillmann, *Du protectorat à l'indépendance, Maroc 1912–1955*, Plon, 1967.

Lucian K. Truscott, *Command Missions*, Presidio Press, 1990.

Hal Vaughan, *FDR's 12 Apostles: The Spies Who Paved the Way for the Invasion of North Africa*, Lyons Press, 2006.

PHOTO CREDITS

Chaoui family archives (used with permission): p. 236, 245
Collection of the author: p. 47, 137, 181, 200, 213
Nelson C. Brown High School - Nouasseur, Morocco – www.nouasseur.com: p. 60, 161